THE CHRONICLES OF THE ADONAI:

THE ISLAND

Braxton Hunter

TRINITY LIVING PRESS

THE ISLAND

Trinity Living Press
(an affiliate of Trinity Academic Press)

©2018 by Braxton Hunter

ISBN-13: 978-0692045091

ISBN-10: 0692045090

Printed in the United States of America

Library of Congress-in-Publication Data

Hunter, Braxton, 2018-
   The Chronicles of the Adonai: The Island/
Braxton Hunter.
   p.   cm.
   ISBN 13: 978-0692045091
   ISBN 10: 0692045090

      1.   Survival - Fiction. 2. Mystery - Fiction, Adventure - Fiction.
   3. Religion. 1. Title.
2016907104

10	9	8	7	6	5	4	3	2	1

For

Sarah: my Hope

THE FOLLOWING IS A WORK OF FICTION

None of the characters represent actual personalities. Nevertheless, scientific, philosophical and historical facts mentioned by those characters *are* true. Evidences referenced are also real, and are used by working professional philosophers to demonstrate the truth of a particular worldview. The author has written on each of these subjects in several non-fiction books at the popular and scholarly level.

THE ANTAGONISTS IN THIS WORK
DO NOT REPRESENT ALL WHO SHARE
THEIR WORLDVIEW

There are many unbelievers in the world today. The vast majority of them are as opposed to the actions taken by the villains in this work as would be any Christian. That the antagonists in this story happen to hold to non-Christian worldviews should not be taken to indicate that the author is describing what he believes to be the typical non-Christian's morality, or the actions to which all other perspectives lead. Non-Christians are often heroic. Professing Christians are sometimes villainous.

HELPFUL TERMINOLOGY

THE APOLOGIA – Meaning "to defend," or "in defense of," the term is ascribed to the fictional group of young people whose responsibility it is to defend The Colony.

THE ADONAI – Meaning "masters," the plural term was used by Hebrews as a name for God, but it is the self ascribed label blasphemously used by the leaders of The Colony.

ADON – The singular form of Adonai used for an individual leader of The Colony.

THE GREAT DIVIDE – The term for the great separation between The Colony and the world of suffering.

THE VERITAS – Meaning "truth," the term is ascribed to the group of young ladies whose job it is to explain the "truth" of The Great Divide.

CHAPTER ONE

Justin

The drop seems to last forever, then I find my footing in the tunnel. I stand in the shallow water and scan for the Adon. After dusting off my Apologia jacket, I zip up the front so that only a few inches of my sleeveless red T-shirt are exposed. The stubble on my head matches that of my face. I haven't slept in two days, my muscles are aching from too many fights, and my head is spinning from the lust for the truth about the second Colony. Hope is somewhere close. But, Damian Yukimura is in these tunnels, and I will find him - *today*!

Arvin is close. Louis is close. I worry a moment for Hope and then comfort myself with the knowledge that she is safe on a rooftop a half-mile away. She's watching and she knows how to stay hidden. She'll be fine.

Slowly opening and closing my hands I creep through the tunnel that is about eight feet high at its peak. The centuries-old stone would be fascinating if I were here for any other purpose. This predator will not escape.

"Yukimura," I shout as my echo reverberates through the space, "you're caught! Just give up!" Suddenly I hear the consecutive splashes of footsteps in the sludge and I rocket through the tunnels toward my prey. Approaching an intersection I round the corner tossing caution to the wind. He was this way.

Turning a second corner I see him. He's approaching an exit. Picking up the pace my muscles scream with pain. My calves feel like they are about to burst. Failure. He's out of the tunnel. Reaching the edge I see the slums of Rio de Janeiro gain focus in my eyes. We are fifty feet up and Yukimura has leapt a good 10 feet forward and five feet down onto the roof of a nearby residence. Structure after structure. They are so close together that a blanket of dilapidating buildings covers several blocks. I'm not going to make it.

Closing my eyes for five long seconds to muster some resolve, I take a short run and make the leap. I land running and am soon hopping from rooftop to rooftop - keeping Yukimura in my line of sight. "Soon," I remind myself. "Soon he will run out of steam like me. Soon he will reach a point of no escape." Only . . . now I've lost him. Bystanders look on from the street below and the windows all around as I contemplate my next move.

Fortunately, a small child with raven hair and a boyish grin, giggles a bit as he points toward an almost hidden window. Yukimura! He's struggling to pull himself inside. Resting my hands on my knees I breathe heavily three times before sprinting to the ledge of the roof and hurling myself over the alley and toward the enemy. We collide as our bodies collapse into the opening and onto the floor of a remarkably well-decorated apartment. We both moan as I pull myself

2

together and grab him by the collar.

"Get up, Yukimura," I growl.

"You finally did it boy," Yukimura dejectedly comments. "You got me. The last Adon of The Colony."

"Problem is, Doctor," I sarcastically reply, "I don't want you. I want the second Colony." I restrain his hands and sit him in a wicker chair that is positioned in the midst of the room next to its twin and a large ornate desk. No AC. It's hot. The room is maroon with pictures covering most of the walls. Cultural artifacts are prominently displayed all around and palms make up the rest of the décor.

"You won't find it," the Adon assures.

"At least not the way you suppose." Arvin! In a corner of the room I suddenly become aware of the headhunter from Porcher Island. And with him is the only remaining member of the night watch Apologia, Louis. Louis has Hope in a sleeper hold. Frostbite! Arvin has a gun and it's trained on me.

"As he said, boy, you won't be getting to that Colony the way you'd like. I'll gladly send the two of you there in body bags. But since this just got interesting, why don't you loose these hand restraints and we'll have a chat." Realizing I have few options, I retrieve a switchblade, cut the bonds and Yukimura rubs his wrists.

"Hope," I begin, "it's going to be alright."

"No," Yukimura says in a deep and breathy manner, "it will not be alright." Standing, he moves to a wet bar and mixes two drinks. I can't see well, but it looks as though he is adding something foreign. Approaching, he sits the two heavy glasses on the desk, each one with a rich thud.

"You have a choice to make, boy." He's enjoying every second. "You'll decide your own fate, and of course the girl's fate too. I don't care much about her. She wouldn't be chasing old professors around the globe in search of a rabbit hole like our Colony if it weren't for you. I'm happy to let her go and let Arvin, here, put a bullet in you to ensure this is all over. You'll be dead, but she'll go free." Without altering my stern expression, I shift my eyes around the room and catch a glimpse of Hope, jaw pushed forward in anger slowly shaking her head. "Or . . . I'll let you follow me down this rabbit hole, but on my terms. You and the girl will go with me to the second Colony alive, but unconscious. You'll be risking her life, but you'll get your answers. All you have to do is drink. Poetic, isn't it? Like Alice in Wonderland or something."

Running my finger around the rim of the glass I inquire, "Wait . . . what would it profit you to bring us to The Colony even unconscious and in bondage? How do I know it's not a trick and the moment we drink, we'll keel over?"

Shaking his head in faux confusion he sits back in the chair comfortably and says, "Well, I could kill you now if I wanted to. My reason for taking you to The Colony is an Adonai secret. You don't need to know. Still, let me assure you that I am utterly indifferent as to the choice you make."

I roll it all around in my mind. Even if he does take me to The Colony, it could be a death sentence for both of us. I'm not afraid to sacrifice myself here, anymore than I was when knelt before Tristan in the snow. But I know the truth. Hope will seek revenge. She will revert to the reckless vigilante she used to be just after Noah died. There's only one logical choice. Swiftly I reach for the glass filled with bluish liquid and stand. At this Arvin aims his gun. I must have startled him. Yukimura quickly holds out his palm to calm the monster. He watches me with anticipation. Hope's eyes are wide and her lips are apart.

"Yukimura," I say, "you better live up to your end of the bargain."

"My boy, you are in a position entirely unsuitable to give orders."

I take one final glance around the room and shake my head in frustration. Tossing back the drink I wait a solid ten seconds before my vision begins to cloud and I crumple to the floor.

"I'm with you," a voice says. "Do not be afraid." Then it all goes black.

CHAPTER TWO
Julie

"So, Julie," the interviewer says, "you're telling us that an entire civilization . . . uh . . . a Colony, I think you said, was developed by your father and based on the dream of a world without the belief in God. Is that right?" The stage lights are hot on my face. Rose Bellet agreed to do this interview based on my claim that I had solid evidence. However, I can tell by the expressions I see in the faces of the in-studio audience that my pants suit and glasses aren't bringing the credibility I had hoped for.

"Yes, Rose," I answer. "The planning of The Colony was phenomenal. It was a work of incredible strategy. Moreover, the young people of The Colony were made to believe that their outpost home was all that was left of humanity. It was like some dystopian wasteland covered in snow."

"But," Rose breaks in, "when the authorities traveled with you to the site, there was no trace of it - just the wreckage of an old ski resort. Isn't that right?" The question catches me off guard even though I had prepared myself for it.

"Well, yes . . . but . . ." I begin to say, but Dr. Ben Ruth cuts me off.

"Ms. Bellet, you have to conceive of the intellectual prowess of those involved in this."

"The ones you are calling the Adonai," Rose clarifies.

"That's right," Ruth answers. "The Adonai represent some of the most brilliant minds of their time. Just as great planning went in to the exodus *to* The Colony, great planning was clearly put in to the exodus *from* The Colony. How it was done is a mystery to us, but it is a fact all the same." It's clear that Rose Bellet wants to believe us. She runs this program for the purpose of demonstrating the Christian worldview and typically has Bible scholars and Christian philosophers to interview. Yet, I can tell that this one is hard for her to swallow.

"Facts," she says as the word floats through the air as if on display for the audience to examine, "are undeniable truths. What evidence can you offer us that what you are saying is true?"

It's my turn now. I say, "We have several witnesses. My husband and I were there, as well as a young lady named Hope and my brother, Justin. Hope and Justin were both raised in The Colony. On top of that, the people of Endville can testify to the plan." She's scanning her notes.

"We tried to get a response from the minister and his wife in Endville . . . a Rev. Dan and his wife Gracie," she explains, "but they were unwilling to comment." She removes her glasses as the words trail off and squints her eyes, ready to judge my response.

"That's surprising, I have to say." It's not though. Dan and Gracie are probably fearful of legal allegations if they speak out. They could be charged for something related to their involvement. I'm just glad they turned it around. "But those of us here are willing to die for the belief in the existence of The Colony. Isn't that one of the great Christian answers to why we should believe the disciples of Jesus were telling the truth about the resurrection? Men will live for a lie, but they will not die for one. You have scholars on your show all the time who talk about that, Ms. Bellet."

"True, Julie, but you have not been put in a position to demonstrate that devotion before us. Furthermore, your husband is in the audience and we would expect him to back up your claims. This Justin and Hope are not even here for us to interview. Dr. Ben Ruth believes you, but he never saw The Colony active. So, it sounds like we're supposed to just take the word of you and your husband on this. Am I missing something?"

Rob can't take any more. He stands on the front row of the audience and demands, "Now you listen here! I saw it with my own eyes! It was chaos! I flew the chopper out of that rat hole! You make it sound like we're both crazy!" There is commotion in the crowd and security tries to quiet Rob.

Rose thumbs the mute on her microphone and whispers, "I believe you, but you aren't giving us much to work with here. People don't like conspiracy theories and you've got to bring me more than this."

***

As we exit the building in downtown Chicago and enter a limo provided by the studio, the world seems twisted. No one believes us. We sound deluded.

"If I had just taken my camera to The Colony all of this would be proven," I say in frustration to Ben.

"I'm not so sure," he replies. "Rose Bellet would believe you. She's a good woman. The problem is that there are certain people who have decided that no matter what evidence they are presented with they simply will not believe. You can't do anything with people like that." His words ring true, but they do little to calm my raging emotions.

We position ourselves in the car. Ruth is in the front seat and Rob fumes next to me in the back. He isn't used to any of this. The city is a jungle compared to his quiet life in BC. In his world a man can defend his wife's honor without having to take on a television studio to do it.

"Rob, It will be okay," I assure him.

"How can you say that, Julie?" he asks with a raised voice. "It ain't right! Our lives were on the line and a generation of teenagers have had their youth stolen."

Ben speaks with the voice of mature wisdom, "Rob, you are in an impossible situation. Julie is your bride and you want to protect her reputation, but she has taken this burden on herself. She is the primary voice of advocacy for those who have none. You must prepare yourself for hard times to come."

"Look," I suggest, "honey I love you, but maybe it's time for you to take a little break. Go back home and spend some time with your plane. Go fishing. Get out into the wilderness . . . at least until this all dies down."

"You need me now, Julie. I'm not just gonna take off for 'me time,'" he says with air quotes.

"We're not getting any quality time anyway, flyboy," I explain. "I'm not going to rest until I convince someone. It's going to be interview after interview for a while. Besides, I want to think of you in your natural habitat. That's where I fell in love with you. That image gives me strength. I just want to know that you're riding on the wind, calm and cool." I'll convince him. I feel a little strange, though, not telling him the full story. Justin and Hope are out there somewhere and I've got to find them.

Darkness. It's black and . . . muggy. Opening my eyes I expect the darkness to be chased away. It remains. Rolling onto my belly I feel the ground with my hands. Gritty concrete glides across my fingers as I explore the foreign surface. Struggling to stand, I hear my every movement echoing in what must be a hard and confined space. As I recognize the unmistakable sounds of my own cracking joints, I stand. The repetitive and rhythmic dripping water fills out the damp environment, and I move through it with outstretched arms. Three paces transport me to what feels like a rough cinderblock wall. Moving along its surface my thigh finally nudges a movable object and the sound of wood screeching against smooth cement violates the space. A table. Seconds later I locate an old oil lamp and a book of matches. Performing the action briskly, light floods the room and I see that it's worse than I imagined.

The room looks to be about twenty by thirty feet. The ceiling is a good fifteen feet up. There is a vertical tunnel of sorts in the center of the ceiling that stretches up another thirty feet to a hatch that is closed. It looks as though there was once a metal ladder comprised of rungs that arched out from the rock. They are all absent now with the exception of one mangled bar left protruding five feet inside the orifice. There are no windows. There are no doors. My guess is I'm underground. None of this seems too surprising though. I expected to be restrained or imprisoned in some way or other. What shocks me is the sight of the walls themselves. At one end of the space, etched deeply into the stone is the Creed of the Adonai, which reads, "Freedom to Think – Freedom to Live - Hope to Seek – Hope to Give." Yet, it appears as though some poor soul has violently scrapped away at the inscription with a loose stone. The scrapping did not end there.

The walls are covered with strange etchings no doubt left by the same culprit. They don't make a lot of sense.

"The word of God – The Lord is a man of war."

"The word of God - It were better for him that a millstone were hanged about his neck, and he cast into the sea, than that he should offend one of these little ones."

"The word of God – And my wrath shall wax hot."

Scanning each section of the walls reveals more violent scribbling. Some of it seems to imply God commanding or glorying in killing. Yet, in the center of them all, in larger words, is the phrase, "The Adonai imposters must die!" Whoever was down here before sure didn't have any love for his captors.

On the table is one book that appears to be

some form of diary. The pages have more of the same esoteric statements, but there are also several paragraphs related to the author's time in this hopeless pit. It is written in archaic wording.

"Here in this hellish prison, my purpose has been revealed. Vengeance shall be brought on the blasphemous fools. I shall be the blade that strikes from the darkness. I shall be his prophet. He wills it. He has delivered this truth to the ears of mine heart. His vicar shall I be. A vision and prophecy has been given. He will raise me up to smite the false Adonai."

Eerie does not begin to describe the feeling this experience produces. Tilting my head slightly up as if to force my thoughts elsewhere, I consider the dripping water and rush to its location. Falling from the opening overhead is what almost amounts to a trickle of life-giving fluid. I open my mouth and let the cool liquid pound against my tongue. Somewhat refreshed I rotate examining the room again. "I've got to get out of here," I say out loud.

Despite that the opening has no ladder, if I could get inside its lip it wouldn't be too hard to climb up, one foot on each side of the space. The problem is, there's no way to reach the height. Though I already know it will be an exercise in futility, I drag the table to the middle of the room, climb on top and jump. Too high. Eyeballing the chair, I develop a slightly less ridiculous plan. Placing the chair atop the table, I again climb the wooden precipice. Knowing what might happen I leap again. The chair falls away and I slap the interior of the opening. Not good enough. Without time to prepare myself, I land on the table and it shatters beneath my weight.

"Frostbite," I shout as I recover from the fall.

***

What feels like four hours passes as I consider my meager options. Yukimura, or someone, might show up eventually. After all, they brought me here for a reason. If the Adonai just wanted me dead, they could have handled that in Rio. On the other hand, if they don't show up I'll starve to death in this cavern. I can't trust that they'll return. With the table now collapsed things seem even more grim. I could try to scrape around the edges of the cinderblocks in the walls. If I could get several of them free I may be able to stack them, but that could take days . . . or longer. Slowly my eyes drift down to the sleeve of my jacket and I thumb the material. Neurons begin to fire in my brain. An idea. Not a bad idea.

***

Having worked on my new plan for several more hours I must have fallen asleep. However, regrouping I completed my work. It was harder than I thought it would be to scrape, bite and tear away the leather of my Apologia jacket into long strips. The sharpest rock I could locate revealed itself to be pretty dull as I tried to penetrate the tough material. A small amount of pride trickles in like the water from the ceiling as I admire the makeshift rope I've fashioned. Now it's time to see if it's all been worth it.

Tying the leathery band to a piece of wood from what had been the table, I again examine the deformed bar inside the overhead tunnel. Hear we go. Tossing the homemade grappling hook through the air my eyes are wide with anticipation. My raised eyebrows relax again as the creation bounces around in the opening and then lands with a wooden rattle on the floor. Five more attempts produce five more failures. No surprise. The seventh toss makes contact with the rung, and the eighth even gets wedged a bit. Unfortunately, the slightest of tugs brings the tool rattling down again. Number nine gracefully wraps around the pole with centripetal force and the wooden chunk wedges itself between the metal and the rock.

"Got it," I shout before placing my hand to my head in surprise and backing to the wall. Observing the hanging leather I slide to the floor almost afraid to disturb the situation. Breathing a breathy prayer of gratitude I drag the palms of my hands across my face as if to wipe away the frustration of the work done over the past several hours. As I stand and approach the rope, I look back to the graffiti on the walls and speak to its author as though he has been my unwanted companion in this musky tomb, "See ya, weirdo!"

I stretch out my fingers and wiggle them in preparation before wrapping my palms around the rope. Blowing out forcefully three times to relieve anxiety I try a firm tug. Stable. I try again adding more weight and again it doesn't budge. "This just might work," I encourage myself. Beginning a free climb, I chuckle to myself as I ascend from the room. Once my entire body is in the tunnel I place my feet on either side and begin to climb. If I fall . . . don't think that way, Justin. Reaching the hatch, I find that fortune has smiled on me. A rock protrudes enough to get my footing so that I can leverage my body to lift the lid. It's chained, but it opens enough that I may be able to wriggle through. The sunlight is offensive and squinting, I claw at grass and mud like some mindless zombie emerging from the earth. Finally, my foot is out and the hatch slams shut with a horrid thud. Rolling over with my forearm covering my eyes, I lie on my back and catch my breath. My head lying on the earth, I look to the right and allow my eyes to adjust. High heels strut past. High heels?

CHAPTER FOUR

It is only now that I realize the grass upon which I rest is a finely cut lawn that is the deepest green I've ever seen. The hatch sits in the midst of a wall that is curved in a semicircle around the opening and stretches up ten feet or so. The stone of the wall is beautifully cut and arranged. Vines and brightly colored flowers weave their way up its surface and contribute to the aged beauty of the scene. The wall then continues in either direction some distance. Yet, before aesthetics arrest my attention, I flash to my feet and stumble away from the high heels that wander past.

The world materializes and turns upright as I stand in shock. An Asian woman dressed in a green sundress continues to walk away from my direction taking no thought of my sudden appearance. She carries a beautiful ceramic watering pot and moves about the grounds caring for the exotic blossoms. Gardens with ornate renaissance style sculptures stretch for at least seventy yards before me. A ten-foot wide stone walkway lined with oversized potted plants and more of the same statues stretches from my general area to the other side of the yard. More beautiful young ladies of various ethnicities are moving about the environment in the same green sundresses and high-heeled sandals. They are all performing tasks related to the upkeep of the grounds. My first impulse is to run, but I'm strangely mesmerized. None of them seem to care that a muddy straggler has just struggled for his life up and out of the belly of the earth and into their presence.

At the far end of the walkway is a historic looking robust white Mansion that is half eaten by foliage. Only . . . the foliage is visually appealing and adds to the effect. Somehow the combination of the hole, the apathy the women seem to have about my presence, and the beauty of the stately manor all hit the brain in just the right way to cause a deep creepiness to emerge.

I half stagger and half walk the distance of the yard and realize that another character is present. A man who looks to be about twenty-eight years old is the centerpiece of the servants' efforts. He sits amidst the antique outdoor furniture with his left leg crossed lazily over his right. His maroon pants fit tightly and black military style boots reach halfway up his calves. A leather vest, so brown it wants to be black, covers his torso, but he wears no shirt. On his left bicep is a tattoo of the Adonai emblem complete with what seems to be a human eye set in the letter "A." He's tall. I'd say he's an easy six two. He's also fairly muscular and his tan skin is covered with brass and silver jewelry. Shoulder length hair hangs freely as his head is leaned over the back of the chair in a posture of extreme relaxation. The fingers of his left hand dangle off of the chair's arm and his right hand grips the handle of a German stein. As he lifts his head upon hearing my approach, raised eyebrows and a deep frown portray a textbook image of confusion. His face completes the profile.

Reaching into the left breast pocket of his vest, he retrieves a pair of thin dark-rimmed glasses and raises them to his face to get a better look. Without standing, he addresses the nearby woman watering the flowers who is now carrying out her task in our vicinity.

"Bailee," he begins in an Australian accent, "who is this fellow?" He asks the question as though I'm not present. She approaches and whispers in his ear. With her head still next to his, he opens his mouth as if he suddenly remembers. She moves away and he briskly stands to his feet. Slapping his hands together in enthusiasm, he approaches with a smile. With the glasses he looks like some sort of overly attractive librarian pirate. Weird as that image seems, I immediately conclude that it would be in my best interest to prevent Hope from seeing this guy. Once he is uncomfortably close, with his fingers laced together at his chest, he looks me over and laughingly says in an embarrassed low tone, "I completely forgot." His hand goes to his mouth for a moment.

Not knowing exactly what's going on, I begin to say, "I'm . . . uh . . ."

"You're Justin . . . Yukimura and some Apologia fellow called Louis brought you here three days ago and put you in that *dread*ful hole. I think they wanted me to make some kind of example of you to the Colonials . . . you know, show them what happens when you double-cross the Adonai," he says with a roll of his eyes. "I don't run things that way 'round here, but it's best to let them think so. The most indispensable question is, *are you all right?*"

21

"Yeah . . . I mean. I guess."

"Ugh," he moans as he places his wrist to his forehead examining my clothing with a look of pity. "You look awful. You simply must forgive me," he says gripping my shoulders. "I had every intention of pulling you out of that dungeon the moment Yukimura and Louis had gone, but the Colonials had a festival planned and there were just so many things to do, and I had to write a speech I'll be giving and . . ." he stops himself and regains his composure before continuing, "None of that serves as a good excuse." Beginning to laugh while he stares into my eyes, he adds, "Just imagine if you hadn't made it out on your own." At this point he loses it and laughs loudly.

Part of me wants to throw him to the ground and demand answers, but his jovial way renders that unnecessary for the moment. At least I'm not imprisoned anymore. He doesn't seem to have any intention of binding my hands. It seems . . . safe.

Removing his glasses he sticks out his hand and announces, "The name's Foley, and I am the Adon of this Colony."

***

Inside the Mansion, gold, marble and intricately designed fixtures abound. A massive staircase reaches halfway to the second floor and then splits off into separate directions. A bust of my father's head sits at the landing, though a beret has been positioned in a silly way on its top and aviator glasses have been affixed to his face. Continuing the ascent, I follow the girl I now know as Bailee through the glamorous estate and into a gorgeous room that facilitates several massive wardrobes. The ceilings must be twenty feet high, and the majestic white and gold trappings are permeated by the tropical vibrant scene outside the windows. Opening one of these I spy a collection of outfits appropriate to the environment.

The delicate features of Bailee's face form an inviting smile and she offers, "Choose," her hands motioning toward the apparel. "Anything you want is yours."

"Thank you," I say in a way that must convey my continuing bewilderment. Looking over the clothes a thought emerges. Dark clothes. For all I know, I may have to sneak, run or hide on this Island. If it's really up to me, I'll make the most of this. There! A black sleeveless tee shirt hangs at the end of the row. And . . . there. Black pants in the snug style Foley wore. I pass on the strange boots and keep my own footwear.

Bailee nods and turns, apparently with the assumption I'll follow. I do. She leads me to one of the most impressive bathrooms I've ever seen and then exits to grant me privacy. The tile is gorgeous and steam billows up all around as I work the shower handle. Whatever is going on, I needed this.

***

Upon leaving the bathroom with my new clothes on, I locate Bailee in an adjacent room waiting loyally for my return. She looks to me and says, "You don't want some color?" Grabbing a maroon neckerchief with no design, she ties it around my neck and it hangs loosely at the collar of the black shirt like a scarf. "There. Now you look . . . handsome," she says, forcing a jokingly serious expression before the flirtatious mock melts away and she gives me a wink.

"Okay, Bailee," I say with a kind, lopsided grin. "If you think so." Again she spins and takes it for granted I'll follow her. Descending the staircase I see Foley patting a male servant on the back and chuckling in a friendly way. His presence does fill the room. He's charismatic and gives you the impression he could be the life of the party or a one-man army.

Spreading his arms to convey a playful sense of admiration he loudly bellows, "Justin Lyn, the son of *the* Adon," placing emphasis on the word "the." He finishes, "The prince of the Northern Colony." If this guy is an Adon I sure can't tell. Is he unaware of what happened? Does he even know that my father is dead? Why is he treating me like an honored guest?

"Foley, what's going on . . . I," he cuts me off.

"Don't worry, young prince. I'm sure you've got many questions, but a picture is worth a thousand . . . no, that's painfully cliché isn't it? Awe, well, let's put it like this - I'll show you." Is it me or is he afraid I'll say the wrong thing in front of the servants? Moving out onto the front porch, two men appear to be standing guard. They wear the same Apologia uniforms I'm used to seeing at the Northern Colony, only their shirts are green, as are the Apologia emblems on the left breast of the jackets and the phrase, "Hope to Give," trailing down the right sleeves. After a second glance, I become aware that the black jackets are a much lighter material and are perforated by tiny holes. This does seem more appropriate to the climate. Strangely, the image of the Apologia and the presence of an Adon produce a cocktail of emotions that is difficult to handle. On the one hand, I am horrified by the idea of a second Colony. At the same time, I have to admit that the familiarity of Colony terms and roles feels bizarrely welcoming. Shaking my head as if to dislodge the confusion, I focus on Foley's words.

"Prince Justin," he starts up, "meet Colin and Paul. They are the only Apologia of this Colony. I trained them myself. Isn't that right gentlemen?"

"Yes sir," the Apologia agree. They must be no older than sixteen or seventeen, but they are certainly athletic. Their skin is tanned by the Island sun, and they both have dark buzzed hair. They could almost be twins. For a moment my thoughts drift to Brent. He would fit in well with these two.

Moving off of the spacious porch and into the yard, I can see that jungle surrounds our location. Behind the Mansion high peaks are visible that reach like protective arms in either direction. I can't see in front of us because of the tall trees, palms and other growth. I begin to head off in the direction of what was clearly once a driveway of some kind, but Foley speaks up.

"Justin," he laughs, "you can go that way if you like, but it'll take you forever. We have more exciting ways of moving about the Island." As he finishes he begins to run. What else can I do but follow?

Racing after the Adon through a well-worn path in the jungle, I almost lose track of him twice. He's fast. Finally, I see him stop at the edge of the tree line. It's clear now that we have reached a cliff. It must be sixty feet down. Jungle blankets the scenery in an ebb and flow pattern all around us. Gripping a zip line that extends to the left, Foley cautions, "Careful, young prince. This is dangerous, but you are an Apologia after all." Tossing me a strange rubbery bar he shouts, "We call it a Hook-Slide. *Hook*, then *slide*, ha ha." His laugh trails off as he begins to glide away on the cable. Examining the bar I see that a vertical opening extends down the length of one side and a claw of some sort is able to slide out. With the hook rotated ninety degrees to the handle, the tool's purpose is clear. Fitting the hook around the cable I stare at the green abyss for ten solid seconds before working up the courage to step off of the cliff.

As the wind hits my face I can't help but recall *the great tramcar chase*, as I've come to call it. At least here sleet and snow are not assaulting my face. The speed increases and I tighten my grip. I subtly giggle with giddiness to myself before feeling guilty for the fun. Hope, Jack and Courtney must be somewhere on this Island and I'm enjoying recreation time. The wind seems to blow my thoughts away as the jungle swallows me up and a rise in the cable slows my descent. It's not enough though. Seeing the end of the cable embedded in a tree before my eyes, I drop in an ungraceful roll and sprawl in the leaves and twigs. Brushing the debris out of my hair I begin to sit up. Suddenly the rubbery handle of the Hook-Slide is in my face as Foley hands it to me.

"You're going to have to do better than that if you're to make it here for very long." I grip the handle and Foley pulls me up. "Don't worry Prince Justin. You'll get the hang of it." Why does he keep calling me that? My father's fame is well known among the Adonai.

Ten paces move us to the other side of the small hill and the view of the Island opens up. "You see that?" Foley asks, indicating a distance of at least 600 yards out from the beach. "That is one of the most obvious reasons our Colony is hidden from the outside world." Stretching out from the body of the Island is the shape of a crescent moon and the tips almost meet. High rocky cliffs all but complete the circle and what appears to be a long opening provides a narrow waterway through to the ocean.

"There," he says, pointing to the plaster and rock homes with red clay roofs, "is our Colony itself." It genuinely appears to be a small town. Small homes even speckle the hillside reaching up from the beach. Fishing boats clutter the closest region of the cove. "We catch or grow our food. We are completely self sufficient."

"Where did all this come from?" I ask. "You didn't build all this, did you?"

"I promise you'll get your answers in just a few moments. Try to land more gracefully this time." He winks and flicks out the hook before sliding away for the second time. Again, my only option is to follow.

CHAPTER FIVE

I hit the ground and run along a bit to avoid a fall. Snapping the hook together with the handle I shove the Hook-Slide into the back of my pants and jog with Foley toward the bustling secret community. He high-fives two Colonials and playfully tousles the hair of a third. They all seem excited to see him. Music that has that record player hiss is heard coming from old loud speakers set high on poles or attached to trees. The seventies rocker dryly chants, "We don't need your rules and rulers." With the crashing of waves and the trudging guitar song, it is a festive atmosphere. My host hops onto a porch and guides us into a thatch-covered structure as casually as one would his own kitchen.

In the shallow room I hear the sizzle of meat and Foley sits us down at a table. A few moments later a tin plate of fish and corn is brought. "Eat up, my friend. You must be famished," the Adon urges. I do. "Now," he finally allows, "you have some questions."

"Okay," I speak with determination, "first of all, Yukimura should have brought someone with me – a girl named Hope." He nods his head as he removes a glass from his mouth and places it with a thud on the table.

"Yes. A red head if I recall," his eyes squint as if he's concentrating on the memory. "She got loose once you all arrived and ran off into the jungle."

Standing I shout, "The jungle?"

Hands up in a cautioning way, Foley encourages, "calm down, Justin. She can't get far. We *are* on an Island after all. Committing Departure here is out of the question." As he speaks, I glance around the room considering the information. I slowly sit back down and pick at the fish with a fork.

"It does sound like Hope," I assure myself.

"Yeah, course it does, mate. She'll be back. After all, she'll be looking for you, right?" He is right. Just like before, Hope will be trying to sneak *into* a Colony. At least she has experience. "The best thing you can do, young prince, is to enjoy Colony life and wait for her."

"Okay, well, what about the other Northern Colony Apologia, Jack and Courtney? Are they here?"

"Yeah, dark haired brainy fellow with a receding brow line, and a mouthy blonde, huh?" He said a mouthful.

"That's them! Where are they?" I stand and shout again.

"They're fine," the Adon urges. "I've got them out on a camping expedition with some friends on the outer edge of the Island. Didn't want them seen while Yukimura was around. They were going to be gone for a week. That means they've still got three or four days, and they'll be back too." He leans in for effect and attempts to comfort me with, "Justin . . . I know you'll feel better when you can lay eyes on your friends, but they're all here on our Island and they're all fine. We've just got to wait." His attempt at comfort works. We stand to leave the makeshift restaurant and I only now notice a sign that reads, "The Circle Island Café." Suddenly, flashes of the Circle of Life Café invade my thoughts and I strangely begin to feel at home in this alternate Colony. It is complete with shades of my old life.

***

With our feet in the clearest and bluest ocean, I could imagine my thoughts are drawn to the descriptions I'd read in encyclopedias and novels at the Inquiry and Enlightenment Academy of the Northern Colony growing up. Those authors meagerly tried to harness the English language to capture the reality I'm now experiencing. They failed. It wasn't their fault. The beauty of the Maker's design must be seen to be appreciated. How could anyone doubt God's existence with this breathtaking vision?

"Foley . . . where are the Colonials from the Northern Colony?" Looking around I notice that everyone here seems to be between the ages of ten and twenty-two years old. "Is there another section to the Island where they are, or something?"

"Oh . . . no, my friend. They aren't here." Not here? What's he saying? They have to be here. "Jack and Courtney were sent here to be killed as examples," he says again rolling his eyes. "Then you and the redhead showed up and the same marching orders were given. Naturally, I agreed, but hopefully I've demonstrated to your satisfaction that I've no intention of any such thing."

"Okay," I say while trying to process the information. "Then where are they?"

He smiles and again chuckles in his jolly fashion before answering, "I've no idea. Not here. That's all I know."

Two kids play what looks like hockey with a coconut and it rolls into the water in front of us. We pause to let the kids clear away. Looking Foley in the eyes, I ask the most direct question. "Alright, I've got to know. Why are you being so cool, Foley? I mean are you unaware of what happened at the Northern Colony? I assumed you knew if you had orders to kill us, but if so, we should be enemies of the Adonai state or something."

As if dismissing my question, he responds, "You wanna see my favorite part of our Colony?" He takes off running from the water toward the base of a cliff at the edge of the beach. Raising my head a Chapel comes into view. It looks to be about three times the size of the small wedding Chapel at the Northern Colony. Frostbite! I'm in the same predicament I've been in since we left the Mansion. I have life or death issues on my mind and this playful joker keeps sliding away. Like a dope I again do the only thing I can . . .

follow.

***

Ascending the vine-covered stone stairs, the aged chapel fills my field of vision. Foley works the iron handle and the oversized doorway swings open. Inside the structure the ambiance of stained glass benefits from the view of the cove visible through missing or broken panes. Streams of light cast an array of colors on the aged white walls and hard brown pews. Foley moves for the first time with a posture of respect. His hands are folded at his chest with both index fingers resting on his chin. There, before him, is a large open Bible. What's going on?

"Prince Justin," he addresses with a sincere grin and joyous eyes, "there is a reason I did not kill you or your friends. I couldn't kill my own family." As he speaks, his meaning doesn't set in at first. Did my mother and father have another son – one with an Australian accent?

"What . . . what do you mean?" I ask. "Foley, this is weird."

His mouth stretches into a wide, openmouthed grin as he declares, "Justin, I'm a believer!"

CHAPTER SIX

Looking through one of the missing panes I roll the thoughts around in my head. This sounds too good to be true. Frankly, there's a lot I don't know. Why is there a second Colony? Where did the first Colony go? Why would the Adonai place a believer in leadership instead of killing him? I'm not satisfied with all of these answers, but I am happy with Foley's news. Can I trust him?

"Wait a minute," I demand. "How can this be? I mean, how did you get here? Why are there two Colonies? How can you be a believer and an Adon at the same time? None of this makes sense." He nods slowly and begins to back away toward the last window on the jungle side of the Chapel. It has no glass at all.

"I'll tell you, young prince. I'll tell you . . . everything." His hands motion in front of his face with the last word as if he's a stage magician ready to dazzle. Lifting one foot and placing it on the sill, he launches away . . . again.

Rushing to the opening I see that there is another zip line attached to the exterior of the building. Flicking the hook out . . . again I make connection with the cable . . . again, and slide after him . . . again. The fear of the action is fading and if I'm honest with myself, it's starting to be fun. Entering the tree line the heat from the sun vanishes and the cool of the jungle wraps around my speeding frame. It is a welcome sensation. I'm not used to the heat. Unlike most people, I long for the snow sometimes. This, however, I could get used to.

As green and brown blurs past all around, I notice a fifty by fifty foot pool of blue. I drop toward a mossy knoll just short of the water imagining what fun it would have been to just land in the center of the pool. I'm not getting my clothes soaked again. The entire area is surrounded by jungle and a thirty-foot high waterfall plummets into the inviting pool. No sooner do I get my bearings, then I notice the Adon diving from a rock, having kept his maroon pants as swim wear. The rest of his outfit is casually laying on a nearby rock. I suppose I'm meant to do the same.

***

Gripping a rope swing above a small boulder, I fly out over the water and drop. The pool is refreshing, but it ruins the clean feeling gained from the shower. I suppose it doesn't matter in the bohemian lifestyle of this island. Allowing myself a bit of indulgence, I enjoy the moment and move to the waterfall allowing the cold liquid to spill over my scalp. Foley smiles, clearly content that he has impressed me with the undeniable paradise. He has. Now my questioning must continue, but with the most pressing concerns answered, I find myself less and less diligent in the investigation. I'm more and more seduced by the beauty and pleasure of the Island. Curiosity persists though, and I do want to have all the facts.

"Okay, Foley, you've got nowhere left to run."

"Ha ha," he says in a you-caught-me sort of way.

"Give me the history of the Island . . . in . . . uh . . . including your personal story."

"Right. Well, after World War II, Nazi troops, fearing prosecution for crimes against humanity, took their families and established their own Colony here on this Island. None of it lasted very long. Some left, and the rest died, but the secret remained. Of those who left, they were caught and the secret died with them. One ten year old boy, however, survived to tell the tale." His eyes widen to accentuate the mystery as he speaks. It's clear he's told the story many times, and has the drama down. "It was a family secret, and after living a full life, the boy, then a man of sixty years, told his son. That son helped in the plan of the Adonai."

While Foley explains the island's history, I tread the water and consider his words. It makes sense of the architecture, and the Chapel did have German text on the stained glass. The Adon's strange boots, glasses and vest may have been found in the Mansion. They match the period and nationality as well. "So," I ask, "this Colony was always a part of the plan?"

"No. This was intended to be the site of the original Colony for your father and the other scholars. After all, if you want to set up an unbelieving utopia, it's hard to get people on board with the idea of living in that *dread*ful tundra up north . . . er . . . no offense. But, you see, certain problems emerged."

"Problems?"

"Yes, despite that this strip of land was chosen by the Nazis and then chosen again by the Adonai because of its location far outside of shipping lanes, the fear persisted that it would be easily discovered. Also, as the vision of the Adonai grew, so did the desired size of The Colony." His face turns to disgust and he announces, "This island would have easily been big enough," in an offended tone.

Draping my arms spread eagle along one rocky edge of the water, I continue my interview. "But that doesn't explain how *you* got here."

"Ah," he adds with his head tilted back. "Five years after the Adonai established the Northern Colony, things were rolling along so well that ten families were chosen to relocate and populate this Island as the Southern Colony." He laughs and jokes, "Adonai franchising!" He shakes off the attempt at humor and continues, "I was fifteen years old. My family, along with the others, was chosen because there were three children. Ten families of five made for fifty original colonials here. More children were born as time went by, and The Colony was a success."

"So where are the parents?"

"Deportation is the best way to describe it. The Adonai moved them to an undisclosed location a couple of years ago. I imagine they've gone wherever your Northern community is now. The idea, as it was explained to me, was that this would become the first Colony to be run completely by a generation with no knowledge of God. As the oldest and most appropriate for the duty, I was made the sole Adonai of The Colony with instructions to make contact with Malory Lyn, regularly." I now recognize his voice from the strange phone under the map at the Administrative Lodge. "Upon my installation as an Adonai, they filled me in on the reason for all of this. They made the mistake of telling me about what they described as the myth of God."

"Okay," I say while nodding my head with squinted eyes.

"You haven't heard the best part yet. Stuff washes up on the beach from time to time, and on one occasion, a suitcase was found. In that suitcase were two, large family Bibles. One of them, you saw in the Chapel. I then had the word of God. I de-voured it," he reminisces with affection on his face. "Embracing its message, I proclaimed the truth to The Colony. What's more, I proclaimed the truth about the outside world. These Colonials do not believe in the Great Darkness anymore."

"That's incredible," I shout.

"Right. This means if a plane ever did fly overhead we wouldn't need to make up some illogical lie. What they do believe in is The Great Divide," he says with passion in his voice.

"Wait, what?"

"The Great Divide is the principle that our Colony should remain separate from the outside world. Think, mate, of all the pain, heartache, unbelief, war and destruction that rages across the ocean. Here, we are preserved from all of that. This Island was once a monument to, and home for, genocidal monsters. Now our Colony is like a flower that has blossomed in the midst of a battlefield. Before you ask, yes, I keep the Adon title and my two Apologia serve to keep order in the tradition of the Northern Colony. This is all really just to keep the Adonai happy and disinterested. For all they know, we are still living in the godless utopia they constructed. We let them believe this because they are our only real threat."

The Colony *is* paradise. I understand why Foley wants to preserve it. The only part of the story I take issue with is the insistence on what he's calling The Great Divide. Still, since I don't know any different, I'm assuming all of this is a blessing from God. It's certainly not the certain death I expected.

With this, Foley announces, "Class time is over," and splashes water in my face.

CHAPTER SEVEN

Brotherhood is a powerful thing. It is much more than crude biological similarity. When two people agree on something as powerful as patriotism, a humanitarian cause, or a worldview, a closeness takes hold that can be more inseparable than common ancestry. For those who share in the one true faith, scripture describes a deeper unity. They are part of one race, one priesthood, one holy nation – one body. It is an invisible Colony. It is a Colony that can never be destroyed, scattered or conquered because it has no walls, geographic location or borders. If The Colony of God is stamped out in one place, it springs up tenfold elsewhere. All colonies made by man will one day fail, but The Colony of God will never be defeated. In that Colony, two men are brothers before they ever meet. Once they do, the roots of brotherhood grow fast and deep. Such is the case with Foley and me.

Having become more confident with the zip lines, I chase the Adon through the forest only five feet behind him on the cable. We yell as the moonlight pierces the trees and the cool wind wisps past our ears. The lights of the Mansion's rear yard come into view and we drop in rapid succession. We both land and roll before posturing ourselves legs wide in fighting stances.

"Don't try it, Foley," I warn. "I'm an Apologia of the *Northern* Colony. Where *I* come from we don't lay around all day eating mangos."

"OOhh, I wouldn't dare, young Justin. You are the legendary prince of the Adonai." Relaxing his stance and laughing as he catches his breath, he finishes, "I'm sure I wouldn't stand a chance." Somehow I think he probably would, but I follow suit and we casually stride toward the Mansion as though we are conquering heroes returning from some nonexistent battle. The garden is striking at night. Mosquitos hover around the bright lampposts, wind causes a stir among the leaves of the trees, and Bailee waits dutifully with refreshments at the door. She is clearly of Asian descent, but her accent doesn't reveal it.

"Adon Foley and Apologia Justin, return from their adventure," she says with cheer. Her hair is down now and hangs straight and loose.

"Drop the formalities, dear Bailee," Foley says as we both retrieve glasses of freshly squeezed orange juice from the girl's ornate silver tray. "Justin, I'm going to retire for the evening. Bailee, here, will show you to your room. My house is your house." He turns to enter the Mansion and then stops, looks back and adds, "Listen, mate, . . . you were sent here for a reason. There are big things in store for us." With that, he vanishes into the structure.

***

The quarters I am provided are toward the back end of the house. It would have been the farthest room to the left from my original vantage point in the rear yard. Everything is aged, but rich. A bed with a decorative mosquito net is facing out from the wall on which the door is positioned. Another interior wall houses a large closet. Four large windows are on the other two walls as this is a corner room. Between the windows opposite the bed is a doorway that leads to an upper level porch. With the glass of juice in my hand I cross the room and exit onto the long balcony in a relaxed manner and Bailee follows.

"You like it here, Apologia Justin?" she asks as we gaze on the gardens. Only now do I really pay her any attention. When I first clawed my way out of the hole I was so obsessed with answers that I all but ignored her presence. She's stunning. It's weird, though, that she keeps referring to me that way. Even at the Northern Colony, no one ever referred to me with my Life Role before my name.

Biting my lips for a few seconds before nodding my head I look at her and answer, "It's growing on me, I have to say. I do like these accommodations a bit more than the ones I was given for the first part of my stay." She gives a tickled and squeaky chuckle as we both look back to the hole across the yard. I take a drink and ask, "Do you live at the Mansion, Bailee?"

"No, I live near the beach on a cliff above The Circle Island Café. I will be going back there soon." She's soft. She is the essence of femininity. Her delicate movements and careful words are unusually subtle compared to Hope, Courtney and Julie. Freckles fleck her cheeks and long lashes frame her gaze . . . what are you thinking, Justin. Hope would be horrified. "I work

here most of the day. I'm in the Veritas Life Role."
Veritas?

"I don't know that one, Bailee. What's the
Veritas Role?"

Giggling she replies, "You are Apologia – I am
Veritas. The Veritas role exists to support the true way.
It was instituted by Adon Foley as a way of clarifying
his teachings to The Colony."

"His teachings?"

"Yes. The Adon pours through the scriptures,"
she answers, motioning with her hands, "and discerns
the truth. Then he speaks it to The Colony at the Life
Circle Chapel. Then the Veritas serve food, drinks and
answer questions for the colonials. It is a great honor."

"So . . . what . . . does he let you hear his
message ahead of time?"

"That is why we Veritas spend our days here at
the Mansion. We practice our serving with him, and
listen to his teaching." She instantly seems shyly
embarrassed like a star-struck fan and finishes, "He's so
wise." Shaking off the composure, she beams at me and
adds, "but you are too. I just know it. You are the
liberator of the godless Colony. You will teach me
much . . . I can tell." Suddenly, all the admiration she
was pouring on Foley has spilled over onto me. My ego
is soaring.

"Well . . . I don't . . . I mean, Bailee, I . . ."

Raising her eyebrows she adds, "No, it's true. Adon Foley wants me to spend all my time with you. You are to teach me about the evils of the false Adonai, and I am to teach you about The Colony." As she finishes she takes my hand and briefly leans her head on my shoulder before backing to the doorway. "Apologia Justin, I will see you in the morning at Life Circle Assembly."

"Okay, Veritas Bailee," I respond with a playfully mocking tone. "Just drop the title and go with Justin."

"You got it . . . Justin." She says my name with a faux stern face and a teasingly low voice.

***

I wait a solid hour before I make my move. It feels wrong to sneak around without telling Foley, but I came here for a reason. I have no cause to doubt him, but I've been fooled by the Adonai before. I'll feel better about things if I can check this place out freely, without an escort. Slinking along the porch I approach the edge. With a grassy crunch my feet hit the ground and I creep back toward the jungle. This place is a network of zip lines. Locating the nearest one I attach the hook, now with familiarity, and begin the slide.

Landing on the first hill I can spy the spot, about sixty yards away, where Foley had to help me back up after my initial attempt at the exercise. I begin again on another cable and continue toward the beachfront majority of The Colony. This is a particularly long slide. Wait, what's happening? I see The Colony to the right and realize that I'm not heading in its direction. I'm heading into . . . a cave. Rock surrounds me and so does darkness. Fighting the urge to release the Hook-Slide, I grip more tightly. The rope slows and blindly I feel for the ground. Got it. Slowly removing the hook I crouch and begin to creep through the darkness. It's getting brighter.

Exiting the tunnel I realize I am in a reasonably large cavern that contains an underground cove. I am high above the room and a climbing rope hangs from the mouth of my entry tunnel to a surface next to the water. It is not well lit here and stalactites obscure my view. Gripping the rope I cautiously descend one hand after the other with my legs wrapped around it. When my feet reach the bottom I hunker next to a large rock and watch. The two Island Apologia are examining a . . . it's a boat. It's like a fishing boat or something. And there's someone else wearing a black robe and hood of some kind with lettering that matches the color of the green on the Island Apologia jackets. The small strangely clothed figure is reading something aloud and the Apologia dutifully stand listening. As she finishes they grab sledgehammers and . . . whoa! Okay, that'll do it. The vessel begins to sink as they continue their work.

Creeping to another nearby rock I get a better view of the room. Filling the cove behind the sinking boat are half sunken crafts of various sizes. When they finish their work, the two stand before the robed character and the three of them shout in unison, "The true way - the true way - The Great Divide - to stay we pray!" This is weird. Where did these boats come from? If they're not from here, where are the passengers? Wait . . . I can almost read the lettering on the strange figure's robe. "Hope to Seek" is written down the right sleeve just as "Hope to Give" is written down the sleeve of the standard Apologia uniform. On the left breast of the robe is a "V" that almost appears to be the exact inverse of the "A" on the Apologia jacket. She lowers the hood and I begin to catch a glimpse of her face. What! It's Bailee. This . . . this doesn't make sense. Turning in my crouched pose I place my back to the rock and slide into a sitting position to consider the scene I just witnessed.

Confident they've left, I stand and freely move about the cove. Unsure if it would do much to disguise my identity, I pull the neckerchief Bailee gave me up and over my nose so that the bottom portion of my face is concealed by the maroon fabric. Each boat is from a different place . . . no, a different country. How is this possible? As I crouch to dust away a portion of the lettering, I sense another presence and immediately stand looking around. Silence. Beginning to doubt my intuition, I start to look back at the vessel when a subtle movement catches my eye. There! Standing at the back of the cove, opposite my entry, is the image of darkness. The outfit is difficult to specify. A black, long-sleeved shirt blends into black pants and black gloves. From the stance, build and posture I'd guess it's a man. Long black hair down to the jawline spills over a dark face. What is that . . . face paint?

Locking eyes with me he begins a run. I run in the opposite direction toward the rope. This isn't good.

Ten seconds transports me to the lip of the entry tunnel and I clamber toward the exterior. He's on my trail. Thirty more seconds and I reach the opening as fresh jungle night air fills my lungs. Sprinting deeper into the woods with everything I've got, I feel as though I'm outpacing him. Racing through a narrow valley, to my right and left the earth slopes upward at a steep incline. If I attempt to scale either side I'm going to get caught. If I had to, I may be able to take him down, but I'd prefer to keep my anonymity. At this distance he wouldn't be able to confidently identify me. Glancing over my shoulder I see the persistent runner silently giving chase. He's fast.

The trail remains a valley but begins to slope upward at a gradual, but significant grade. My calves burn and I sweat profusely. He's gaining on me. I need a game changer. Perfect! After ascending what must have been a slow sixty-foot rise, I spot a zip line.

Latching on I push off and begin a much slower slide than I've become used to. The line doesn't slope downward in the typical dramatic way. I'm moving, but not very fast. Digging into the handle with all of my might I glance over my shoulder and see that the dark figure has stopped. He's working on the cable with some sort of tool. I feel reverberations in the line and suddenly I'm falling. *He cut it loose!* The trees below begin to rush up toward me before I wrap my hands around the Hook-Slide and the cable and swing hard against the grassy slope, the top of which would have been my original destination. The slope is steep. I don't have much time. Releasing the cable I slide into the jungle below. Before the trees mask the scene I notice my enemy climbing down the opposite slope into the other side of the wooded area. Dusting off my arms I begin to run to the right along the valley floor and slide beneath a fallen mossy log. Controlling my breathing consciously, I wait.

The repetitive crunching of grass draws closer as boots pound against the jungle floor. I'm still. My lungs ache as I long to fill them with life-giving oxygen, but I've got to mask my breathing. As the mysterious figure wanders out of the area, I roll onto my belly and stand. I've got a long sneaky hike back to the Mansion. Hopefully, no one has been alerted to my absence.

CHAPTER EIGHT

I awaken and cross the room toward the closet. Opening its large wooden doors I find that Bailee has had it stocked with two more outfits identical to the one I chose, as well as several more colorful options that she would clearly like me to consider. I don't. In the Northern Colony I didn't have many options. Almost everyday meant wearing my Apologia uniform with either a red or black shirt. On my day off I would choose among three other ensembles. Such was life at my Colony - old habits die-hard. I reach for the duplicate apparel and dress myself.

Knowing that I'm heading for the daily Life Circle Assembly feels oddly familiar. However, I will not be standing in a lazy posture considering my daily activities the way I did for years at the Northern Colony. I will be attentively scanning the crowd as I consider last night's activities. Perhaps the faceless dark figure will be there. His body language will give him away. No doubt, he'll look different, but one benefit of Angus Clancy's Apologia training at the Northern Colony is my education in investigative detective work.

Impulse nags me to simply explain to Foley what happened and listen as the jolly Adon explains things in a cool manner. Caution prevails, though, as I think of my options. If I reveal my nocturnal adventure

Foley will presume that I don't completely trust him. Maybe I don't. I feel a strong and immediate bond of friendship with him, but I've been burnt by the Adonai before. Second, the scene at the cove and the chase through the jungle was unsettling. It's entirely possible that there is an acceptable explanation for the sinking of the boats. I saw no crew. No one was harmed. They've made no secret of their strange commitment to this Great Divide. Further, while I was seen with Foley by many colonials at the beach yesterday, my jungle foe could be an unmentioned night watch Apologia who was unaware of my presence. That would explain the chase, but then . . . he tried to kill me on the zip line. At the very least he *could* have killed me. These concerns are enough to stir my caution. I will continue to trust Foley, but at arm's length. The same goes for Bailee.

***

Approaching what I now know to call the Life Circle Chapel, I find a relatively large crowd assembling. Bailee guides me through them and toward the front of the old church. There is electricity in the air. The Veritas girl motions for me to sit on the front pew and then ascends the platform taking her place among two other Veritas-clad young women. Three other Veritas sit on the far side of the stage and they are all wearing the black and green hooded robes I viewed in the cove. They are the same girls I saw working in the garden after emerging from the hole. Foley rests on a large wooden chair directly behind the lectern between them. My creepiness radar is blaring in my head. There is a great rabble in the Chapel as everyone waits, and I turn to get a view of the sanctuary behind me. The youthful crowd is made up of laughing boys, whispering girls, and a few young mothers holding infants. Framing the twenty-foot high ceiling are German words "GOTT MIT UNS." I don't know what it means. Just before the assembly time begins, two boys clamber into the window where the zip line starts and grab a seat, playfully punching each other in their arms. It all has a lost-boys-of-Neverland charm to it. Foley chuckles in amusement as he watches them. There is no sign of my enemy.

Suddenly everyone stands and the Veritas each raise both arms in a worshipful posture diagonally upward. This apparently signals the entire congregation in unison to chant, "The true way - the true way - The Great Divide - to stay we pray!" Startled, I spin. A boy on the second row giggles as does Bailee when I look back to the stage. The crowd all sit and I follow their lead. The Adon stands to address his Colony and the subtle whispery chatter ends.

He begins, "Our Colony is blessed to be beyond The Great Divide from the dark world of wickedness across the sea. Do you hear it Colony? Do you hear the breaking of waves on our beach?"

Several voices shout, "The true way!"

Another voice is heard saying, "The Great Divide!"

"Yes," Foley continues with somber passion, "Each time you hear the sound of breaking waves it is a reminder that we have been delivered from the land of pain, evil and destruction. We have also been delivered from the godless Adonai. *I am* your Adon, and *I* will teach you *the true way* to the *true* Adonai.

"The true way," another colonial shouts.

"Friends," the Adon says, "I want you to meet someone who has, in the space of one day, become like a brother to me." As he pauses his presentation Foley looks to me with a sympathetic smile. "Join me Apologia," he says as I begin to climb the stage. "This young warrior is Justin Lyn. He is the son of Malory Lyn of the Northern Colony!" Gasps and rabble arise from the crowd. "Never fear colonials. He is a liberator. It is by his hand that the Northern Colony has fallen. He is the prince of the Adonai, but he is the avenger of God. Justin Lyn is a hero. He joins our Colony as a living legend. He is now your brother too!" Cheers begin and the crowd starts to shout. Much of what Foley says about me is either exaggeration or requires further explanation. Nevertheless, I can tell this is not the time to clarify. I produce a confused grin and the Adon motions for me to return to my seat.

Once the chatter trails off he begins again proclaiming, "God has visited death and damnation on the godless Colony, my friends. Such is the way of God. He will not stand for injustice. He will not stand for mockery. When the wicked crowd, led by a man named Korah, rose up against Moses the text explains, 'And the earth opened her mouth, and swallowed them up together with Korah, when that company died, what time the fire devoured two hundred and fifty men: and they became . . . a sign.'" He walks about the stage looking on the crowd, examining their faces. As his speech ramps up to a climax, the crowd shouts their approval. The celebrated Adon demands, "*I* . . . am your leader. *I* . . . am your Moses! *I* know what is best for you! Follow my teaching! Follow the true way! OBSERVE THE GREAT DIVIDE!" This is too much. He's giving them the impression that he cannot be questioned. Even the Adonai at the Northern Colony weren't this domineering in their speeches. I've got to say something . . . but . . . wait, it's Bailee.

As Foley exits along the center aisle, Bailee raises both hands again and the crowd chants, "The true way, the true way, The Great Divide, to stay we pray!" Upon finishing this creedal response everyone begins to exit. I follow at the back of the group and Bailee locks arms with me and guides me out the door. This would *not* be a good time for Hope to arrive. Descending the stone staircase of the Life Circle Chapel, I see that the entire Colony is spreading out in six large circles. They hold hands and sit on the beach. Bailee escorts me to the nearest group and I sit alongside a skinny, bearded fellow with long blond hair and a Jamaican looking guy with dreadlocks. She leaves momentarily and then returns along with her five fellow Veritas girls. Each of them approaches a different group with a silver tray and a metallic goblet of sorts.

Bailee sits at our circle next to me and passes the drink around to each of us. Everyone takes a drink in turn. I'm not sure what's going on with these strange rituals, but Bailee's presence calms me. Maybe the best thing to do is just play along. I don't want to rock the boat until I'm back at the Mansion. After all, it could just be the way these Christians participate in the church tradition of communion. As it is my turn to drink from the community beverage, I hold it for five solid seconds looking it over before taking a sip. Bailee pats me gently on the back as I hand the vessel to her. It isn't until she places it back on the silver tray that I notice the color of the liquid. Blue! Moving my tongue around on the roof of my mouth I recognize the faint aftertaste. It's the same drink Yukimura gave me before this adventure began. Though it's a lighter color and more diluted in flavor, it is unmistakable. This is not good! I look around and run my fingers over my scalp as the other colonials squint at me with concern.

"It just helps you focus, Justin," Bailee assures with a kind smile. "You will learn to look forward to it." Expecting to topple over, I lean back on my hands. Suddenly I feel a tingle run over me from the top of my head to the tips of my toes. My head is swimming, but . . . wait. I'm clear. Everything is suddenly clear! The beach is fantastic. The subtle breeze is exquisite! Bailee is gorgeous! Wasn't I just about to make a scene over something? Yeah, Foley was talking crazy. I've got to say something, but . . . I don't know. Is it that big of a deal? Why bring everyone down when this place is so . . . happy?

"What did we learn about the breaking of waves today, colonials?" Bailee asks.

"That they separate us from the world," a younger girl says.

"No," Mr. dreadlocks interrupts. "The waves

are a blessing from God." I must be smiling like a jerk. I can't help it. Foley couldn't have been more clear.

"Sorry, guys. I know I'm new to this, but wasn't the point that because the waves separate us from the evil world that the sound of them kind of represents God's blessing of deliverance for us?" Why am I expounding on Foley's words. I have big problems with Foley's separatist ideas.

"Apologia Justin is right," Bailee says with determination. "And what happens if you speak against Adon Foley according to the message?"

"God will destroy you like he did the Northern Colony and like the man who spoke against Moses," a colonial dutifully answers.

The beard adds, "I think his name was Korah. Is that right?"

"That's right," Bailee confirms. "You all seem to be getting it. Have a good day and we'll learn more tomorrow. As Bailee's trademark smile stretches across her face, the group stands and begins to splinter off in different directions. Some head toward the fishing boats, some follow a path into the jungle and a few approach The Colony buildings that line the beach.

Considering the events, I feel confused. I know that Foley has just ripped a biblical story out of context and applied it to himself. I know that the idea that this Island's separation is a good thing is highly questionable. The whole ordeal seems downright cult-like, and the Adon was the stereotypical charismatic cult leader with a messiah complex. Yet, as these thoughts shoot through my mind I find myself not caring that much. I just want to have a good time. This place is great. Bailee is great. Foley's great. Zip lines are great. I'll worry about the rest later.

***

Jogging barefoot through the Mansion I feel the deep and fibrous rug beneath my feet. At the bottom of the stairs Bailee waits for me wearing a modest one-piece green bathing suit under a black sarong. We walk together out of the far side of the home and follow a wooded path away from the yard in the opposite direction from The Colony. She laces her fingers through mine and walks close beside me.

"Justin," she nervously asks, "do you like me?" For a half-second, my thoughts go to Hope, but then quickly evaporate.

"Uh . . . yeah. Is it that obvious? We didn't learn to mask our feelings very well at the Northern Colony." She's beaming.

"Good . . . I like you. I like you very much." She's adorable.

We come to a break in the forest and there is at least a thirty-five foot drop to the water below. It is a rocky alcove and narrow walls flank the water as it continues to the left and around a bend. In the water below are Foley and two other Veritas girls swimming and laughing.

"Don't be a sissy, prince Justin," Foley shouts. "Jump!"

"You can jump . . . or walk with me down the path," Bailee gently offers.

"Do the men ever take the path?"

Raising her eyebrows, she answers, "No."

Hearing this I jump. Under the water I hear a voice in my head say, "Be sober, be vigilant." What does that mean? No matter.

When I emerge I am next to Foley who is treading water. The Veritas girls are gently stepping across the rocks toward Bailee as she descends on a path that wraps around the water toward our location.

Foley congratulates me and boldly asks, "Are you having fun with Bailee, mate?"

"Yeah, she's pretty incredible."

"You know . . . the two of you would make a powerful couple in our Colony." My prepared reply is to insist that I have no intention of staying at The Colony, but why shouldn't I? Issues with Foley's preaching and the weird stuff I witnessed last night aside, I like it here. I'll need answers at some point, but I'm not writing anything off.

"She isn't . . . with . . . anyone?"

"Mate, she *wants* to be with you. We do have rules at the Southern Colony. We marry, commit to one other person and stay monogamous for life. The Veritas Life Role requires a lifetime of singleness and devotion to the true way, but I'd make an exception for Bailee. I've got big plans for you, Justin."

"What plans?"

"The world is getting smaller, Justin. In order to maintain The Great Divide I will have to leave at some point and ensure that the Adonai never again disturb this place. They believe I'm still loyal to them. I can make arrangements to meet with any remaining leaders and . . . convince them."

"Fat chance," I sarcastically remark.

"You let me deal with that. The important point is that I'll be gone, maybe for a long time. The Colony will need a new leader. It will need a new Adon."

"I've got no desire to go by that title."

"I get it, mate, but don't let that stop you from enjoying its benefits. You can make of this Colony whatever you like. However God leads you to rule will be no concern of mine." I stare at Bailee as she giggles with the Veritas. "Just think, Justin, the idea of The Colony wasn't the problem. What the Adonai got wrong was the deception and the purpose. They had the wrong worldview, but their organization was good."

He pauses to gauge my reaction. "I saw the look on your face, mate. You have issues with my leadership style." I begin to feign protest, but he starts again. "It's fine, Justin. You can do it your way. You and Bailee together. When I return, I will support you."

The thoughts are washed away when Bailee, followed by her two compatriots, splashes into the water dousing us. It's as if the world is in slow-motion and Bailee and I lock eyes. She winks. There is an obvious connection. It can't be denied. In this moment I don't want to leave. I don't care if the whole world dissolves. What we have is more than enough.

7

Be sober, be vigilant. I consider the words while I slide through the darkness. Even though I can recall every minute detail of my day, it is still a blur. It would be far too soft a statement to say I wasn't myself. Idiot! Why wasn't I thinking of my friends? Why wasn't I focused on the mission? I can't deny the affection developing for Bailee. Nor will I lie to myself about my bond of friendship with Foley. It grows stronger each day. In spite of that, Hope is out in that jungle and the thought of what she may be experiencing is too much. Courtney and Jack are out there too. Worst of all, a black clad nightmare is on the loose. What if he has already done away with them?

Rummaging through my clothing options at the Mansion, I discovered a solid black ski mask. I don't know that it's worth it, given that I stand out like a sore Northern Colony thumb here, but it gives me more confidence. With the low budget mask my emotions are hidden. The covering is like a shield. I've got to move past the central structures of the beachfront Colony and along the path that I know leads to the fields where they grow their limited assortment of vegetation. Hopefully no one notices.

I land running and maneuver through the overgrowth behind the buildings. Whoa! Halting next to a window and just short of being seen, a baby is crying and a mother is mothering. Ten seconds pass and the young woman leaves the room with the child in her arms. Time to move. Footsteps land softly beneath me as I exercise Apologia techniques to move stealthily on the balls of my feet. Midway through the tiny civilization I notice two couples sitting at a bonfire with heads lovingly on shoulders across from a single longhaired guitarist gently tabbing his acoustic instrument.

> *"Circle Island is heaven on earth,*
> *across the sea a world of black crows and dearth*
> *here the true way,*
> *the black crows can crow where they stay."*

The lyrics are soft and would be relaxing under other circumstance. It's momentarily mesmerizing. Keep moving, Justin. Everything about this Colony is intoxicating. Be sober, be vigilant.

The moonlight illuminates the grassy worn path that winds up a hill between The Colony and the Life Circle Chapel. Hugging the edge of the woods, I rush up the trail with my head down. Three minutes place me at a plateau and footfall field sized clearing complete with sections of rows. It begins to mist, but there are no solid drops of rain. I scan the area and see nothing. If Hope is here wouldn't she have signaled me by now? In the distance I can hear the muted tones of the musician's strings. The darkness, the mist and the music create a peaceful loneliness in the field. Thunder rumbles distantly on the sea. Then I see him. The black hair, midnight clothing and painted face are unmistakable. He's watching me from a crouched position at the back of the field not knowing I've located him. Slowly I walk and slowly I scan the area as though he is not there. Peripheral vision reveals that he is prowling along the tree line toward my location. Capitalizing on the situation I pace toward the back of the field stopping on occasion to look around. He moves when I move. Ten minutes have passed and I'm at the back of the field. He's twenty feet to my right in the bushes. It's time. With my right hand I grip the Hook-Slide to the left of my torso. In one swift motion I cast it through the air and into his skull.

Recovering against a trunk the figure rubs his head and glances toward me. He's too late. My foot is in his chest and he's against a tree, spread-eagle but standing. The stalker knows he needs to recover. Turning, he runs. I give chase. Launching around a boulder he vanishes. I make the turn, but he's nowhere in view. There! A sadly dilapidated old building resembling a schoolhouse is positioned nearby with German lettering above the door. He's got to be there. Rain begins to assault the jungle with violence. I make no attempt to hide my presence as I gingerly approach the front door. Broken glass and small pools of water cover the tile floor. A bulletin board hangs by one corner on the wall and derogatory caricatures of various ethnicities are seen on pages cornered with swastikas. The boldness of the twentieth century racism is shockingly eerie. Water drips breaking the silence. I see it almost too late.

A leathery boot flies off course as I deflect it with my right forearm and the assailant spins to regain his footing. I slap away two punches and dodge a knee before grabbing his head and thrusting it through the rotten wood of a classroom door. Somehow his movement is both complex and predictable. It's not that he's less than advanced, but that I know what he's planning before he does. How? "*Argh*," I howl as his gloved knuckles meet my jawline. Okay, maybe he isn't completely predictable. The successful punch apparently invigorates him enough to attempt a tackle that places us on the floor at the back of the room. Rolling onto my back with my right foot on his chest, I propel him with force past my body and flailing out a window. Glass shatters as though the old panels welcome the destruction. On my feet I hop through the opening and see *this* black crow is on the run again. The words of the song arrest my attention as I run. "The black crows can crow where they stay." Focus, Justin. Be sober, be vigilant.

He's on a zip line and is flying away. Without the hook I've got no choice. I don't think. I run . . . and jump. My arms are around his waist and we sail together for a moment before he releases. Under the water we wrestle for a moment before we reemerge. Shaking my head I recognize the area where Foley and I lounged and he explained the history of The Colony. We continue our hand to hand in the water. Gripping each other's clothing, we are under the waterfall. Wait, what! No wonder his fighting style was familiar.

Tossing him against a rock I shout, "Jack?" in a questioning tone while emitting a surprised chuckle. I quickly remove the ski mask.

"Justin," He responds with the face paint running down in black streaks.

***

Inside the Chapel, Jack sits on the steps of the stage while I pace the width of the room and the storm rages outside. "So," I explain, "that's why I was searching the Island. I was looking for the three of you."

"Justin, I can't tell you how great it is to see you again, man. I never thought I would. Did it work? Did you see the message I left at the Northern Colony Chapel?"

"I saw it," I say with an emotional grin, "and I found you."

"I was terrified. We were thrown into that dungeon. The darkness was thick. Later I found out we had been down there for a week," Jack explains.

"A week? What did you eat and drink?"

"They lowered fish and we drank the Ocean's Wave, although, Courtney wouldn't take it. She thought it might be poison or something, but what would be the point of that?"

"Ocean's Wave?"

"Yeah, you know, the blue stuff from Life Circle Assembly here." Gears begin to turn in my brain as I consider his words. I'd give anything for an Ocean's Wave right now. It's like an intense craving. "They had to leave us there to make sure we weren't with the Adonai. We both flat near went crazy."

"Yeah, especially with that dark scribble everywhere," I remind him. "What was it . . . I shall be the blade that strikes from the darkness?"

His face looks solemn and he finishes, "He will raise me up to smite the false Adonai." It looks like the weird text made a different impact on Jack. "Justin, once you've been down there for a week, the quotes begin to make sense. They . . . change you." There is a long pause as my fellow Apologia stares in thought at the nothingness toward the back of the sanctuary. Shaking it off, he concludes, "It was all worth it, though, when we were pulled up in the Mansion yard."

"Jack, I have to tell you, I'd give anything sometimes if we could just be back home at the Northern Colony. I mean, I couldn't handle the murderers and liars once I knew about them, but the ignorance had a certain bliss didn't it? Wouldn't you give anything sometimes to just sit at the Circle of Life Café after Apologia patrols drink tea and joke – just you, me, Courtney and even Brent?" For a moment, I see his old self coming out.

"Yeah, I would, you frostbitten jerk," he playfully answers. "If you hadn't taken us on this frostbitten adventure, none of this frostbitten mess would have ever happened." We both spare a moment to laugh.

"Okay, buddy, I've told you my experience at The Colony so far. Is Foley lying? Can I trust him?"

With his left index finger he drapes his hair over his ear and out of his way. After thinking through my story he exhales through puckered lips and says, "Foley told you the truth. They are believers. He is duping the Adonai in order to keep them at bay. Courtney and I were sent to the other side of the Island, but it wasn't to avoid being seen by Yukimura. We were sent to scout out another beach."

"Okay, are the colonials planning a move or an expansion?"

"No, there is something else. There is another group there. They are faithful to the Adonai, and hostile to Foley. They believe in the original mission of the Colonies." I slowly sit on a pew facing my friend in awe of the revelation. "Foley wanted information on them. Obviously, they are a massive threat to Foley's vision."

"Another group . . . It makes sense, but I don't get why you would be running around in the woods at night. Why haven't I seen you during the day, and where's Courtney?" He looks at the floor with agony in his eyes.

"They took her, Justin," he whimpers. "We were discovered. A fight ensued. We ran. She was behind me and we were running through the jungle toward a zip line. I jumped, she was caught and I slid helplessly away into the darkness. The last thing I remember hearing was her screams."

"Look, let's tell Foley," I demand as I stand. "We can go after her right now!"

He stands too and calmly explains, "We can't. The reason I've been staying hidden is because you're right. Foley *would* mount an attack. He'd take the two of us, his own Apologia guys, a few capable colonials and head off after them. The other group would kill Courtney, or . . . at least they might. I'm not willing to risk it. I'm here now because I saw an outsider's boat near shore. Now I know it was actually Yukimura, Louis, Hope and you. You can imagine, though, that I thought the Adonai had sent a team here. I guess I thought they might have figured out the truth about Foley and were here to kill him. I thought they might exterminate everyone. The last two nights I thought you were from that team."

"Yeah, you could have killed me last night, Jack. What was that about?" I give him a harmless shove.

"You need to know, Justin, that the past several months has changed me. My belief has grown . . . . but so has my anger against the Adonai. I'm willing to go further, be more reckless, I'm willing to . . . to . . ." It's clear he doesn't want to say it, whatever *it* is. He doesn't get to finish. Lighting strikes powerfully outside and we both rush to the window. On the beach I see that a few colonials are heading this way. It makes sense. This is probably the best storm shelter they've got in the lower section of The Colony.

"Jack, we need to go, they'll be . . ." turning, I see that I am alone. My fellow Apologia disappeared through the window. Rushing to that side of the sanctuary I peer out at trees swaying and waves of intense rain billowing down. I barely make out the image of the black crow sliding into the obscurity of the jungle.

I still haven't found Hope. Now I'm terrified for Courtney. Tomorrow morning I'll talk to Foley. I'll explain Jack's concerns about an obvious intrusion of the other group's camp. It's time to find out for myself if I can trust the young Adon or not.

CHAPTER TEN

Desire is a powerful force. It can lead to obsession. Obsession can lead to addiction, lust and abuse. Desire in and of itself is not an evil. It is a part of man's design. Just as it can lead to wickedness, it can likewise provoke ambition, devotion, obedience and loyalty. Some have adopted the falsehood that desire must lead to suffering. This has led some religions to prescribe the removal of all desire. According to them, one must transcend desire and reach a state of ultimate contentment. In that state suffering ends. Foolishness! How can one desire to remove all desire? If such a state were reached, how could one desire to stay in the absence of desire? It's all self-refuting. No. Desire is not wrong. It can, however, lead to that which is wrong. At this moment I am filled with desire.

I awake in my quarters at the Mansion thinking of Hope. My desire is to be with her. I also long to see Courtney safely at Jack's side. These desires are good. These desires are pure. Suddenly another desire, of another type creeps organically into my field of vision. A tumbler is resting on the nightstand containing the bluish fluid I now know is called Ocean's Wave. Time seems to slow down. Someone, likely Bailee, has left it here for me. I stare at it for thirty seconds allowing the temptation to dig talons into my will. No. I wrap myself in a bathrobe and slide to the shower room.

Steam fills the air and I inhale deeply. Leaning with my right hand against the yellow tile I begin to rationalize. The Ocean's Wave is simply a calming agent. It could be useful for clarity. Jack's been here longer than I have and he didn't warn against drinking it. After all, I've been filled with anxiety and confusion without it. When I had tasted the substance before, everything made sense. No! Be sober, be vigilant. Be sober, be vigilant. Desire is a powerful force, indeed.

Drying off, my thoughts wander to Bailee. As much as I want Hope at my side, I indulge the possibility of a romantic future with the Veritas girl. I struggle to recapture the fleeting thoughts I should not be having. "God please help me to stay strong," I whisper aloud. She's entrancing. Again, I wrap myself in the terrycloth and slip back into my room. The Ocean's Wave has a presence in the room, like Bailee herself were here smiling in that alluring way. I've got to get dressed and leave . . . fast.

With my typical ensemble I confidently stride out of the room and five paces down the hall toward the staircase before I halt. Standing in the hallway I grind my teeth and make fists of my hands. It's like I'm in a fog of confusion. I've felt this before, with other vices. It's like there is a metaphysical chain drawing me back into the room. The glass is in my grip. My shoulders shrug and I drink . . . every . . . last . . . drop.

I turn to see myself in a full-length mirror across the room. I know what I've done. The desire won. I let it win. It was a choice for which I instantly feel remorseful. Such is the way of sin. There are always influences, but there is always a free choice. Falling to my knees I pray, "Father, please. Forgive me. I don't know what I was thinking." Inside I know it's too late. The sin will be forgiven, but the consequences will probably remain.

For a moment I think I've gotten a reprieve. Has God supernaturally prevented the Ocean's Wave from overtaking me and dragging me into its undertow? No, I feel it seeping in. It's working its way through my veins. I turn to leave. This was the battle. I've lost.

Halfway down the hall my sadness dissipates. I don't know why I get so bent out of shape over stuff like this. Life shouldn't be so serious. It's too short. Chill out, Justin. It's no big deal. I'm not even sure this is the drink talking. I was just being dramatic.

***

I'm down the stairs in no time and Bailee is nowhere in sight. It's early. Perhaps she's at the Life Circle Assembly getting things ready. At first I am let down, then curiosity captivates me. I should explore the Mansion. Beginning down the hall toward the wing of the house opposite my little apartment, I notice portraits lining the walls. Each of the Northern Colony Adonai are pictured along with a few others I don't know. Doherty, Walker, Parson, Yukimura, Clancy, Lyn - even Wynfelt is included. A large room opens to the left through double doors. It is a library of German titles. It looks as though Foley has devoted a special place of prominence to the theological works. I knew he was a good guy. Why would someone be so interested in Christian theology if they weren't genuinely Christian? Carved into a second doorway are the strange words from the Chapel again: "GOTT MIT UNS."

I wonder what it means until another presence speaks from behind me. "God with us." It's Foley. I turn and tilt my head up with my mouth open indicating my confused attempt to understand. "That's what it means. Gott mit uns . . . God with us. They were monsters, but they understood Christian theology."

"My understanding is that they were more interested in Germanic occultism and world domination than true faith."

"You're not wrong," Foley says as he pulls a strip of leather from a display case. "See this? Gott mit uns. It was on the belts the officers wore. They thought they were doing the Lord's work."

"But," I add, "they did not represent true Christianity. They were using it to manipulate order. In fact, their thinking relied on existential atheistic beliefs."

"Young prince, you're right. I would never defend the Nazis. That said, like you've heard me say about the Adonai, it wasn't their structure or firm grip that was wrong. It was the underlying philosophical beliefs." Okay, he *says* he's not defending the Nazis, but his words sound too close to it for my liking. On any other day, I'd have the zeal for a debate, but as it stands, I'm just glad to see my friend. Clearly he feels the same as he finishes, "Listen to us, discussing the ethical implications of leadership strategies among long-dead ideologues. Talk about boring. I've got something much more interesting to discuss." His speech intensifies as he moves across the room. "Check this out, mate." Apparently Nazis loved secret passages.

The bookshelf slides to the left and an old iron ladder is visible disappearing into a stone passage in the floor. I feel a delighted smile stretch across my face. "Oh, frostbite! That's awesome!"

"You haven't seen the best part, my friend." He's as giddy as I am, seeing it through my eyes.

Sliding down the ladder I look to my right and see that I am in a stone passage with piping lining the corners of the ceiling. My first inclination is that the old passage merely serves the purpose of plumbing work. That wouldn't make sense, however, of the secret entrance. We follow the long passageway and for a moment I think of asking him about the opposing islanders Jack mentioned. The impulse fades when I hear a ripping sound ahead of us in the tunnel. Foley slaps my bicep and shouts, "C'mon!"

The tunnel ends and we are on a platform above a circular room of the same greyish smooth stone. Ten feet below us, on the floor of the room are the Veritas girls working next to a stockpile of large crates. Each crate bears the Nazi swastika. Along the walls are two-dozen aged black and white photographs in simple wooden frames. I don't take time to look at them. I'm fixated, instead, on the contents of the crates.

The Veritas use small knives to extract tiny amounts of baby blue powder and place it on their ornate silver trays.

"Foley, what's . . . what's happening, pal?" My eyes are focused on my two obsessions at the same time. Bailee looks up at me with a flirtatious wink as she separates the powder with some sort of measuring device.

Whispering, he confirms, "It's exactly what you think it is, mate."

Overhearing our conversation, Bailee smiles and says, "Ocean's Wave."

Desire is, indeed, a powerful thing. Desire is not evil. Yet, somehow in my haze I know . . . the battle is lost. Desire has become lust.

CHAPTER ELEVEN

The Veritas leave the room the same way we came in and Foley begins to explain. "Can I trust you, young prince?" Expressionless, I stare at him for a moment and then scan the scene considering the whole thing. "This will stretch you, Justin, but trust me when I say that your whole world is about to change." Another wave of apathy shoots through my veins and it's as if I can feel the fizzing of a chemical reaction in my brain.

"Trust me, Foley, I'm getting used to world changing revelations."

He smiles wide and says, "Get ready!" The Adon places both hands on a section of the stone wall and pushes forcefully. Slowly a six by three foot portion of the stone sinks into the surface enough for passage. Inside is a shallow room with a track, a cart of some sort and a cramped hole into which the rails lead. The hole around the track is small enough that one would have to lay flat on the cart in order to roll through. On the alternate side of the rails is what appears to be a pulley system complete with a lever.

In a low and somber voice, Foley says, "You're up, mate. Take this." An old-timey lighter lands in my palm. Is he crazy? I feel like I would normally protest, but today I don't. Maybe it's the Ocean's Wave. Who cares? Lying on the cart I rest my head on the wood and flatten my body as much as possible while holding onto the edges. Foley begins, "One . . . two . . . three . . ." (CACHUNK). The cart begins to slide as dust puffs into the stuffy air.

It's pitch black and the speed is surprising. Wind rushes past my face and I don't dare move for fear that some jagged rock might crack me in the head. As quickly as the ride began it slows to a finish. I'm no longer in the tunnel. I'm in a larger space. Crawling off the apparatus I stand and thumb the lighter. The room materializes around me.

It's plush. The rug is deep and red, like the long runners in the Mansion. A small mahogany bed is present, but is speckled with mold. Its size was clearly necessitated by the width and height of the entrance tunnel. A miniature cabinet stocked with books sits in the corner and a pipe sticks out diagonally upward from the wall. That's how the guest is to relieve himself I suppose. In the ceiling is another pipe, clearly meant to introduce outside air. The room is small. It's only about ten by five feet and the ceiling is low enough that my head nearly touches the stone. Rotating with the outstretched lighter, a horrifying sight comes into view. In a chair at the back of the room are the remains of the room's former inhabitant. A skeleton is sitting with its skull leaning against the wall. What's left of nondescript clothing decays on the bones. Only a buckle with an embedded metal swastika remains completely intact.

The purpose of the small underground cavity is obvious. This was a secret bunker meant to allow its guest to remain undiscovered by invaders and safe from bombings. Whoever this was must have been extremely important. Could it be . . .? No. It's impossible. Without moving, I attempt to appreciate the possibility. With a deep stale breath I ignore the thoughts and look to the cabinet.

The assortment is bizarre. A Bible, a couple of atheist works, and a few Germanic occult texts. Some of them are in English. Others are in German. I spend a little time examining them out of curiosity before noticing an open journal on top of the small cupboard. Respectfully opening the leather cover I see that there is only one entry. It is thankfully written in English.

A Prophecy
Here I will die, far from the enemy. One day two saviors will come to this spot of land and produce a race of perfection. The first will purge the enclave of its deceptive rulers. Then the young prince will join him and vanquish the Unbelieving Tribe. Together the two saviors will birth a paradise safe from the world across a great divide.
Gott Mit Uns!

Without moving my head my eyes rotate upward above the cabinet. Whoever died here was a painter. Blowing away the dust, I see two figures. One with long blonde hair and glasses. Next to him is a black clad figure with a shaved head and maroon scarf. They each have their hand on levers of some kind. I stumble backward and fall sitting onto the bed as the room seems to spin. It's Foley . . . and . . . it's me.

***

Safely back from the belly of the Island I roll off of the cart and onto my feet. Walking through the secret door and into the chamber with the concentrated Ocean's Wave powder, I find the prophetic Adon looking over the black and white framed photos on the wall. Though his back is turned to me he is aware of my return as he speaks.

"It was all waiting, young prince. It was waiting for us." Still confused, I cross the expanse of the room and stand at his side. Perhaps I was always meant to be at Foley's right hand. Joining his gaze at the wall, only now do I pay the images attention. Each photograph pictures a group of Nazi refugees. I recognize the image of the beachfront buildings behind them. They still stand today. They appear to be annual shots taken to document their Colony's existence. Scanning the wall the subjects look older in each frame. Suddenly, a newer image appears and it is in muted colors. It's the current Colony dressed in more modern clothing. They picked up where the Nazis left off. Looking to me, the Adon drops the somber atmosphere and projects sheer enthusiasm. "Us, Justin! We are the saviors from the prophecy!"

"Hold up, Foley," I say with closed eyes and an unpreventable smile. "How is all of this possible?" Holding up my hands in a let's-figure-this-out sort of way, I continue, "Even if that's us in the picture . . . and . . . even if the prophecy is somehow true, how does all of this square with the Christian faith? I get free from the domination of the Adonai and you want me to trust Nazi prophecies?"

"Hey, I know how it sounds, but I think there's a bit of truth in all of this. The Nazi prophecy *has* to be right. We are the proof, I mean, there's a picture of us . . . in what we're wearing right now. We both already accept Christianity. What I'm doing at this Colony is taking the best of both of these worlds and bringing them together. Even monstrous villains can get a few things right." He briskly removes his glasses and grips my shoulders before demanding, "*We* are the chosen ones!"

We stand in the subterranean fortress and I run my fingers through my very short hair. The temptation to just take it all on board and go with it is strong. I can't deny what I saw. The feeling that I was meant for something great in God's plan has been lingering in my mind since the fall of the Northern Colony. "Do you think . . . I mean . . . Foley . . . do you really believe this?"

He pours a glass of the Ocean's Wave and hands it to me assuring, "Mate, it's undeniable." I take it and make my decision. Drinking the fluid I decide to trust my new friend. For a brief moment I hesitate as thoughts of Hope, Jack and Courtney scream for my attention, but the Wave crashes and the worries drown.

***

Back in the Mansion Library, Foley closes the double doors to the hallway and we recline on oversized lavish chairs opposite from one another. I ask one nagging question that even the blue addiction doesn't wash away. "What's up with the Ocean's Wave? Why are we drinking decades old Nazi chemicals? I don't get it."

"Simple," he answers with a shrug. "The Ocean's Wave is a decontaminant that keeps the body clean from infection. If you haven't noticed, our crops and drinking water are not processed. We have no filtration system and sickness can mean death. Our forbearers knew this too. It also contains a number of vitamins and minerals that we need."

"Maybe it's just me, but if I'm honest, it seems pretty addictive . . . and . . . this is gonna sound crazy, but I think it makes me a little too relaxed. Do you know what I mean? Like, I don't worry so much about things. I'm talking about things I *should* be worried about."

"Calm down, mate. You're not crazy. It *is* addictive, but that's because your body is addicted to the vitamins and minerals it needs. You don't worry as much because malnutrition brings on stress. Ocean's Wave solves that problem." I take another sip and roll the thoughts around in my head. It does make sense. Foley's answers usually do. It's easy enough to see why The Colony trusts him so much.

"Hmm. You know, Foley, I think you've finally won me over." I want to bring up Jack and the opposing group of islanders that has kidnapped Courtney, but as if reading my thoughts, *he* makes the move.

"Only now?" he asks in a faux offended tone. "Honestly, Justin, there is one item I feel a bit ashamed about. I don't quite know how you'll feel when I tell you, but I . . . I may have stretched the truth a bit about your friends. What I told you about the redhead is true. I haven't got a clue where she is, but she can't have gotten far. Jack and Courtney, however, ran an errand for me. More like reconnaissance, I suppose. You see, mate, there exists a ragtag group of dissenters on this chunk of heaven."

"You mean, like, a second Colony?" I ask while keeping up the routine. If he finds out I saw Jack and didn't tell him, he may not trust me. If he learns that Courtney was taken, Jack's fears may come to pass.

"That's right. We don't exactly see eye to eye. They are Adonai loyalists. Jack and Courtney have not returned. I expected them to be here by now. Their absence is disconcerting." He's being as open as I could have ever hoped for. "Justin, I believe the other group is the 'Unbelieving Tribe' from the prophecy. If that's right, then you are meant to 'vanquish' them, whatever that means."

"I'm not gonna kill anyone."

"Oh no, no, no, no, no. Of course not, don't be daft."

"I guess 'vanquish' could just mean sending them away or something."

He lights up, "Yes, or it might even mean

reaching them with the message of the truth and vanquishing their old ways. Whatever it means, I think you and I have enough trust in each other for some collaboration."

"What do you mean?"

"Justin, it's time for you to spread your wings as the young prince you are prophesied to be. During Life Circle Assembly you stay here and gather equipment. You've been held back too long. Go and get your friends. Go to the Unbelieving Tribe."

CHAPTER TWELVE

Clasping a utility belt to my waist, I slip the Hook-Slide into a leather loop and attach a small pouch full of the Ocean's Wave powder. If Foley is telling the truth about the substance, I'll need it to keep healthy – at least, that's what I'm telling myself. My hosts left me a black machete that fits nicely under the belt. Another small pouch holds a lighter and a folded up hand-drawn map of the Island. It's bigger than I thought. While the beachfront I'm familiar with looks out toward a large cove surrounded by increasingly bear rock that almost meets in a circle around the water, the jungle extends in the other direction for several miles – five, if the map is correct. I could traverse the distance in an hour if it were not for the thick foliage. However, the hike will last for the better part of the day considering the elevation change and the overgrowth.

Before leaving my quarters I notice a handwritten letter resting on the nightstand. It's from Bailee. Suddenly, I have a flood of excitement as a fourteen year old would at the sight of a note from his crush.

My prince,
I know of your journey and I trust you to come back to me. A
girl should not be so forward, but I think you feel the same. God
wants this for us. I have only known you a short time, but I
think of you throughout my day. We should be together. You are

*my match. I don't know what you want, but I want my future
with you. Please come home to me safe!
Your princess, Bailee*

My breathing increases as I consider her words. Things move much faster here than at the Northern Colony. How can I ignore my feelings for Hope? We've overcome the world together. Still, Bailee is special. I can imagine the future that is already beginning to take shape. It would be nice, though, if the pace could slow a bit. I don't know exactly what's going on in my head lately, and I need to think things through.

***

Launching out the back of the Mansion I race to the rear wall of the yard. An iron gate swings open in the stone barrier and I'm suddenly in another world, almost untouched by the hands of men. In the distance, maybe two miles away, a peak is visible. According to the map, it represents the middle of the Island. To get there, I'll need to cross one gaping river and five zip lines. It's time. I flick the claw from the Hook-Slide and begin my descent. The whole Island is a network of these cables. I suppose that's what happens when teenagers run the show.

For the first time in three days I actually feel free. I'm not hiding from anyone. It's not as though I have to be back to the Mansion before somebody notices. There is a healthy fear of the Unbelieving Tribe, but aside from that I actually think this should be fun. I land running and slow to a jog. "Pace yourself,

Justin," I remind myself out loud. Holstering the Hook-Slide and retrieving the machete, I begin to hack away at the world before me as I steadily progress. A sweat quickly covers my skin. Maybe this won't be as fun as I imagined.

Barely a quarter of a mile from the Mansion, I sense a presence. Looking over my shoulder I see nothing, I grip the machete more tightly and squint my eyes before turning back to my work. Five more paces and I hear footsteps behind me. Once I'm confident the tracker is near, I spin with the blade high. Nothing. Ten solid seconds of observation passes before I resume the labor, but when I continue it is with ever increasing suspicion. Then I hear it.

"Hee, hee, ho, ho," a high-pitched voice emits. It sounds a bit raspy and . . . maybe male. "Ho, ho, hee, hee!" There it is again, now in front of me in the tangled jungle. My eyes cast back and forth until I rush headlong into the overgrowth with no concern for the discomfort resulting from the uncut foliage. "Ha, ha, haaaa," The laughing man vocalizes again. I'm annoyed by the jovial unseen stalker. Finally, I rip through the wall of vines and palms into a . . . clearing.

"*Ahhh*," I holler. Only it wasn't just a clearing. It was a trap. I now dangle by one foot above the very small clearing and my machete is on the ground, one foot out of reach. In this humiliating circumstance, the source of my irritation is revealed. As if he is a natural part of the jungle, the oldest man I've ever seen sits with a toothy grin on a nearby rock. His hair reaches to his shoulders, his beard extends to his belly and his modest brown robe stretches to his shins. He is barefoot and holds a cane. Yet, his most striking feature is his stature. The character can be no more than five feet tall, maybe a little less. "Hey, who are you? What are you doing? Let me down from here!"

My captor rhymes, "The *foot* is in the rope – the rope is in the *tree* – the tree has caught the *dope* and the dope he shouts at *me*!" He laughs as he finishes. His accent is German.

"Yeah, yeah, very funny. Can you get me down from here now? You've had your fun!"

His high voice and childlike way would likely be charming under other circumstances. The old man responds, "Not yet. Hee hee! Dope hasn't met me yet."

"C'mon . . . sir. I . . ." he cuts me off before I can finish.

"My name Aldo," he says with somewhat broken English.

"Okay, Aldo," I respond with sarcasm. "Why are you following me? Are you from The Colony?"

"Ha ha, ho, ho," he laughs before abruptly straightening his face to a grim expression and saying, "No." He then continues as if he tickled himself with the answer and laughs again. Finally, he grows calm enough to say, "I came first. My home before it become their home." He smiles revealing teeth that need work. As if he knows what I'm thinking, he finishes, "I am old. Dope old one day too."

"Yeah, I hope so, but I *won't* be if you don't get me down."

"The dope need *advice* – but first must be *nice*!" Now, frustrated doesn't capture it. I'm mad. Unfortunately, an angry stare is all I can produce.

"Okay, if it'll get me out of this tree, what's the advice?"

"Dope is angry with Aldo, but glad with Colony. This foolish. Take Aldo's advice. Tell no one we meet. If dope tell, dope no see Aldo again."

"Suits me just fine."

He smiles and replies, "Dope need see Aldo again. *Mockers resent correction, so they avoid Aldo.* Aldo only come out to see man open to change mind. Man not open to change mind, Aldo stay hidden." Slipping his cane through a loop on the handle of the machete, my new friend raises the blade to my hand. I snatch it and begin to cut. The funny little man disappears into the bushes chanting, "The foot is in the *rope* – the rope is in the *tree* – the tree has caught the *dope* and the dope he shouts at *me*! Hee, hee, hee, ho, ho." I hit the dirt and rush in his direction, but Aldo is gone. I can't focus on him anymore. I have a mission.

***

It was about ten o'clock when I left the

Mansion and an hour seems to have passed. I drop from another zip line and approach the sound of rushing water. The river! I jog a bit in anticipation and the jungle releases me. There it is, wider than I expected. I shake off the thoughts of Aldo, but feel compelled to take his unwanted advice. I won't mention him. I don't want to ruin his solitude. He's harmless. For now, I'm on a mission that involves somehow getting across this river. It must be fifty yards to the other side. Above me I notice a cable attached twenty feet up in a tree, but it is not at an angle. Sliding will be difficult. Worse, in the tree I will not be able to get the necessary running start to sail all the way across. No matter. I have no other options. Time to climb.

Standing on a branch next to the cable I see that the tree has grown around the man-made line. Rust covers the metal fibers. Attaching the Hook-Slide, I lean my back against the tree and prepare to kick away. Now! I take two short steps on the branch and launch. At first it seems to be working well, then despair overcomes me as I begin to slow. I'm hanging like an amateur halfway across. The water rages beneath me. Reaching up, I grip the line with my right hand and struggle to fit the Hook-Slide back into my utility belt. With both fists squeezing the cable, I rotate and slowly replace my hands so that I'm facing the direction from which I came. With what strength I have I raise my legs and wrap them around the cord and begin to crawl. "*Arrgh*," I yell. The metal is blazing hot. I can't hold it. For seconds at a time, I move a few feet and then hang by my legs for a rest. I'm two-thirds across and I can go no more. Hanging upside down with my eyes closed I hear a familiar voice.

"Weird scarf, hero!" Startled, I open my eyes and see the unbelievable girl I fell in love with. Only, she's upside down from my perspective.

"Hope," I holler with desperate joy. She smiles with an expression that returns the affection.

"Put the scarf under your grip, you big, gorgeous dummy."

"What," I ask in a confused daze.

With eyes wide she says, "The cable is hot right?"

"Yeah."

"So take off that ridiculous scarf, wrap it around the cable and pull yourself into my arms."

"Oh . . . Yeah . . . That makes sense." She shakes her head and rolls her eyes in disbelief as her arms are out in an exaggerated shrug.

Taking her advice, I begin to climb again. As I traverse the distance I reflect on her appearance. Her hair is in a billowing ponytail. She's still wearing the black tank top she had when I last saw her in Rio. Her jeans are rolled up to just below the knee and there are distressed holes emerging in various areas of the denim. Her shoes are flat canvas and colored cream. Insect bites are visible on her arms and legs.

Dropping to the earth, I embrace Hope. Her playful banter crumbles. Sobbing into my shoulder she whimpers, "I thought we'd never see each other again. Where have you been? Where'd you get these clothes? Where did you get this girly scarf? Never mind. I don't care. I'm just glad you're here now." Her words trail off as she wipes away tears.

"Hope," I say running my fingers through her hair, "It's crazy. I've gone out each night looking for you . . . Jack, Courtney . . . but mostly you." Torrents of emotion spring forth from both of us, and it feels good. Stepping back, I hold both her hands as I face her. "There's a lot to say, but this," I insist, adorning the fabric around my neck, "is a neckerchief . . . not a scarf." We both begin to giggle. The giggle becomes a chuckle, then we laugh loudly.

***

Following Hope along the river's edge, I explain the events of the last few days, stopping occasionally to answer questions or clarify important points. I'm beginning to stress about the dynamic that will exist when she meets Bailee for the first time. How am I going to explain this? Sweeping the thoughts under the rug of procrastination, I just keep telling the story, making sure to sidestep my infatuation. "So," I finish, "that's why you found me dangling from a wire."

Shaking her head as she stares at the ground she worries, "Justin, I'm glad you're safe, but I'd almost prefer it if they had been like the Adonai from the Northern Colony."

"What are you saying?" I ask, taking shocked offense. "They're believers! We've been delivered from certain death!"

"It just sounds like a . . . like . . ."

"Like a what," I say, cutting her off.

"Well, like a cult!"

"Look, I know how it sounds," I passionately admit, "but it's not what you think." She stops walking and looks at me nodding sarcastically, her tone more and more aggressive.

"Oh really? Nazi prophecies, robed figures, a charismatic leader who thinks he's a savior – no that doesn't sound creepy at all."

I begin to respond when a rustling begins in the trees and Hope loudly shushes me. Tilting my head to indicate we should move along, we hunker and rush a good thirty feet up the river before ducking into the tree line. We sit in the bushes for a few minutes before it seems safe.

Picking up our conversation, I teasingly whisper, "So enough about me, how've you been?"

Eyeballing me dryly with a look that could freeze lava, she answers, "Come on, Mr. Chosen One, I'll show you."

CHAPTER THIRTEEN

The tree is massive. It looks like something out of a storybook. High above the riverbank an old sail boat sits positioned in the midst of multiple thick branches. It's a good forty feet long and has clearly been embedded in the giant wooden nest for decades. The tree is close enough to the deep river to imply that a flood carried the long-forgotten vessel along the water to its current resting place. Thick fuzzy vines wrap around the timber's trunk and form an unlikely ladder stretching upward to the awkward tree house.

"Time to climb, hero!" Hope grips the organic webbing with familiarity and starts to rise. I follow. It's no surprise she's found a way to live in the wilderness. A survivalist lifestyle is all she's ever known.

"You know, sometimes . . . just sometimes . . . I think the Adonai were right. You are crazy!" A chunk of bark hits me square in the forehead. Yep, she meant to do that.

As we continue to climb she asks, "What's the deal with the rubber handlebar thing?"

"They call it a Hook-Slide."

"What?"

"You know, for the zip lines all over the place . . . like the one you found me dangling from."

"Yeah? How's that been working for you?"

We reach the deck and slip on board. It feels solid enough. Opening a hatch, Hope slips inside and indicates for me to follow. Broken windows supply enough light to see fairly well. The interior is shallow but lengthy. There is a small kitchenette, two benches along the walls and a fold out table at the back of the space.

"Well, what do you think?" Hope says with a reasonable amount of pride.

Looking around the room I notice some freshly carved graffiti at the top of the back wall. "Wynfelt Manor?"

"What can I say? I got bored out here. At least, I was bored at night, during the day I spent all my time searching for you." Guilt shoots through my body as the blood rushes from my face. She's been vigorously looking for me out of concern for my life. I've been living at the Southern Colony beach resort.

"Okay, Hope, tell me everything."

She takes a deep breath in preparation, leans back on the bench and begins, "I woke up in a wooden box."

"Like a coffin or something?"

"Same shape, but more like a crate. It took me a minute to remember what was happening. The gaps in the wood were wide enough that I could see the deck of the ship. I must have watched for hours. Yukimura and that Louis guy occasionally trotted past, but I couldn't see what they were doing. Maybe five hours passed and I heard them shouting. Then I saw the Island – a strip of black on a sea of grey. It was getting dark and would be night soon. When the ship was in the harbor I heard children laughing and people singing. I knew it was all real. They hadn't just taken us out to toss us overboard. This was the sound of an Adonai Colony. The lid of the crate began to rattle and I played dead. Louis lifted me out and dragged me to the beach. I didn't dare open my eyes. I can only imagine that Yukimura was towing you along. The sounds of the beach died down and I knew we were alone."

"Don't tell me you attacked a trained Apologia."

"No." She looks a bit offended. "I could have though . . . I could have. Seriously, I could have taken him."

"I believe you," I say laughing.

"Anyway, they laid me down for whatever reason and when they weren't looking I ran. I ran with everything I had. It wasn't easy after being cramped in that box for who knows how long? By the time I stopped running I didn't know where I was."

"The Departure girl got lost? I can't believe it."
Seriously, it's hard to believe.

"I didn't sleep that night. It was a nightmare."
Suddenly I feel bad about teasing her. In a second I'm
at her side, on the other bench, with my arm around
her shoulders.

Leaning her head against my neck, she
continues, "Finally, midmorning, I found the river. I
guess I figured, a river is what first brought you to me,
maybe . . . I know it sounds silly, but . . . maybe one
would take me to you." Looking up she affectionately
determines, "Eventually it did I guess. First, it brought
me to this thing."

"Weren't you scared to climb up here?"

She sniffles and answers, "What choice did I
have?"

"I feel bad that I was at The Colony while you
were suffering out here." For a moment, she snaps out
of the emotional state. I've always loved this about her.
One minute she's the soft porcelain image of
vulnerability, and the next she's ready to pounce.

"Yeah, about this Colony, you need to know
some things."

"Like what?"

"Let's get back to the cult thing."

"It's not a cult, Hope. These people do things a little differently. Maybe they even believe a little differently, but they're sincere." My indignation rises again. "You should just see these people when Foley is preaching at Life Circle Chapel. They're devoted to every word."

"Justin, I don't want this to sound condescending, but you're still what we might call a babe in the faith. I watched you devour the Bible when we were in Chicago, and I'm proud of you, but not everyone who has beliefs based on the Bible actually has biblical beliefs."

"What, like church denominations? We've talked about this. You yourself said that most of the disagreements groups have with each other are of secondary importance and don't affect the core Christian message."

"That's true, they don't, but some do. If someone else claims to be a savior, or gives credence to false prophecy . . . let alone false Nazi prophecy, they're twisting the message into something completely different than the gospel. Listen, there are two things my father taught me that he said would be trustworthy guides in this area - things that I should remember if I ever escaped the Northern Colony. One, people can be sincere and be sincerely wrong, and two, if you're wrong about Jesus it doesn't matter what you're right about. You said everyone at the Southern Colony was sincere."

"Yeah, that's gotta count for something."

"Not really. A lot of people who are Muslim, Mormon, Hindu, or even atheist, are among the most sincere you'll ever meet. That doesn't mean they're right."

"Okay, well I see what you mean, but . . ."

Cutting me off she finishes, "And as for Jesus. It remains to be seen exactly what this Southern Colony Adon says about Him, but if it isn't what orthodox Christians have always believed, preached and defended, then it has to be rejected. Justin," she focuses more deeply into my eyes and her gaze intensifies, "it doesn't matter how practical his ideas are, or how much of the truth he does proclaim. If he's wrong about Jesus, it just doesn't matter about the rest."

"Yeah, but as I was trying to say, sweetheart, we don't know that for sure." She sits back pursing her lips and shaking her head in disagreement. "Alright, you tell me. As I've explained their beliefs, what about it is definitely, for sure, without question, false doctrine." She licks her lips and opens her mouth to answer, but I speak first, "Bear in mind, too, that when Foley talks about us as the two saviors of The Colony, he might not . . . scratch that . . . he almost certainly doesn't mean 'savior' in the way we mean it about Jesus."

"Okay, fine, this Nazi prophecy stuff is way, way, way, out there. I mean, Justin, I can't even believe you would give that a thought."

"I understand, but you didn't see it, Hope. I mean the picture was us . . . *it was us.* The prophecy looks right."

"You sound just like a lot of other religious people outside of Christianity."

"What do you mean?"

"You know, Hindus, Mormons, New Agers, whatever . . . they say things like, who are you to deny my experience of the supernatural? How can you tell me that I didn't have a real encounter? Who do you think you are to question my experience of faith? The thing is, we don't. I believe that some Nazi guy's prophecy could have an element of truth. I believe that Mormons experience what they call 'the burning in the bosom,' and I believe that the Muslims are right about one thing. Muhammad probably had a real experience in that cave where he supposedly had a vision. But just because someone has a supernatural experience doesn't mean it's a *good* supernatural experience. The demonic are at work deceiving people all over the world. They're having experiences. The question is, how do they know who or what they are experiencing." We stare at each other as I mull over what she has explained. Finally, she breaks the silence, "So, a so-called prophecy that seems supernatural . . . doesn't prove a thing to me. What I want to know is whether your Southern Colony is true to the revealed message of God. But you know what? You're right that I can't prove they aren't teaching the truth just yet. As you said, they may just be a weird group of believers with some weird practices. There are a lot of people like that who are truly saved in the world. We'll just have to wait and see. And for the record, Justin, I hope you're right. Like we always say . . . *truth will triumph*." We sit awkwardly for a few moments before I change the subject.

"Hope, what did you eat out here? What did you drink?"

"I know a few things about surviving off of the land. Dig a hole next to the river and the soil works as its own filtration system. It's not ideal, but it's all I've had. As far as food, like I said, I foraged for whatever berries or . . . grubs, I could find." Her face looks disgusted at the memory. "I tried not to drink much though. Getting sick out here . . . alone . . . I just might not make it."

"Oh, man, I can help." Reaching into my bag, I retrieve the Ocean's Wave powder. "You got any water up here?" With an inquisitive look, she reaches for an old canister and passes it to me. I mix the substance into the container and the bluish hue becomes visible. For a moment I hesitate to introduce her to this addiction, but Foley's explanation is reasonable. "Here, drink this."

"What . . . what is it?"

"It's just a decontaminant and nutritional supplement." With an impressed turn of her lips, she partakes.

"Justin, this tastes like . . ."

"I know, I know. It tastes like the stuff Yukimura gave us in Rio. I think it is, but it's a much more diluted amount. It's fine. Just wait."

"Hero, why do I feel like this is a role reversal of the Garden of Eden? The only difference is this time it's the man who gets blamed for touching forbidden fruit." I watch her anxious wide eyes stare into mine for ten seconds before she opens her mouth, rolls her head back to look at the ceiling and is overcome with relaxation. She releases the container and I am about to lift it to my own lips when I hear racket on the roof.

CHAPTER FOURTEEN

"It's just squirrels, Justin." Hope is laughing. She's in the midst of the rush of the Ocean's Wave and the calm clarity it brings. Her anxiety is chased away and she's laughing as she watches me peer out the windows. "Hey, hero, you remember that time you and Jack thought someone was laying siege to the train and it turned out to be a deer?" She lays on her back on the bench and laughs loudly at the memory. "Go check it out if you're that worried about it. We know one thing. It won't be a deer way up in this tree, right?" She laughs more and clears her throat trying to calm herself.

Slipping through the hatch, I look around. Nothing but jungle and the ambient noise it brings. Stealthily, I creep onto the deck of the boat and scan the area. Still nothing. My stance relaxes when I catch a glimpse of . . . awe frostbite! It *is* a squirrel. "Hey, Hope," I shout into the hatch, "Looks like you were right again. I guess you're just always right about every – *Umpf!*" I'm on my chest on the deck before I see my assailant. He's wearing the Southern Colony black and green Apologia uniform, but it's not either of Foley's guys.

"I am an Apologia officer from the True Southern Colony. I am placing you under arrest and returning you to our camp." His words are familiar. I said them myself when I first attempted to capture

Hope and Noah. So, this is how it feels to be on the other side of the declaration?

Standing, I reply, "Okay, okay, . . . you got me." I feign my recovery. Rubbing my head, I add, "Just calm down and let me . . ." Kneeing him in the stomach I grab the back of his neck and toss him toward the front of the vessel. Whoa! Did the boat just rock or is it my imagination? Probably my imagination. Crouching next to my enemy, I explain, "I didn't mean to hurt you, but you gotta understand, I'm on an important mission here." No sooner do I finish the statement than I hear the slam of boots behind me and a second Apologia knocks me to the deck. (CREEAAKK). Okay, now I know the boat is rocking. The second attacker looks around and in his hesitation, I kick hard upward against his chest. He staggers backward four paces and lands on his back against the slanting roof of the cabin. I chuckle at my surprising success as I reach my feet, but then I hear the first guy groaning to his stance and gripping the rail to steady himself. I slap away two jabs and block a kick while shouting, "The boat is going to sink, I . . . I mean fall. You guys wanna die today?" It's clear that the more weight that is added to the front of the apparatus, the more it begins to creak. Ignoring my warning, number two comes running at me to join the fight. Holding up my hands I shout, "No, wait!" He kicks hard against my waist and his run, my body and the first Apologia's dodging of the whole ordeal causes the craft to tilt dramatically forward.

"What's going . . . oh," Hope screams as she emerges from the cabin. "Hold on, Hero, I'm coming."

Now realizing the situation, my two opponents drop the struggle and join me in shouting, "Don't," as we all stare at her. She was the redheaded straw that broke the treetop camel's back. The boat begins to slide for the first time in decades and we all scream in unison as it falls from the tree. This is it.

Opening my eyes from a squint I notice that we are not dead. We are in fact still moving. Of all things, the boat slid right out of the tree and into the river. It won't last long with the holes in the bottom, but for now it seems okay. We all look at each other with glee, realizing the death we were spared. Helping each other up, hilarious laughter breaks out all around, and begins to lessen as Hope and I nervously eyeball each other between glancing at the Apologia. Finally, the laughter is gone and our faces all become stern. One of them shrugs at me and I respond with pursed lips and a solemn nod. With that, our battle picks up where it left off. Hope begins to block, dodge, jab and kick with number one and I defend against number two. Two and I battle to the back of the vessel and as it hits a rock, I fall to my back grabbing an old oar. I hold it horizontally to protect against his kick. He looks to his right and grips another oar. On my feet, we begin swinging the unlikely weapons in the most ridiculous fencing match ever.

Catching me in the face with the wooden paddle, I stagger to the other side of the roof and nearly fall overboard. The boat is beginning to sink. Hope is on all fours crawling away from her foe. I've got to do something. Straightening up, I grip the middle of my oar like a javelin and hurl it thirty feet toward the Apologia standing over his prey. Success! He grabs his chest and falls overboard, but remains in play holding the rail. He's in trouble. The craft is half submerged now. A second later I charge the remaining soldier and we wrestle as each of us grip the wooden oar between us. We spin, jerking at it until he shakes me loose and I'm on my back next to Hope. We're moving fast now. We're also sinking fast. We have almost reached the spot where the cable crosses the river. I review my options but can't come up with much.

From our right and the Apologia's left, I see the old crow sailing along the line. It's Jack! He drops to the deck knocking the Apologia spinning over the edge and into the river. Sternly he marches to the spot where the first is still clinging to the boat. Yanking his hand away in annoyance the guy joins his buddy in the rough waters.

"What are you doing, Jack," I demand. "They could die!"

"They'll be fine," he answers in a dismissive way. "And even if they don't make it, they're from the Unbelieving Tribe. Who gives a freeze what happens to them?"

"I do." I answer, "We don't kill people, Jack!" His eyes look as if shame is attempting to fill them, but fails.

"They're faithful to the Adonai. The . . . the Adonai ruined our lives."

Hope speaks up, "They're crawling onto the bank. I can see them, they're fine."

Looking back to my companion, I instruct, "That's not us. That's how *they* are. We're not them."

"We may not be them," Hope announces, "but we're gonna be in the river just like them if we don't do something!" Water is spilling over the rails and onto the deck. It's time to disembark. As the river curves around a bend, a low hung tree is visible on the right hand side.

"Get ready guys," I say as we all realize the plan. "Now!" All three of us are in the tree and clambering up to straddle its thick outstretched form.

"Why?" Hope asks as the boat disappears.

"Why what?" Jack inquires.

"Why is it," she continues, "that every time I find a safe, respectable home, you Apologia guys come along and ride it into the ground?"

CHAPTER FIFTEEN

"We've got to move quickly," Jack warns as we hack our way through the overgrowth. The two Apologia guys from the Unbelieving Tribe, will be on our tails.

"Reeelaax, guys," Hope suggests. "There are three of us and two of them." I don't notice it so much in myself, but seeing her experiencing the effects of the Ocean's Wave, I wonder if this calmed clarity is a bit too calmed.

Speaking over my shoulder as I swing the machete, I answer, "No, Jack's right. It's not about our ability to overcome *them*. It's about approaching the Unbelieving Tribe without being expected. The Unbelieving Apologia don't even know why we were out here. They don't know who we are. I'm sure they assume we're with Foley, but then, they used to be at the Southern Colony. They knew everyone there."

"They didn't know me and Courtney," Jack reminds us.

"Good point," I admit.

"I'm telling you, Justin, you've got to be more ruthless with these guys."

"Is this the Jack I remember?" I ask. "The Jack that was terrified of the outside world? You've certainly toughened up over the past few months."

"I have. It only took losing my entire way of life and having the girl I love ripped away! We can't be taking a soft hand to the Adonai. They need to be decisively dealt with. You guys might not understand, but Foley gets it."

"This Foley seems charming," Hope sarcastically murmurs. "Speaking of the girl you love, has she realized you're the better Apologia catch?" I stop hacking for a moment to look back at her with mild irritation before wiping my brow and continuing the work.

"It happened." His face is melancholy as if remembering an old flame. "It was bound to happen. The only constant either of us had out here was . . . each other. We spent a lot of time alone together. I consider myself indebted to Foley for that. One night, on the beach, she kissed my cheek. It was simple enough, but it was a long kiss. She's the first girl who ever kissed me. Whatever feelings I had for her before are now intensified ten-fold. It was like she woke up to me. She hadn't really ever noticed me before . . . I mean, not really. I became her world in the way she was mine. We only have one difference. She's never fully accepted Foley's vision for The Colony. I have. So, Justin, have I toughened up? Yeah . . . I had to. I already wanted vengeance. Since they took her . . . I want blood." We all stop moving.

"Jack," Hope says, rubbing his arm, "Do you still believe?"

"I do."

"Do you still believe *truth will triumph*?"

He grits his teeth for a moment and then answers, "I do."

"Vengeance is mine, says the Lord." She stares sincerely into his eyes with tears brimming. He stares back, but there is only a hint of emotion. She hugs him, but he doesn't respond. Hope is caring, but this isn't like her. The Ocean's Wave has loosened her inhibitions. Nevertheless, he needs this now.

"C'mon guys," I instruct.

***

Another hour of hacking places us at the base of the peak that marks the halfway point to the Unbelieving Tribe's beach.

"What do we do, Jack?" I ask, "Do we go around?"

"Nope. The other side of the peak is littered with landmines that the Nazis dumped when they settled here. The idea was that no one would be able to approach them from behind on foot. Halfway up the peak, on the other side, a zip line extends over the area. That's how we get across."

"Land mines? Surely, they aren't still active," I contend.

"Actually, the ordinances can remain active for decades. These old models have wicks, but they've rotted over time. This means that they can be set off very easily."

Hope squints and asks, "How do you know all this?"

"Simple. I took one apart."

"Hope, Jack had the highest intelligence scores of our Apologia crew back at the Inquiry and Enlightenment Academy. He'll take anything apart to figure it out."

"Yeah, I should have been in the research group, but they needed someone in the Apologia Life Role who would be especially adept at investigatory work. The bottom line is, you don't want to go anywhere near the landmines."

Eyeballing a wall of black stone in the midst of the green and brown landscape, I ask the obvious question. "Okay, so there's a zip line on the other side that extends over a mine field. How do we get up to it?"

Jack walks along the side of the rise with his gloved hands hanging at his side. Finally, he reveals, "Here . . . here it is." A cord hangs against the rock.

Instantly, Hope and I understand the idea."

"You expect me to climb that thing?" Hope asks in doubt.

"Don't worry, snowflake," I encourage. "Just pretend it's a Colony you're trying to break into."

She looks at me with sudden adoration, likely induced by the Ocean's Wave, and asks, "Awe, snowflake? Is that like a pet name or something?"

"Yeah," I answer while looking around with a frown of consideration. I look to her with a lopsided grin and decide, "I think I'm gonna stick with it." She leans against my arm to show her affection. What would Bailee think?

"Okay, lovebirds, can we start climbing?"

***

Above the treetops I can see the topography of the immediate area. We're at least one hundred feet above the jungle floor and still climbing. Jack is higher up on the line, Hope is climbing after him and I bring up the rear. The ordeal isn't that challenging for any of us, despite our groans of complaint. Black and grey rock makes up most of the surface. Our feet locate crevices and outcroppings and our hands grip the cable. It's clear that another fifty feet will transport us to whatever's at the top of the line.

"*Arghh,*" I yell as the nerves in my right

shoulder blaze with intense and unexpected pain. I hang by my left arm and rotate on the line, my back against the rock. Grimacing, I notice the two Unbelieving Apologia in the forest below. Jack recognizes the dilemma and explains what I cannot see.

"Small blade in your back, Justin. Can't be deep. Can you climb?"

"Yeah," I grunt. "Keep moving!"

We reach the top of the cable as several more throwing knives clang against the rocks all around us. Reaching the top we all roll onto the surface exhausted. I sit as Hope extracts the blade from my back; and knelt behind me she presses hard with both palms against the point of impact. There she remains to stop the bleeding.

Cautiously peering over the edge, Jack reveals, "Their climbing the cable."

"What do we do?" Hope wonders aloud.

"We just have to keep moving," I typically respond.

Jack kneels in front of me and says, "No, Justin. There's a more sure way." He prepares himself to dislodge the cord.

"Jack, how far up are they?" I demand in a gruff voice. "If they're high enough it could kill them!"

Looking back to me he answers, "You mend your wounds! Someone's got to handle this!" Realizing his lack of concern, I launch from my position to stop him, but it's too late. The three of us watch as the line slides effortlessly over the cliff. Hope gasps. I stand wide-eyed and in shock. Jack looks at each of us in turn with pursed lips.

"It's done," he calmly says before walking away. Rushing to get a view, Hope and I see the two Unbelieving Apologia lying on the forest floor motionless.

"Hey," I shout to them. "Are you guys okay?" Nothing.

Standing, I rush to Jack and toss him against a rocky wall. "What are you thinking, you frostbitten numb skull? Have you lost your mind? They're dead!" As I hold his shoulders to the rock he reaches up under my right arm and digs his fingers into the wound. "*Ahh!*" I'm on the ground in a moment and I kick against his legs sweeping *him* to the dirt too.

"Stop . . . just stop," Hope pleads through tears. I'm on top of him now with my hand around his throat. He coughs and gags. What am I doing? This is my best friend in the world. He's the one I dragged through the snow to the Northern Colony Chapel when we both committed Departure. He's the one I've seen as a younger brother all my life. Battle-hardened, longhaired killer he may be, but I can't do this. Releasing him I stand to my feet and back away with a cold stare. He leans on one hand and coughs aggressively, gripping his neck.

Peering again over the edge I stare at the two bodies. Hope is next to me and whispers, "I'm not comfortable with how he's acting, but it does seem like some kind of self-defense or something. I mean . . . right?"

"I don't know." The image of the two Apologia bodies meets my vision again and I insist, "But this . . . this just isn't us."

CHAPTER SIXTEEN

Is killing wrong? The Old Testament of the Bible seems to imply that killing, perhaps even capital punishment, is often necessary and permissible. Moses records God telling Noah, "Whoever sheds the blood of man, by man shall his blood be shed, for God made man in his own image." In the second book of the scriptures, he again commands, "Whoever strikes a man so that he dies shall be put to death." Yet, Jesus says, "You have heard that it was said, 'An eye for an eye, and a tooth for a tooth.' But I say to you, do not resist an evil person; but whoever slaps you on your right cheek, turn the other to him also.'" My time in Chicago was spent spilling over these concepts. How are the words of Jesus not in conflict with the commands of the Father through Moses? The answer is simple enough. Eye-for-eye punishment *is* undeniably *just*. There is no indication that Jesus did not think that sort of justice is exactly what judges *should* dispense. On the other hand, the Savior was teaching that His people, in their interpersonal dealings, should not kill or harm. It seems consistent with His message that killing is sometimes unavoidable, but followers of Christ must be willing to be personally defrauded. Still, I have questions. Is it not right to fight when the protection of innocents is in view? Should we not fight to save Courtney now?

My mind has been plagued by these theological

conundrums all afternoon as we have sat on the ridge of the peak catatonically considering what we . . . what Jack has done. There has been no motivation to move on. Our world has changed now that one of our own has spilt the blood of an enemy. Can I find a way to justify what my partner has done?

Distant birds are all that can be heard as we solemnly sit speechless. Standing, I dust off my hands and return to the edge of the cliff to view the bodies once more. I suppose I'm hoping that at some point I will see them rouse and know that this nightmare has been chased away.

Jack breaks the silence with, "Isn't it necessary?" We both stare at him as the distant sun begins to set. "You know . . . I mean, Foley says that in the past Christians have waged wars to ensure belief."

"Yeah," Hope knowledgably answers. "There were - the Crusades, the Spanish Inquisition, along with other Inquisitions. They killed for unbelief or the protection of 'Christian Holy sites,' but that's not what Jesus taught. Proper belief does not come at the end of a sword, Jack." Looking down, he has lost the fervor to fight. We are all worn out from an eventful day, but there's something else. Something is missing.

"Look guys," I begin, "we can't change what's been done, but we still have a mission. Our Courtney is at the Unbelieving Tribe and we have to save her.

"There's nothing we can do today, hero," Hope urges. "It's almost night." Reaching into her pocket, she retrieves a flask containing water. "You got any more of that blue stuff?" The moment she mentions the substance, Jack's head tilts up and my eyes widen in anticipation. We are both filled with desire. Hope probably doesn't even realize it yet, but her request may be a subtle indication that she too is experiencing the effects. Jack fiddles with his utility belt, as do I. We both produce small packets and Hope stirs it into the water. In turn, we each sip lustfully from the container. Now, nothing is amiss. Everything is falling into place.

It is only now that I am able to rid my thoughts of the day's tragedy. Looking around, I notice the surface of the ridge for the first time. We are situated high above the jungle on a black and grey area two-thirds up the peak. At the back of the natural shelf is a shallow cave only deep enough for shelter from the rain that is now beginning.

Jack moves into the concave area and begins a wrestling match with a large somewhat rounded stone. Hope and I exchange confused looks until the stone is removed and a two by four-foot passage is revealed. Hunkering down he slips into the opening before motioning for us to follow. I grip the lighter and wave my hand toward the spot in an "after you" sort of way.

Inside we find a room of sorts that is large enough for us to stand. The circular space is probably fifteen by fifteen. Two candles sit on either side of a rock on which a large Bible rests. It is open and the pages have been discolored by time. Etched into the walls are some of the same strange phrases I saw in the hole at the back of the Mansion yard. Above the Bible, one quote takes prominence. It says, "The Word of God - And they utterly destroyed all that was in the city, both man and woman, young and old, and ox, and sheep, and donkey, with the edge of the sword." Black ink underlines verses in the sacred text that involve God's commands to do violence to unbelievers.

"How did you know about this place, Jack?" Hope asks.

"Foley told me an old hermit used to live here that survived from the Nazi group. He thought Courtney and I might need it if we were followed. I stayed here the first night on my way back. The Unbelieving Tribe doesn't know about it."

Losing interest in his words I ask, "Hope, what is this about?" Looking up from the Bible to the words on the wall, then back to her I continue, "why are these violent commands in the Bible?"

"Justin, there are some hard teachings in the Old Testament. God commanded Joshua to go into the land of Canaan and lead a military conquest to overthrow the wicked cities inhabiting the land."

"That doesn't sound like Jesus," I contend.

"I know it's tough. I don't deny that. What you've got to understand is that the Bible indicates that these people were involved in incest, idolatry, child sacrifice . . . they were terrible."

"Okay, but that doesn't mean we have the right to slaughter people like that."

"You're right. We don't. But this was a judgment from God. It would be wrong for man to decide on his own to do these things, but the Maker and perfect Judge can bring judgment if He chooses."

"So, is it right for any army to do these sorts of things?" Jack asks, looking a whole lot more comfortable with the idea.

"Not necessarily," Hope articulates. "Under Joshua, Israel was in a unique position that modern armies are not."

"How so?" I ask with deep interest.

"First, the Israelites had absolute assurance of what God wanted them to do. No modern army has that sort of specific military instruction from God. Second, modern soldiers may be fighting alongside Muslims, Satanists . . . whatever, and firing across the battlefield at a Christian brother or sister. In the time of Joshua, the Israelites were the believers on earth. They could be confident that everyone they were attacking under God's direction was an unbeliever who was ripe for judgment. He makes those judgments . . . not us."

Weighing the concepts I press, "But doesn't that just seem . . ."

"It's like this, guys – If you don't believe in God, then, yeah, it just sounds like an ancient army justifying their violence based on their own cultural religious junk. But . . . if you believe the arguments and evidence for God's existence work, then it's God's decision when and how He will carry out His judgment." Somewhat sated by her explanation, I stare expressionless at the cave wall. "When you get down to it, there will always be things in Scripture that we don't like, just like there are things in the rest of life that we don't like. I don't like that people get cancer. That doesn't mean that cancer doesn't exist just because I don't agree with it."

"Well," Jack adds as he spins his Hook-Slide in his right hand, "that doesn't tell us why this place is filled with these quotations."

"If a Nazi hermit lived here, he was probably misapplying the passages to their wicked ideology." We all sit silently thinking things through for thirty seconds or so.

"I'll tell you what, snowflake, too much has happened today to dig any deeper. Time to sleep."

CHAPTER SEVENTEEN

Morning light pours in through the small mountainside entrance. Hope is still asleep. Slipping outside I find Jack perched on the cliff, his hair caught in the morning breeze. The fresh air fills my nostrils and I recognize the scent of dewy foliage from the jungle below. My friend is so different now. I want to be proud of the confident soldier he has become, but he's unstable, volatile and angry. We've all been there. It was me when I realized the truth about my father. It was Hope when Noah died. My companion needs me now. If only we could look over the edge this morning and see that . . .

"The bodies are gone." Jack finishes my unspoken thoughts.

"What?"

Turning to face me he repeats, "Yeah, they're just, gone. Either someone came and got them or they picked themselves up and left." As he finishes the words, he sips from Hope's container of Ocean's Wave.

"Or . . . some animal dragged them off."

"Not possible. There's nothing that big out here."

Scanning the base of the peak myself, I

celebrate with, "That's awesome Jack. You just might not be a murderer after all!"

"No, Justin. It's not good. It means someone knows. If they're still alive, *they* know. If they're not, whoever moved the bodies knows. Whichever is true, we've got to get out of here."

Looking around, I wonder aloud, "How *do* we get out of here?"

"Get Hope and I'll show you."

"I'm right here," the girl says as she emerges from the cave.

Gripping the rock, Jack places his left foot on a two-inch wide ridge and says, "This way."

"You've gotta be kidding," Hope responds.

***

We are on the alternate side of the cliff after twenty minutes of vigorous climbing and shuffling. From this new vantage point I am able to see the distant ocean on the Unbelieving Tribe's side of the Island. It looks to be several miles away, but now, with more daylight, we should be able to make it. Unfortunately, a new problem has arisen. Rain. The occasional showers have come again.

"Right, well, that does it," Jack releases in conclusion of the climb. One by one we slip onto another somewhat spacious area and find our footing. No cave exists at this location. I'm glad. Secured to the rock above us, I see the zip line. It stretches like some kind of unlikely telephone line into the green blanket below.

"Wow," Hope emits. "Look at it Justin. It's beautiful." Below us is a large region that looks to be about two hundred yards wide and stretches to our left and right as far as can be seen. Ivy, or kudzu, or other attractive parasitic foliage is so abundant that it renders the entire area the appearance of a leafy green river that divides the peak from the jungle.

Jack fiddles with his Hook-Slide before cautioning, "Yeah, real pretty. You drop into that mess and you've got an eighty percent chance of having your pretty red head blown back to the Northern Colony."

"So, this is the . . ." I start to say, but Jack cuts me off.

"Yep. Beneath that blanket of growth are the temperamental ordinances ditched by the original Nazi Colony. Like I said, we've got to slide across. We could go around, but it would take forever."

"Makes sense."

"Wait," I don't have one of those hook thingies," Hope points out with a hint of worry.

"No problem," says Jack. "I always carry a spare." He tosses her the rubbery handle of an extra

Hook-Slide and she rotates holding her hands at her waist with her chin up and then down.

"You know, this is my first time." Uh oh, she's stressing.

"Look, snowflake," I reply with a comforting grin, "You're the girl I chased over the Northern Colony wall. All you had then were your hands and a cord. You can do this."

"Yeah . . . I can do this," she coaches herself. "Gimme the Ocean's Wave, Jack." He hands her the container and she gulps down what's left of its contents. Wiping her mouth with her forearm she demands, "Okay, let's do this!" Jack goes first.

"See you at the bottom guys!" We watch as he glides through the rain high above the greenery.

"How does this thing open?" Hope asks, nervousness painted all over her face. "Never mind, I got it. Okay, here we go." No sooner does she begin to sail away than I hear voices on the rocky face of the peak. Someone is following us. It's no doubt the two Unbelieving Apologia closing in. Part of me hopes it is. That would at least mean they're alive. Hope made it. Good. I don't follow. Creeping a small distance along the edge of the climb, I crane my neck and spy the pursuers. It's them! Tilting my head down, I close my eyes for a second then open them to stare at the rock and process my relief. Over my shoulder, I peer at Hope and Jack across the green chasm. It looks like they're motioning for me to join them. They're clearly confused. With little time to waste, I slip back to the cable . . . but . . . I was too slow.

"Hey, you sand flea," one of the Apologia shouts. "Get back here!" Moving more quickly now they are almost to the flattened space where they can gain footing.

"Go Justin," I say to myself as I flick open the Hook-Slide and hop onto the cable. I know I'm not free. They were almost there. This is the longest slide I've taken. Two-thirds of the journey has passed when the line falls limp. They cut it! I land tumbling in the eighteen-inch overgrowth. The world goes silent and dark. Then it spins. Then it stabilizes and pain sets in. I lay still until my screaming nerves settle down. "Not dead yet, Justin," I tell myself. Though I'm battered, I carefully stand and recover. Rain pats loudly against the leaves. Then I hear it. (KABOOM!) about fifty yards away, an ordinance explodes, presumably from the fall of the zip line. Rock and dirt fly through the air and then two more explosions violate the eardrum. It's like a domino effect. Looking to Jack and Hope, I quickly consider my options.

"RUN," They both shout from the safety of the trees. I wait through two more detonations, hoping the nightmare will end. No such luck. Run! Half running and half jumping, I tear through the overgrowth with explosions trailing my path. The bad news is I'm hitting the mines with almost every step. The good news is there seems to be an unintended delay due to the aging of the mechanics.

Looking back over my shoulder I see dirt, fire and smoke giving chase no matter where I run. The whole Island is tearing at the seams, or at least that's how it sounds. Approaching the trees my veins pump adrenaline so potent it feels like battery acid. "Go! Run! Back up you frostbitten sand fleas!" They do. Jack and Hope turn to run and I launch into the jungle landing on both of them. For what feels like a lifetime, debris rains down on us as we cling to the earth. Finally, silence again takes hold. All three of us slowly raise our heads together while lying on the ground. "We made it guys," I say with a celebratory laugh. "We're not dead."

Hope winces and asks, "Sand flea?" If looks could kill . . .

"It's what I heard him say," I explain while pointing to the peak.

Jack philosophizes, "Perhaps sand flea is their version of our own makeshift angry slang term frostbitten." He's right that colonials speak differently than most people, regardless of which Colony they inhabit.

"Whatever," Hope starts, "You call me a frostbitten sand flea again and you'll know exactly what one would feel like."

"What?" I ask as she turns to walk away. "That doesn't even make sense." Jack turns to leave too, but not before widening his eyes to express his sympathy and stretching out his hand face down to imply I should let it go. Ah, to be Hope's man. I'd almost forgotten what it was like.

***

As we grow ever nearer to the Unbelieving Tribe my anxiety increases. It reminds me of the occasional presentations we were required to make in speech class at the Inquiry and Enlightenment Academy. I was never nervous until the night before. This entire journey I've been somewhat enjoying myself, especially getting to spend time with my Northern Colony family. In spite of the ordeal with the Unbelieving Apologia, this has been fun. Now, though, it's time to work.

The rain has stopped as quickly as it began. We stand at the edge of a second expanse of kudzu carpet that is about half as wide as the last. In the center is a large ship, or at least what was a ship maybe a hundred and fifty years ago. It's more like rubble now. Lying on its side in broken pieces, one spire extends diagonally sixty feet in the air. An old crows nest is still intact. The base of the ship is little more than a large pile of aging wood and kudzu.

"More bombs, Jack?" I worry.

"No, but we blew our cover with the explosions. The whole Island would have heard it. They'll know we're coming, and they'll be looking for us. On the other side of the clearing there's another hundred and fifty yards of jungle before you hit the Tribe."

With strategy on my mind, I outline, "What if we split up? You could go around to the right, and Hope and . . . Where's Hope?" Apparently having grown tired of our discussion, the redheaded girl decided to live up to her Northern Colony title and depart. She's halfway to the ship before we notice her disappearance.

"Awwww, man," Jack nervously moans while watching. "This isn't good."

"Frostbite! Hope, what are you doing?" I whisper. From running in a hunkered posture, she spins with her back to what was once the hull of a ship and slouches down to rest on her haunches. Staring at us she waves her hands urging us to follow. We do. With caution now to the Island wind, we race halfway across the field in like manner.

"Okay, snowflake, we gotta talk. I promised your old man I would take care of you and you promised that in situations like this you would follow my lead."

Without even making eye contact she peers around a chunk of wood to spy for attackers and dismissively responds, "uh-huh . . . you're right Justin . . ." She's not even looking at me. As I lay into her, she patronizingly continues, "Oh yes . . . you have always done a real good job . . . I'm a lucky girl." She's still not listening.

"You're darn right. Noah said I should watch out for you . . . I watch out for you. You go nuts at the

Northern Colony . . . I watch out for you." As I continue to lecture I pace around the area behind the ship, waving my hands and getting it all off of my chest as I stare at the grass and speak. "I mean, I don't know what else to say . . . every time I think you've learned to follow my lead you . . ."

"Hey, pal," Jack says, punching me in the arm. I follow his gaze upward and find that Hope is halfway up the wooden pole toward the crows nest in the sky.

"Awe, frostbite!" I say. Jack softly chuckles leaning against the wood.

Clambering onto the dilapidated and now slanted deck of the old vessel, we look back and forth between Hope and the opposing jungle. Her climbing skills are impressive. After a few moments of silence we hear, "Come up here guys," as her head pops over the edge of the platform.

"It won't hold, Hope," Jack returns.

"No . . . No, it feels pretty solid," she insists. Looking at each other with a shake of the head, we begin to climb. Reaching the top we both feel the nest begin to creak as if the ship were some ancient monster we are about to awaken. "There," she points.

Cupping my hands around my eyes to shield them from the sunlight, I see a few leaf-covered shelters, a couple of repurposed boats, and three buildings. "They don't look frazzled about the explosions. Jack, the Unbelieving Tribe could make their own shelters and use some of the boats, but why would those three old buildings be here?"

"Foley says the Nazis had an outpost here to keep watch from the back of the Island. Hey, you gotta cover your . . ." He doesn't finish because the mast begins to break.

"*AHHHHHH*," we all howl as the mast folds over onto the rest of the old ship and the three of us crash into the deck. The deck, in turn, breaks and we tumble onto the dirt in the darkened and cramped interior of the boat. Coughing we pull ourselves together.

"You guys okay?" I ask.

"Yeah," Hope answers.

"Been through worse," Jack says.

Crawling out, we set off for the trees somewhat confident that no one is ready for us. Clouds follow us overhead and the rain begins again. It's hard now. Though it is daylight the forest is dim with the overcast sky. Slowly the Unbelieving Tribe comes into view. We've made it, though it has been more of an adventure than Foley imagined. Now a barrier of wood is visible that immediately brings the Northern Colony wall to the forefront of my mind. This one is shorter though. On the other side, we hear the Adonai Colony. The crashing of distant waves is penetrated by rain, voices, the chopping of wood and general movement. It's dark now, as though the atmosphere mirrors the severity of the moment. Getting a boost from Jack, I peer into the camp. It's him!

CHAPTER EIGHTEEN

Why is it that for every culture in the history of man, courage has been regarded as admirable, and cowardice considered detestable? It's almost as if there is a universal objective truth about the matter. Courage is disinterested in self. It gives of itself for the good of another. In this way, it is an expression of love. Cowardice *is* self-interested. It ignores injustice, denies mercy, and is ignorant of heroism's worth. Is it true that courage is good and cowardice bad? If so, then there is a God in whose nature these truths have grounding.

The Ocean's Wave is completely worn off. My fear would be at a fever pitch were it not for my drive to save Courtney. From my perspective, they've got my sister in there and I'll wage war on the whole lot of them if that's what it takes to get her out. Only now I see that there is another familiar face among the tribe. He won't be much of a problem. The old snake slivered away, in fear, at the battle for the Northern Colony. Frankly, I've got more respect for Tristan, Will, Dom and Brent. Cowardice on the other hand, I cannot commend. A coward is here. The fourth and missing member of the Night Watch Apologia of the Northern Colony is here. Louis.

He is speaking with who I presume to be the leader of the Unbelieving Tribe. A shirtless, dark-skinned guy with dreadlocks and a large gauge in his left ear. A nose ring rounds out the picture and carved cuffs hang around several of his braids. Tribal tattoos cover one arm and shoulder as a sleeve. Whoa! How'd he do that out here? At his waist is a curved blade . . . no . . . more like a sword. His pants are dark green and rolled up to below the knee. His footwear looks like handmade sandals secured with braided leather. Next to him, the coward is in his Apologia duds and has the same dumb beard he did when I saw him last. They stand beneath a thatched shelter with four legs and watch the rain.

The thatched shelters line the wall and trail around the outer perimeter of the camp to our right. To the left I see two of the sizeable plaster covered stone buildings. At the other end of the encampment is the third. Littered throughout the area are disassembled boats that have been repurposed as homes.

"Jack, what do you think?" I ask.

"Oh," Hope protests, "I guess the one person here who has actually broken into a Colony undetected and escaped isn't worth asking, huh?" She's playfully teasing. I actually appreciate it in this moment.

"Yeah," I contest, "But you weren't undetected were you?" Though we were adversaries at the time, the memory of chasing her out of The Colony and down to the river is a fond one.

"Well," Jack answers ignoring our banter, "Most of these structures are too weak or exposed for imprisoning someone. I'd say she's in one of the buildings."

"I agree."

"Exactly what I would have said, Jack," Hope agrees with a look of faux seriousness.

We move along the exterior of the wall until we are directly behind the old stone architecture. With a boost, I straddle the wall and reach down to help Jack, then Hope over. Dropping to the other side, we sneak along the framework until a window is located. Inside there is one guard. I'm through the opening and across the floor before he realizes my presence. Wrapping the inside of my elbow around his neck, I squeeze according to my Apologia training until he passes out unharmed. There is a stone staircase that winds to an upper level. Otherwise the room is vacant.

"I wouldn't think they'd have her upstairs," Jack reasons aloud. Moving around the room there isn't much to see, then the answer reveals itself.

"Here," Hope directs with a shouting whisper. On the floor behind the stairs is a large metal ring bolted to a hatch. With a sturdy pull the hatch rises and a ladder is visible. Stretching into the earth.

"Courtney," Jack grunts as he pushes us out of the way. Hope stands watch and we slide down the ladder into a small space no larger than ten by five feet. At the back of the short tunnel we find her - our fellow Apologia, our sister, our . . . each other. Courtney wears a dingy white tank top and form-fitting black pants.

She's covered in dirt, and looks fatigued if not delirious, slumped on the floor with her legs chained to the wall. "Courtney, hey baby, we found you," Jack says through tears. It is the first raw emotion I've seen from him since arriving on the Island.

"J . . . Jack," she questions with a breathy voice.

"Yeah, baby, I'm right here. And look . . . look who I brought with me." She rotates to see my face.

"Justin. It can't . . . it can't be you." The rumble of thunder can be heard from outside. The claustrophobic dungeon, the raging storm, the desperation of the situation and the reunion create an otherworldly atmosphere as though we are in some hellish oblivion.

"I'm here, Courtney," I say with unexpected tears running. "I couldn't leave you here. We can't fight the Adonai without you, right?" I smile wide, but am broken to see my dear friend in this state. "I . . . I've followed you to the ends of the earth to drag you up out of the pit, out of the miry clay. It's all going to be alright." She places one hand on each of our cheeks. There was a time when I was perturbed by her affection. It was misguided. Now, here, it bears the warmth of family.

She is rousing now and says, "I never thought I'd see either of you again. You . . . you shouldn't have come. He'll kill you." Jack is working on the metal cuffs attached to her legs as she explains.

"Who? You mean that big guy outside?" Jack asks.

"Yes . . . his name is Adon Oleth. You can't stop him."

"Listen," I say with haste, "Don't worry about it, Courtney. We're getting out of here. Nobody saw us come in." No sooner do I say it than I hear Hope's scream. For a half second I lock eyes with Jack and he nods.

I'm up the ladder in five seconds and it feels as though the world has tilted on its axis. Hope is on the ground backing into the corner and the formerly unconscious tribe member is approaching with aggression. He must have caught her off guard. Kicking against the top rung, I hurl myself across the floor and jerk his leg, dropping him. Hope grabs him around the neck and puts him out for the second time in ten minutes.

"Twice. You don't think that'll do any permanent damage do you," Hope says.

"Right now I can't think about it." Through the front window I see the ocean to my left and the beach in front of me. Louis is striding toward the front door with two other islanders in tow as Courtney and Jack worm out of the hatch. "Hope, take Courtney and get out through the back window. Don't stop until you at least get to the clearing."

"You got it, hero! Come on doll." She wraps Courtney's arm around her shoulder and they move across the room to the window.

"Ready Jack?"

"I'm ready."

"Just don't kill anyone, okay, buddy?" He just rolls his eyes.

The door flies open and the room fills with combat as we spar with two Unbelieving Tribe members. Louis watches in horror at the revelation that the Day Watch Apologia have arrived in full force. These guys are nothing compared to the two Apologia clad gentlemen we left stranded on the mountain. The room is clear in less than thirty seconds and Louis stands alone. I grab his jacket and toss him against a wall.

"G . . . g . . . guys, just let me tell you what I'm thinking. I'm thinking we just all admit we're in a little over our heads here and try to figure things out together. You . . . you know, we're Apologia right? *Hope to Give,* like the Jacket says. I . . . I . . . mean, really when you think about it we're in this together."

"Shut it, Louis," I grunt. "Why are you here?"

Looking back and forth from one of us to the other in confusion he answers, "What do you mean? Wha . . . what? You don't know? Foley's a maniac. I barely got out alive. I escaped and followed the beach around the Island looking for something . . . anything. Luckily, I found these colonials . . . I mean . . . real colonials. They're rough and tumble, but they're the real thing, which . . . now that I think about it, works for me, but not for you. Justin, Jack, you guys gotta let me go and run away now, or they're gonna kill you. That sounds like a plan, right, guys?"

"I just wanna know one thing," Jack says. "You trained with us as Apologia. We took the same vows and everything. Didn't it bother you to find out the Adonai were killing colonials? Were you just okay with the thought that they were trying to kill us?"

"Jack, c'mon, man . . . you gotta do what you gotta do. Self-preservation. You can't blame me."

"We have to move now," I shout to Jack. Out the window this Oleth fellow is now heading our way as a mob emerges. "Louis, you're a coward. You may survive this thing, but you'll never survive yourself." With that, we're up the stairs and into a smaller room that looks out on the roof. Though it is lower than most, a zip line is attached to the roof of the second floor. At the back of the structure a cable extends over the wall and into the jungle. We'll never make it if we try to run. Courage, Justin.

"What's the play, fearless leader?" Jack asks.

"You go that way, over the wall. Courtney and Hope will need protection. I'll draw their attention on this zip line."

"Into the middle of the camp? Into the lion's den?"

"I'll be fine, buddy. This is a battle. The girls need your help." For a moment, he's the nerdy, helpless friend I knew back home. Only now though, do I realize that it's not helplessness. That's not what I loved about him. It was his humility, and how he loved everyone. Now I see that he's back. He's his old self again. We hug briefly, and I announce, "I'll see you at The Colony. Don't stop until you get there."

"*Truth will triumph*," he shouts as he runs for the zip line that leads over the wall.

"*Truth will triumph!*" I respond as I head for the zip line above the fray.

Latching onto the cord I take off over the heads of the charging horde. If I hit the ground running I might be able to outpace them. Nope! "Arghh!" Someone's leapt up and bear-hugged me around the waist. I'm in the sand and light penetrates the clouds. Standing over me is my captor, Oleth. As I scramble I see him slowly sliding the curved sword from a loop on his belt as he walks casually toward me. "*Umph!*" He kicks me in the face. I roll three times and somehow organize my movements enough to find my feet.

"So, my friend, you are the Northern Colony troublemaker?" he asks with a Nigerian accent. "Louis has told me. You have disturbed the vision of the Adonai. I will kill you, and then I will kill Foley."

"You . . . you're a killer like them, huh?"

"Ahh, I was not a killer. I was a peaceful man, living in paradise. Foley made me a killer. I had to kill to survive. But I am loyal to the Adonai. If they too decided to kill to protect their Colony, I will succeed where they failed." There's no way out of this. I'm trapped. I've got to fight.

Retrieving my machete I stand ready for certain death. He swings and I dodge. He swings again and I deflect his blade with mine before attempting a kick to his gut. I miss and stagger four paces past him before spinning to get a punch to the face. I spit blood and then look to him again. He swings with all his might and with a sidestep he misses. I kick against his left calf and he crumples to his knees for a moment before recovering and charging me. Grabbing me by the throat, he tosses me to the sand. A typical move is in order. With a fistful of beach I catapult sand into his eyes and he stops to rub them. A crowd shouts their obscenities, and I stand and speak.

"Listen, the original vision of the Adonai never included murder! This is crazy! You were all duped, or at least your parents were! This is not what your forbearers wanted!"

Oleth laughs, "There is no God here, Apologia. We are not mere unbelievers. We are consistent in our unbelief. No God – no morality. No morality, no problem murdering those who threaten us."

"Then what's the point of loyalty, Oleth? What's the point of anything?"

"You call me Olethron. But, you know something, Apologia? You're right." He begins a laugh, "I don't really care."

He swings again and again, I dodge kneeing him in the stomach. He's not very elegant, but he makes up for it with brute strength. He grips my neck under his arm and begins to squeeze. I don't have a choice. Placing my blade on his thigh I slide it along in a slicing fashion that is shallow and superficial, but enough to cause him to howl in pain and release.

As he stands there holding his thigh he drops his sword and grunts, "Impressive, young fool. I'll tell you what I'm going to do for you. I'm going to let you go. I want you to tell Foley we are coming for him. He will see. First, I want to show you that you can destroy an Adonai Colony, but you cannot destroy the Adonai plan. You were made by the Adonai and I will show you that you are still our property."

Indicating to four colonials, the Adon walks toward the huts. I struggle as the four of them grip my arms and drag me after him. While he inserts a metal pole into a fire I lecture him again, "This makes no sense. This Island is going to be discovered. When it is, you'll all be thrown in prison! You might not believe in right and wrong, but at the very least you should consider your own happiness!"

"We will talk no more, Apologia," he demands

as he removes the long poker. On its end is a brand of some sort. I struggle to get free once more to no avail. Just before the pain I recognize the emblem affixed to the end of the pole. The glowing blood orange symbol of the Adonai moves through the air - the frame of an "A" with what looks like a human eye at the crossbeam. I know it well. Now, though, it no longer represents home, hope, human achievement, protection or family as it did in my childhood. The look of it now matches the reality - pain, slavery, evil, violation.

My heart flutters in my chest as I breathe quickly and wait for the torment. *"Arggggghhhhh!"* My left bicep sizzles, and the scent of burning flesh meets my nostrils. The crowd cheers and I nearly lose consciousness. Neurons rattle, skin burns, tremors overtake me and suddenly I am released. I don't even remember hitting the ground, but I lay there moaning for as long as they'll allow. Searing agony does not leave, but it does subside. Now the earth is moving. Not the earth . . . me. They're dragging me again.

On the outside of the Unbelieving Tribe wall I'm left in the dirt. Oleth's voice interrupts my brief relief when he explains, "You see, my friend, you are a dog. You belong to us. You are not free. You will never be free. Gone from one Adonai Colony and running right to another. So, go tell Adon Foley that I am coming for him. Now leave us, dog . . . or die . . . I do not care," he begins to loudly laugh. "You choose."

CHAPTER NINETEEN

My feet struggle to remain beneath my body and my left hand clutches the brand. Leaning against a tree I affix the neckerchief around the wound and stare at the sky long enough to indulge in a few deep breaths. I'm beaten, bloody and flat worn out. Making it all the way to The Colony is going to be tough.

I'm not even sure exactly where to go. The crew isn't at the broken down ship. I can't cross the minefield again. Jack isn't here to serve as my guide. No doubt, I would have paid more attention on the way here if Jack had not been with us. Stupid, Justin! Left . . . I'm going left, deeper into the interior of the Island where I haven't been. I have no choice. I've got to make it around the minefield.

***

After two hours following the edge of the kudzu-covered field of death, I see that it ends and stone begins. The rock forms a natural barrier to the overgrowth and I am able to cross. This was surely a riverbed at one time. Now distant, the peak is to my right. Before me is a brief row of trees and beyond it looks like a large pond or lake. With renewed vigor, I rush toward the water and don't stop until it is chest high. Ducking under the surface I allow the blood and dirt to be washed away. Stinging, the brand is moistened. Muted joy begins to overcome me as I realize how good it is to be alive. I should be dead! This is all too much. I need the Ocean's Wave!

"A beast you cannot *best*, a friend you cannot *trust*, this no time to *rest*, this no time to *lust*. Hee, hee, ho, ho!" Whirling in the water, I see my jolly stalker again. Aldo sits on a rock next to the shore giggling.

"You again! What do you want?"

He raises his cane and points it in my direction, "Dope not tell of Aldo. This mean dope pass test. Aldo tell dope before, tell no one we meet. If dope tell, dope no see Aldo again . . . dope pass test."

"Great, what do I win, a boat out of this place?"

"Hee, hee," he laughs hysterically before dropping all humor and with a stern look answering, "No." Then, just as before his bushy eyebrows raise and he belly laughs again at himself. "Dope wins advice from Aldo." I roll my eyes.

"Listen, I don't know who you are. I assume you're left over from the Island's former inhabitants, and don't get me wrong, that's really impressive. But, Aldo, you can't possibly understand my situation."

"Hmm. Colony leader act out of what inside," Aldo says, motioning to his heart. "What he do, bad enough. That is not real problem. What he do, he do because of what he believe. Dope need learn what leader believe. Then dope know why he do like he do . .

152

. and why dope cannot trust him. *Listen to advice and accept discipline, and at the end dope will be like Aldo*." As he finishes, he cracks up again. He always looks like he's struggling not to laugh.

"What do *you* know about Foley?"

"Aldo see things. Now listen. This Island strange. The enemy try to speak to dope. Dope, listen me. Do not believe enemy."

"You mean, Foley? Is that the enemy you're talking about?"

"Hee, hee, hee, . . . no."

"Oleth . . . you're talking about Olethron."

"Ho, ho, ho, . . . no. Ultimate enemy. He will try. He will speak to dope. Dope cannot listen. Bye bye, dope!" He gets up to leave and I try to move toward him, but the water slows me. He just disappears into the jungle rhyming again.

"A beast you cannot *best*, a friend you cannot *trust*, this no time to *rest*, this no time to *lust*. Hee, hee, ho, ho!" He's gone.

Moving out of the water I reach for my utility belt and open the small compartment that contains what's left of the Ocean's Wave. I empty the contents into my mouth in its concentrated form and cup my hands in the pond. Water and powder mix on my tongue. There wasn't much left. It'll probably be okay.

". . . no time to lust," Aldo's rhyme had said. Was he talking about the Wave? Was he talking about Bailee? Would he even know about either? Maybe he's onto something. It's too late today, though. Lying back, I allow the Wave to overtake me and then look around for a spot to rest from the afternoon sun.

Wandering around the edge of the water the large mouth of a cave is visible. Approaching the entrance it becomes clear that it isn't deep, but it is tall and wide. I move far enough toward the back to hide me from the sunlight, and in the dim interior, lie down on a rock to sleep.

As exhaustion overtakes me, a seductive message creeps into my mind. "Vanquish them," I sense an inner voice say, "You must . . . vanquish them." In that moment between sleep and awake, I recognize the experience. It is not unlike the strong impulse I felt to trust Hope and Noah at the Northern Colony. This is different somehow. I need to pray, I need . . .

***

"Vanquish them," I hear the voice say again. How long have I been asleep? I wake up and toward the back of the cave I think I see someone. I can't quite make out his frame, but he's definitely there. It's not Aldo. This character is slender, athletic and shadowy. "Vanquish them," he says again, and now it's no longer an inner voice. It's almost audible. Rushing to the back wall of the cave I find no one. Quickly, I reach into my pouch and ignite the lighter. Nothing. A fresh rush of the Ocean's Wave hits me, probably because I stood so quickly, and I'm overcome with confidence and satisfaction. Is this God communicating with me? It must be. "Vanquish them" doesn't sound like what I would expect, but maybe so. Maybe that's the only way.

I should spend some time in prayer, but I've got to move. I'm out of the cave and realize it's morning. Did I sleep all through the night? It is only now that I realize how badly I was beaten. I'm sore. I'm very sore. No more Ocean's Wave. I'll have to try to focus without it. It looks like there is a range of high hills that trail up toward the peak, and a grassy valley cuts through them. That's my best bet.

In the midst of the valley is a sizeable stream that feeds the pond. This area is beautiful. It looks like the images I've seen of Hawaii - colorful flowers, lush greenery and clear water. Gorgeous. The beauty brings a new problem into focus – Hope and Bailee. I've put it off until now, but everyone at the Southern Colony has Bailee and I already engaged or something. Hope, naturally assumes I have eyes only for her. I'm torn. It's like the confusion I felt between Hope and Courtney. Only in Courtney's case I never really felt the same. Shaking my head I tell myself out loud, "Snap out of it, Justin." This is not the time for worrying about crushes and romance. It is, however, time to think about something that involves them. I've got to figure out where my loyalties are. An unnatural movement in my peripheral vision interrupts my thoughts. I'm being followed.

***

Hours have past and I am now almost back to the Southern Colony. I'll be coming in from the Chapel side, along the beach. Whoever is trailing me hasn't done the best job of concealing his presence. It's not the time yet. I've been waiting for the right moment. The beach is in view now and I begin to exit the forest. Large boulders sit along the edge of the beach that will momentarily hide my actions. Kicking against the rocks I position myself seven feet above the sand and wait. I can't see who it is, but his slow movement is obvious. I pounce. He's down and out. It's one of the two Unbelieving Apologia we left on the peak.

His hands are briskly restrained with his own Apologia wrist cuffs. Slapping his cheeks I obnoxiously taunt, "Hey . . . wake up, sand flea." He rouses.

"What . . . I . . ." He is dazed for a few moments before resting his head back on the sand and exhaling with a groan of frustration.

"Come on. Get up. We don't have much further to go." He walks in front of me as I grip the restraints between his hands.

We take a small path that leads around to the front of the Chapel and then down to the beachfront area of The Colony. Several colonials recognize me and begin to shout. Some of them recognize this fellow too. I don't like the way they look at him. A few shout angrily. Uh-oh. Did I just trade one mob for another? They all stop instantly when a Veritas robed angel appears. Bailee! She shushes them and rushes over.

Foley's two Apologia twins take the turncoat and lead him away. Bailee wraps her arms around me and then grips the back of my neck with both hands, pressing her forehead against mine.

"You came back to me," She's crying now. "I knew you would, my prince."

"Bailee, listen I . . ."

"No. We will have time to talk, but we have to get you back to the Mansion. Look at you! You're so banged up."

"Yeah, I feel like I've been through a meat grinder, but listen, have you seen my friends? Did they make it?"

She nods her head enthusiastically with wide eyes for a moment before informing me that, "They are all at the Mansion. Apologia Jack and Apologia Courtney. I'm so glad they are here, and Miss Hope is there too." Time to go all in.

"Bailee, listen, I need to tell you about Hope. I should have already told you. She and I . . . we're kind of . . ." she cuts me off.

"It's okay, Justin. I thought maybe . . . I wondered about it when I saw her."

"What do you mean it's okay? I mean, you were crying just a moment ago for me. I must not be that hard to get over."

"Oh no, no, no, my sweet prince. I know that you and I will be together," she says with determination and a confident smile. "But, you need to come to realize what is *meant to be* on your own. I will not speak of our love to Miss Hope. You will tell her when you realize that our union is undeniable." She kisses me on the cheek and turns to walk away raising the Veritas hood. Wow . . . just . . . wow. Well, that's handy I guess. Following her, I stagger toward the hilly path up to the Mansion.

CHAPTER TWENTY

In the yard behind the Mansion, Jack, Hope and Courtney greet me as Bailee dutifully exits the scene to perform her common tasks. They have all bathed and put on new clothes. Courtney and Jack have been on the Island long enough to have apparently put thought into their own wardrobes. Courtney wears a black tank top that she seems to have designed herself. She has customized it with a large Apologia emblem on the front, tilted at an angle, with bright green dye. She wears jeans rolled up to just below the knee and her blond hair is in a ponytail. Jack is in a black V-neck and one of the lightweight Apologia jackets of the Southern Colony. Hope wears a white V-neck and green tights. Her hair is down. I feel a bit out of place.

"Justin," Courtney shouts as she sees me first. They all turn and come rushing over. Hope hugs me aggressively.

"*Agh!*"

"What? What is it, hero," she asks with a concerned look as she scans my body.

"I'm just a little banged up, snowflake." I see that it now sinks in.

Her jaw gapes and she says, "Come on, we've

got to get you patched up."

"I'm fine," I assure her. "I'll let Foley's crew straighten me out in a bit." I start to stumble as I move for the benches on the Mansion patio.

Jack stabilizes me and says, "Whoa, pal. You sure?"

"Yeah," I grunt as I collapse onto the bench and Hope positions herself next to me cleaning dirt away from the wounds above my eye as best she can with her thumb. "Let me look at Courtney. I want to see my sister." Kneeling on the stone patio in front of me she looks playfully annoyed at the classification. We don't need to say it, though we both know our past. Still, "sister" best describes how I think of her. "You're really here aren't you, my sweet friend?" She tears up and reaches for my hand. I squeeze it gently.

She closes her eyes to let the moment pass and then faking seriousness, jokingly responds, "Yeah, and Justin, just don't even think about following me around like a puppy dog the way you used to. I'm sorry. I know you're infatuated, but me and Jackson are kind of a thing now, okay? You're just going to have to get over me." Hope leans her head on my shoulder as we all lightly chuckle.

"Don't call me Jackson! My name's Jack." Immediately, our chuckles become belly laughs. Here, in this heavenly garden, we're together again. We have our *each other*. My long journey has paid off. Whatever happens next, I know . . .

"*Truth will triumph,*" Jack shouts.

In unison we all respond to the prompt, "*Truth will triumph!*"

***

All afternoon, we joked and caught up with each others' lives. Bailee tended to my wounds while my crew sat around watching. She barely spoke and never betrayed our trust. Courtney has absolutely taken to Jack. My concern that she was putting up a façade has been chased away. I was ready to tell Foley all about our adventure across the Island, and with my injuries I'm sure he wants to know, but he urged me to save it until later tonight. Jack and I have retired to my quarters in the Mansion to prepare for evening dinner. Hope had explained the ceremonial formal dining she and Noah observed on the train, and Foley thought the idea was splendid. So here we are again getting needlessly overdressed in the midst of the most dire of circumstances. That's my Hope.

"We've moved up in the world, huh, Jack?"

He looks at me with a stupid smile and admits, "Justin, I'm happier now than I've been in a long time."

"I'm glad. You and Courtney okay? I couldn't help but see what looked like a passionate disagreement at the back of the yard?"

"Yeah, it's . . . it's nothing."

"C'mon, buddy. Spill it."

"Ocean's Wave," he says staring at the ceiling. Looking back to me he finishes, "She's never touched it. She's been weird about things ever since we got here, and the whole Veritas thing with the Chapel and the Ocean's Wave just creeps her out. She's never made much of a fuss. She realizes that neither of us ever had any experience with religious services. Foley's whole deal seems weird to us, but it might not be weird in the real world." As he speaks I intentionally don't change my facial expression. I know what he doesn't. Normal mainstream Christian services are not like what Foley and the Veritas lead here. Courtney's intuition that it's weird is not wrong. He continues, "So she's never really made a big deal out of things, but she acts like I'm some kind of addict with the Ocean's Wave and thinks I'm too trusting of Foley."

"She doesn't like him?"

"She likes him. She just keeps him at arm's length."

"What about her faith. Does she believe?"

We both sit on the edge of the bed to put on our shoes and he pauses to consider his words. "You gotta remember that she went from the lies of the Northern Colony to this strange place. When I try to explain how God has worked in my life, and all that we learned at the train, she doesn't reject it. She just says, 'Jack, all I know is that I believe in you,' but what does that mean?"

"I don't know. She'll come around."

We exit the bedroom looking like dapper retro fops ready to paint the town red. Tuxedos left over from another time add more elegance than modern clothes can muster. Out on the back patio we find that the evening is lit up with the old lampposts and an elegant outdoor dining scene has been set. The rectangular table is prepared for five and place cards rest on each charger. Foley's name is at the end of the table at the captain's chair, and naturally, I am to sit at his right hand. To my right is a cream card with "Hope" written on it in script. Across from me and to the left of Foley's chair is Jack's spot. To his left is where Courtney has been placed.

Foley glides out of the Mansion in the same clothes he always wears, but now he adorns a black necktie and top hat. Courtney emerges in a black evening gown and large diamond earrings. We all stand in honor of her undeniable beauty. Clearly, my girl has gotten ahold of her. Behind Courtney, Hope follows and it becomes obvious the atmosphere of the garden was incomplete without her presence. She's over the top, but somehow . . . it works. An intricate pastel green dress adorned with pearls and lace spills off her shoulders, but reaches to her feet. She looks like she's ready for one of those otherworldly perfume commercials I saw when I was recuperating in Chicago. The ladies sit, and then we join them.

"Sublime," Foley pronounces. "The Southern

Colony has been impoverished without you ladies . . . in fact, without all of you, my new friends."

I take a sip of Ocean's Wave from an old champagne flute and answer, "We owe you a lot, Foley. I'm sure none of us came here thinking we would be dining in the lap of luxury like this."

"Ah, well, you can thank Lady Hope for that. I love the idea of these absurd evening dinners. I love the history they have with Hope and her father on the train you called . . . what was it? Ah yes, Wynfelt Manor." Hope grins shyly and looks back and forth at the table. "In fact, tonight our Mansion will temporarily be dubbed 'Wynfelt Manor,' and we shall observe this ritual as 'the Dinner of Hope.' . . . You see what I did there, darling. It's an allusion."

Hope responds, "I'm ever so grateful, sir, but I think the word you're looking for is 'pun.' You made a pun."

"Here we go," Jack says.

"Is it?" Foley questions. "I'm quite sure I meant 'allusion.'"

Inhaling through her teeth and shaking her head she contends, "No . . . no, it's a pun."

Jack brushes the debate away with, "Hope, just leave the man alone. You're killing the sense of normalcy we're enjoying."

She winces at him and demands, "Normality . . . normality, normality, normality."

Interrupting the playful banter, the Vertias girls enter wearing their sundresses with serving trays full of food and gather around the circumference of the table. Foley stands and raises a glass.

"Hope, I defer to you, darling. After all, it is your night. And . . . it is a night to celebrate the return of Jack, Courtney, and the prince of the Adonai, my friend Justin. Let us raise our glasses to . . . uh . . ."

"We kind of have a thing for this, Foley," I insert. He motions with his left hand waiting for my answer. "Each other."

"Ah," he agrees. "I like it. *To each other!*"

"*To each other,*" we all say. Only with our glasses raised, I see that Courtney has drinking water. Jack's right. She's staying clear of the Ocean's Wave. Only now do I realize that Foley is drinking from an old ornate German stein. He always does. Because it's not made of clear glass, I can't tell if he's sipping the Wave or not. Nevertheless, I'm too lost in the moment to care.

***

The gentlemen retire to the Mansion library and the girls remain lounging on the patio. Jack, Foley and I sit in the lush red cushioned chairs and sip the Ocean's Wave. Our discussion first centers on the same casual subjects that comprised the evening's careless tone. As the conversation drifts toward serious matters, Jack and I detail our adventures. Jack explains Courtney's captivity and his back and forth attempts to save her. I go into detail about the Unbelieving Tribe, Oleth, and my capture of the anonymous Unbelieving Apologia officer. The cards are on the table.

After listening intently, Foley asks, "Justin, do you trust me?"

"Okay," I grin in a you-got-me sort of way, "I didn't at first. But you've got to understand, I have a lot of Northern Colony baggage."

"No, no," he interrupts, "I do understand. I expected it."

"But," I assure him, "I've come to trust you. I don't know about this prophecy business, but I'm coming around."

"Good. Because what I'm going to tell you will be hard to deal with. Your female counterparts would almost certainly protest."

Jack asks, "It's about the Ocean's Wave isn't it?"

"It's about that and more," he replies. "Ask me what happened to Damian Yukimura."

I feel my eyes shift upward as I consider the strange question, "Okay . . . what happened to

Yukimura?"

"He's dead," the Adon unemotionally reveals.

"Wait," I say, "I thought he came and went. You hid me from him, right? How is he dead?"

"I killed him," he reveals with no more emotion than he would announce that he swatted a mosquito. Then he takes a drink from his stein. "Stabbed him right in the chest." The blood rushes from my head and the room appears to spin. Without moving, Jack shifts his eyes back and forth between us, gauging my reaction.

"Why?" I demand with desperation.

Looking to the hallway as if concerned someone will hear, he answers, "He was an Adon of the Northern Colony. They're killers, mate. Scripture says, 'an eye for an eye . . . if a man sheds innocent blood, by man shall his blood be shed.' Someone has got to do what needs to be done to ensure that they don't ever . . . do it again." I roll it around in my head and attempt to judge whether he's right.

"Did you know about this?" I interrogate Jack.

"It's . . . yeah. I mean, I didn't do it myself, but, yeah . . . I knew. And . . . I can't say it doesn't make sense."

"Alright, Jack . . . now *everything* makes sense. This is why you didn't give it a second thought to try and kill the Unbelieving Apologia!"

"And why should he have," Foley breaks in. "Make no mistake Justin, everyone at the Unbelieving Tribe is a killer. Jack is just living out his faith based on passages like the ones I just quoted."

"How did you come to this conclusion, Foley?" I demand. "Whatever gave you the idea that this was okay?"

"Wonderful question, young prince." He sits up on the edge of his chair. "When this was an Adonai Colony, I was loyal to the Adonai cause. I told you about the suitcase that washed ashore with the two Bibles inside, but I didn't tell you when it washed up. It was while our *parents* were still here. I found the suitcase and kept the Bibles for myself. One of them I hid away in the cave on the peak, knowing it would be taken if found. The other I kept here, at The Colony. If I lost one, I'd have the other, but my secret was discovered by the colonials. Our loyal fathers cast me into that pit at the back of the yard where you both began your stay on the Island. By that time, I had memorized as much of it as I could. They can't take away what's in your head. They left me there for weeks, just tossing down the smallest amount of food and water. That holding cell was meant to correct my thinking. Knelt there everyday, all I saw was the Creed of the Adonai, 'freedom to think, freedom to live, hope to seek, hope to give,' ha! How ironic. And all it did was breed anger in my heart. I thought through the scripture I had memorized. I sat trying to . . . meditate or something. I tried to empty my mind as best I could of all thought.

My goal was to do anything to escape my predicament in the pit even if it only meant psychologically escaping. Then, it happened."

"What did?" I ask, as I drink the Ocean's Wave deeply.

With a look of reverence, Foley continues, "I received a vision . . . a message . . . a burning in my heart. I knew what had to be done. A voice deep within made it known that I had to be the one to smite the false Adonai."

"You're the one who wrote all that stuff on the walls!"

"I am. More than that, I played along and they released me. Then I carried out what the voice commanded." I drink again as he speaks. "It wasn't hard to convince most of the colonials that our parents needed judgment. Together, we banded, and sent them the way of old Yukimura." The Ocean's Wave is at full force in my veins and I know that drinking much more of it will cause me to lose consciousness. "I purified our Colony. I knew it was right. There were dissenters, Adonai loyalists. We drove them out. Setting up the Unbelieving Tribe, they have opposed us violently ever since that day. The story doesn't end there. Ultimately, I discovered the passage," he says nodding toward the secret entrance in the bookshelf. "I learned of the prophecy. I didn't know who the other man in the painting was until you arrived, Justin. Now I've never been more sure." In my bones, I know that I should protest. I don't. The Ocean's Wave makes it all seem sensible.

"What . . . what does all of this have to do with the Ocean's Wave?" I ask.

"Mate . . . I think you already know." I stare into the swirling blue drink and look up to Jack who is expressionless. "The stockpile left over from the former inhabitants was not a decontaminant. It is a mind control drug. They experimented with the idea during the Second World War. Later, their ideas were built upon, but come to find out, they had this all along. It was all I needed. It still keeps The Colony on the straight and narrow path. I teach from scripture, and they drink. Then the Veritas explain my meaning again, and they drink. No one ever questions." I sit paralyzed as his explanation ends. No one speaks for ten full seconds, then a loud scream is heard from outside.

We all rush into the hallway and down the corridor to the foyer. Another scream is heard and we head out the front door where Foley's own Apologia guards circle the source of the action. There, I see the Unbelieving Apologia with a knife to the throat of a Veritas girl. Is it Bailee? No, thank goodness. Bailee is standing by watching the monster holding her friend. The enemy Apologia looks terrified as he clutches the Veritas.

"Where are Courtney and Hope?" I swiftly and nervously ask, gripping Bailee by her shoulders.

"I . . . uh," she can't answer.

"Bailee! Where are they?"

"They went down to the beach," she answers through tears.

"Stop, unbeliever," Foley shouts. "Let her go and you will live. Harm her and you know I will not hesitate."

"Liar," the Unbelieving Apologia barks. "I know what you are! You'll never let me leave!" Foley's grunts creep closer, but the Adon looks calm. "Back away! I'll kill her! I mean it!" He does mean it. Milliseconds later, the Veritas girl falls lifeless to the earth.

"NOOO," I yell, but it's too late. I run half the distance toward them. Suddenly, the Unbelieving Apologia falls lifeless too. Looking back in confusion, I see Foley, arm outstretched, with an antique sidearm raised and smoking.

Lowering the weapon, he looks to us and says, "You see, young prince? How many more innocents will die, before you see what must be done. This . . . is the only way."

Staggering into the Mansion and up to my quarters, I drink deeply of the Ocean's Wave knowing full well what it is, and what will happen. My vision clouds as it did in Rio, and I collapse as everything goes dark. "Vanquish them," the voice from the cave says again. "Vanquish them."

CHAPTER TWENTY-ONE

My head aches as I open my eyes and the room slowly stops spinning. There is another presence standing by.

"Let's talk, mate," Foley says, from a chair near my bed. I sit up in a startled fashion and then rub my eyes, realizing the previous day was not some twisted elegant nightmare. He doesn't encourage me to drink the Ocean's Wave, and despite my addiction, I don't. I need clarity. Real clarity.

***

We walk along the rocky cliffs of the protective natural arms that stretch out from either side of the beachfront Colony and surround the large cove. From the perspective of the beach, we are on the cliffs to the right. The surface of the top, where we walk, is mostly flat and easy to tread. It is a good fifteen feet wide. To my right is open sea as far as can be seen. To the left is the gorgeous beachfront Colony, a good 550 yards away. We are now approaching the end of this peninsula. The circle is broken by a forty-foot gap. Across the gap is the alternate cliffy arm that circles back toward the mainland. The opening seemed so much narrower from the beach. One hundred feet below, the water can be seen moving between the cliffs and into the large cove.

"I love this spot, Justin. It is because here, I see how separate we are. I can look to the Island and see all that I love, and the bright future we have in this paradise. I can also look to the sea, and thank God that we are so divorced from the world of pain and suffering."

We are both silent, considering his words before I ask, "Foley . . . What do you think it means that the prophecy calls us 'saviors?'"

"Well, simply put, we are to be gods."

"What do you mean, gods?"

"You know like, Jesus. Jesus became a god. We will be like him. Isn't that what every Christian intends to do . . . be like Jesus?"

"Sure, but, you're saying Jesus wasn't God in the flesh? You're saying he became a god?"

"Of course. He's the Son of God. It's not like God is split into two or something," he laughs.

"Well, the way I've always understood it, most Christians believe in a Holy Trinity – God the Father, God the Son, and God the Holy Spirit."

"I do too. I just realize that Jesus was a man about whom certain prophecies were made. Those prophecies were fulfilled and he became a god."

Flicking me in the chest with the back of his hand, he adds, "That's just like us, Justin. We can become gods too. We have prophecies. We will fulfill them. It's a high, high calling, mate." What he says doesn't sound right, but then, there's a lot I don't know about the faith. Maybe Foley *is* right. I don't know.

Walking to the edge of the cliff I look out at the open sea and answer, "There's just so much I don't know. What you're saying now, the Unbelieving Tribe, the Life Circle Assembly . . . the killing."

"I believe what I've told you is based on scripture. And as for the killing, well, look at the horizon, my friend. Do you see anyone coming to our aid? Is anyone on their way to imprison and give fair trial to the Unbelieving Tribe?"

"No, of course not, but . . ."

"That's right. We're alone. With all the possibility that brings, there is also responsibility. Justin, Oleth is organizing to attack, you told me yourself. That was his message for me. Once again, an Adonai is planning the slaughter of innocent believers. What are we supposed to do? Wait to die?" His passion is increasing, and his voice rises. "There's nothing wrong with self-defense, and here it's kill or be killed!"

"Yeah, but . . ."

"Do you plan to let them slaughter Hope? What about Courtney?" I don't respond. How could I? I would do anything to protect my friends. He grips my bare arm where the fresh Adonai brand is burned into my skin, and says, "They're making their mark with no regard for flesh and blood!"

***

Approaching the Life Circle Chapel alone, I know I have hours of study ahead. The sanctuary is quiet and bright. Lifting the aged leather Bible from its holder, I move to a pew and begin searching. Everyone tells me that if I want to understand the message, I should start in the Gospel of John. I read all of the scriptures during my time in Chicago, but the finer points of doctrine require specific research. I barely begin reading before I see it. There, on the first line it reads, *"In the beginning was the Word and the Word was with God and the Word was . . . a . . . God."* I know from my previous reading that the 'Word,' is Jesus. I must have missed the one letter word that changes the entire meaning of the passage, and perhaps the entire proper understanding of the Christian faith – 'a.'

Hours later I find another hint. Colossians 2:9 says, *"- because it is in him that all the fullness of the divine quality dwells bodily."* Huh. That just doesn't sound right. Before I can continue my investigation a loud creak disturbs the silence.

"Hey, hero," Hope says in a cheerful voice that echoes off of the stone walls. "You trying to hide?" I make a personal commitment not to tell her about the violent events of the night before.

"I'm not the one who ran off with Courtney

after dinner," I kid.

"She wanted to show me her little shack just off the beach. It's so cute, Justin. This place really is paradise." I'm glad she's enjoying herself, but I now know that were it not for the Ocean's Wave she would be skeptical of everything about this place.

"Hope, we've got to talk." Her cheerful demeanor fades to seriousness. "Have you had the blue stuff today?"

"Ocean's Wave? Not since breakfast. Why? Now that you mention it though, I wouldn't mind it."

"Don't . . . Just trust me. It's some sort of intoxicant. It . . . messes with your head."

"Okay. Justin, are you all right? You're worrying me." I'm worrying myself too. The very mention of the Ocean's Wave is driving me crazy with desire.

"Forget that for now. What do you make of this passage?" I indicate first to John 1:1.

"Uh . . . uh, oh," she says.

"It sounds weird right? And look at this in Colossians."

"Justin, I know what this is. It's a translation of the Bible that has been edited to present Jesus as a created being, and not God incarnate. I forget what it's called. The New . . . globe . . . earth. No, I don't remember. Bottom line is, it's bad news. It was put together by a worldwide cult. What would be funny if it weren't so dangerous is that no one even knows who the translators were. Most modern translations have a page in the front that tells about the translation team, and their credentials. It's a big secret within some cult organization who these translators were."

"Well, what's wrong with it?" I demand.

"Okay," she begins. "'*In the beginning was the Word, and the Word was with God and the Word was God.*' That's how it's supposed to read. They have it '. . . *the Word was . . . a . . . god.*' That's the textual manipulation. My father made sure I knew about this and a few other cults so that if I ever made it out of the Northern Colony region, I wouldn't fall right in with another weird group."

"What about this one," I say, showing her Colossians 2:9.

"Yep. Same thing. This translation has it, '*because it is in him that all the fullness of the . . . divine quality . . . dwells bodily.*' It should read something like, '. . . *the fullness of the Godhead dwells bodily,*' indicating that Jesus doesn't just possess a divine quality, but is God in the flesh. If this is what Foley's been reading, and teaching from . . . he's going to have some weird beliefs."

"He does."

***

After twenty minutes, I've caught Hope up on my morning conversation with Foley, the truth about the Ocean's Wave, and Foley's willingness to kill. Her indignation has risen slowly as the Ocean's Wave has worn off. Two things I kept from her - The death of the Veritas girl and the Unbelieving Apologia, and the dark visitor from the cave. Now it's time to get an answer.

"Hope," I say, with my hand on hers. "There's one more thing. Sleeping in a cave on the way back from the Unbelieving Tribe, I heard a voice. I think it was God speaking to me. You know like . . . a revelation or something. It said, 'vanquish them.'" She recoils her hand from beneath mine and stands in disgust. I stand to meet her line of vision and ask, "Is it possible? Is God telling me to help vanquish the Unbelieving Tribe and fulfill the prophecy?"

Looking utterly distressed she answers, "No! This is frightening, Justin, but remember what I told you at the peak. Not everything that is spiritual is good. The leaders of some of the most influential false religions in the world claimed to have had experiences like that. Some of them outright said that they thought they had encountered a . . . a . . . demon." I walk to the window and the world seems somehow grim. She approaches me from behind and with her hands on my shoulders rests her forehead on my back. "Justin, the enemy, the ultimate enemy, has been laying this trap for a long time. The prophecy, the voice, Foley, the false doctrine about Jesus . . . it's all a part of a strategy that has been planned for decades."

"I don't know what to think, Hope. It all seems to fit so well. The worst thing of all, I guess, is the killing, but is it really wrong if it's in defense of innocent people? I mean, look, Foley is right about one thing. There isn't anyone else here to stop the Unbelieving Tribe. There are no prisons to put them in even if we could capture them all . . . and we couldn't anyway. Would God hold it against us if we killed to protect others?"

Looking hopeless as she slumps onto a pew, she answers honestly, "I don't know." Looking up at me she says, "I love it here. I love the tribe. I love that we're all together. I even like Foley . . . but . . . I won't remain silent about the truth, Justin. What Foley is teaching about Jesus is false. If we really believe truth will triumph, someone has to actually give and defend that truth."

Since our somewhat contentious conversation is already happening, I decide to lay it all out. "You're right. The truth matters, but . . . I've got to tell you something Hope that I'm afraid will change things between us. It's . . . uh . . . I don't know if you'll . . ."

"Hey," she says taking my hand, "it's okay. You can tell me anything." With a cock of the head, I give her a skeptical look.

"I want you to know that I love you. But . . ."

"I love you too, Justin."

"Just . . . let me finish. I love you, and nothing is going to change that. But there's a girl here on the Island." Her façade markedly changes as she slips backward into the pew. "Maybe . . . maybe it's the Ocean's Wave, but I developed . . . feelings for her. She's not . . . I mean . . . she . . ."

Breaking in with sudden anger, Hope asks, "You mean to tell me that while I was out there lost in this hot, muggy, dangerous wilderness, you were back here at Club Foley living out a romance story with some colonial flirt?" This isn't going well.

"No, Hope! I mean . . . yes, but . . . sort of," I utter with a nervous smile.

"Your attempts to look cute and charming won't help!" She starts to walk away and then comes back and shouts, "You know what? That's fine! You just go have your Island life. Fall in love with the Island girl! Join the Island cult! Hey, why not trade Jack in for a new best friend! Oh wait, you already did that!" She turns to walk away.

"No, Hope wait! I love *you*! I'm telling you this because the truth matters! I'm telling you, I've chosen *you* . . . not her!" She turns again to aggressively address me.

"Oh, what a lucky girl I am!" Sarcasm. "The chosen one has chosen me! Did you ever stop to think I could have chosen someone else?"

"Like who?" Immediately I realize the stupidity

of the question.

"Like *who*? I don't know! I could have fallen in love with *Jack* on the train!" She ends with a what-do-you-think-of-that sort of look.

"Jack? Come on snowflake, that's just ridiculous."

"Don't you 'snowflake' me! I'll tell you what, hero, we're stuck out here on this chunk of sand!" She takes two deep breaths and attempts to calm herself. In a much more relaxed voice she says, "You and I will meet with the others. We'll work as a team to get out of this mess, but just know that I have to rethink everything. I thought we had a commitment to each other. I guess I was wrong."

CHAPTER TWENTY-TWO

Fish sizzles in the Circle Island Café. Jack, Courtney, Hope and I sit in the corner looking out on the beach. Jack wears his Southern Colony Apologia uniform with its green lettering. The girls wear two more of Courtney's homemade Apologia tank tops, One black and one grey, both with green tilted Apologia emblems. Whispering, we share all our information. Well, neither Hope nor I mention our little spat. Our food is served and Hope begins to drink from a thick metal cup. Courtney covers the brim with her palm just before Hope drinks and presses the container down to the table. "Don't," she firmly says.

Hope looks momentarily surprised and responds, "Yeah. Yeah, I don't know what I was thinking." Of course she does. She was thinking exactly what Jack and I are thinking. Every cell in our bodies is raging for the stuff. Jack's eyes speak volumes to me. Neither of us likes keeping secrets from our Adon friend. Neither of us is comfortable with the upheaval of our new existence.

"What do we do, Justin?" Courtney asks. Suddenly, it's like we're in our former Apologia group at the Northern Colony. She recognizes my role as the leader.

Looking out the window I respond, "We explain the truth to Foley. He's got to understand that out here on this Island he hasn't had any proper mentoring in the faith. He'll take it in."

"Yeah," Jack agrees nodding his head rapidly. "I think he'll listen, especially since Justin and Hope have been living in the real world with all its resources for the past few months. He's not the type to ignore this sort of thing."

Shaking her head, Courtney replies, "No. I . . . I'm still working through what I think about all that faith stuff, but my real concern is the killing. You're not gonna convince him there. But since we are on the topic, how do you guys explain all the bloody details in the Bible. Is he making it up? Is it really in there? Is it more of that bad translation or whatever? That can't be what this God is like or else you guys wouldn't be into it. He sounds like . . . well . . . like the Adonai."

"He is the Adonai," Hope urges, "but not these murderous leaders who call themselves the Adonai. He's the true Master. They blasphemously use the word."

"You're not answering my question, Hope," Courtney says with an annoyed expression.

"Yes," the redhead answers. "Yes, that stuff is in the Bible – the actual Bible."

Looking around the room at no one in particular, Courtney rolls her eyes and says, "Okay, well there it is. God *is* like *these* Adonai. Appropriate."

"No," Hope says, "He's not. He's nothing like them. They had no right to execute judgment, and especially not for people who believe in God. Look Courtney, if someone doesn't believe in God, then yeah, some stuff in the Bible is hard to swallow. But if you do believe, then you acknowledge that He's the Maker of the universe. He's the ultimate judge. Those who carried out His orders had direct commands from Him. The Adonai, nor any other human leader, has that. And the people that were judged were ripe for judgment."

While Courtney thinks things through, I demand, "We talk to Foley. We tell him where he's wrong on the Jesus questions. As for the killing, I'm still on the fence. This is self-defense, not murder. There's got to be a difference." Hope abruptly stands and begins to head out the door, her nerves on edge from the discussion, and the lack of Ocean's Wave. She stops and turns before exiting.

"I won't be silent," she says. "I'll speak the truth no matter the cost." With this, she disappears around the corner. Jack and Courtney leave to continue their patrol of The Colony in true Apologia fashion. No one else speaks.

***

I sit on the beach watching the ocean to collect my thoughts as seventies rock echoes with a fuzz in the background. Footsteps pounding the sand trample those thoughts as a colonial woman shouts, "they got her . . . THEY GOT HER!" colonials scramble and I'm on my feet in an instant.

"What's happening?" I demand in a gruff voice grabbing the girl's forearm.

"The Unbeliever," she says in distress. "In the field! He got Veritas Bailee!" Time seems to slow as I rush up the path toward the field. One other Veritas girl is knelt in the midst of the crops and I race to her location. Then I see it. Bailee is on the ground, badly injured with a wound to her abdomen. I don't have to see anymore to put together what happened. Stupid, Justin! The other Unbelieving Apologia was on the hunt. He couldn't return to his tribe without a kill.

Kneeling, I cradle her head and demand, "Bailee! Bailee, I'm here!" Then looking to the other crying Veritas I shout, "Go get help!"

"Prince, Justin," She moans squinting in the sunlight to see my face. Her hand softly rests on my cheek. "I'm glad it's you . . . I'm glad it's you with me here."

"Bailee, hold on. They're coming with help, we'll fix this." My heart pounds and tears begin to stream.

"I don't want to leave you, my prince, but I can't stay." Tears stream down the sides of her face as fear sets in.

"You *can* stay, Bailee. I'm right here. The Veritas need you. I need you."

"At least now," she says through coughs, "you and Miss Hope can be together."

"Bailee. Bailee! Stay with me, sweetheart!"

She's fading fast and I look around for help, but it isn't coming. With what energy she has left, she groans, "The true way . . . the true way . . . The Great Divide . . . to stay we . . . pray."

"No, don't, Bailee. You don't know the truth. I didn't tell you. I . . ." She's gone.

Immediately behind me I hear the remaining Veritas running and I tightly clutch Bailee's body, knowing it's too late. Then movement creeps into my field of vision. Raising my head from Bailee's sweet face to gaze with anger toward the back of the field, my mission becomes clear. Foley has been right all along, at least about the need to kill. Call it self-defense, or call it vengeance, but I know what I have to do. I stand as the Veritas abruptly bump past me and land next to Bailee, but my eyes never leave the tree line. At first I walk as I struggle to process my emotions, then running, I disregard my thoughts. Sprinting, my face bends toward rage.

I'm in the trees at a faster pace than I've ever made. Green and brown blur around me and I vault over rocks. I see him. "Run," I shout. "Run as fast as you can, Unbeliever!" I keep racing through the forest and gaining on him. "What's wrong, sand flea? You can run faster than that," I taunt. He looks back and I recognize absolute terror on his face. "You scared? You should be! You'll get no mercy from me!" We approach the top of a hill that trails off at a moderate grade. He drops on his back and begins to slide. I follow. Halfway down I grip his uniform and as the slide ends we tumble together to the ground. He's knocked out.

Standing, I breathe heavily from the chase and with my hands on my hips I prepare myself to satisfy my violent desire. "Vanquish them," the inclination comes. Pursing my lips, I grip one of his hands and begin to drag the unconscious murderer back toward The Colony.

**

Crossing the Mansion yard, I carry the enemy perpendicular on my shoulders as a hunter would a buck. Kicking the doors open I enter the back of the structure and stride down the hallway toward Foley's library. The Adon sits reading a book when I carelessly drop the intruder on the rug at his feet.

"Bailee is dead. Here is her killer," I say gritting my teeth.

Removing his glasses he folds his book and places it on a side table. He decides, "Then he must die, young prince." I nod. The Unbelieving Apologia rouses and stands attempting to figure out where he is.

At the sight of Foley standing by, the young man shrieks, "NOOO!" and backs away as though he's seen the devil himself. He stumbles backward over a table and struggles to find his feet.

"Apologia," Foley hollers. In seconds the twin Southern Colony Apologia appear and straighten the frightened soul out.

"Let me," I say, grabbing the base of his Apologia hood.

"Right, well, . . . to the cliffs," the Adon pronounces as though it were commonplace.

CHAPTER TWENTY-THREE

The black and green robe of a Veritas girl wildly flaps in the wind as she follows me, Foley, the two Southern Colony Apologia, and the killer from the Unbelieving Tribe. We approach the spot where the circle of cliffs breaks and I view the distant drop again. I position the captive on his knees facing the ocean and see that if pushed over, the rocky slopes will mean his death. To my left, the space between the cliffs that serves as a massive gateway into The Colony cove does not have the jagged rocks, though it would be a long drop.

My resolve is strong as the Veritas girl speaks in a ceremonial fashion, "The true way, the true way – The Great Divide, to stay we pray."

I position my foot between the shoulders of the Unbelieving Apologia, prepared to release my anger when . . .

"Justin, don't," I stop and look to Jack and Courtney rushing along the cliffs toward us. Of course they would try to stop me. The whole Colony must have been notified of the day's events by now.

"Everyone calm down," Foley directs.

"Think of me what you will," I growl. "This

man is a murderer! He can't be allowed to do it again! I'll do whatever it takes to protect The Colony from the likes of him!"

"You sound like your father," Courtney screams. The statement is jarring. She's right. She wasn't even there when I knelt over Noah. My father was willing to kill to defend his little kingdom. But this is different. I'm nothing like he was!

"Justin," Jack shouts, "They took Hope!"

"Okay," Foley breaks in with a chuckle. "This is getting out of control. I would think you two would know better than to think you've got all the details. Let's just get back to the business at hand. Justin, would you please execute this man's . . . well, execution," he says with a laugh. He's nervous about something. Jack and Courtney have reached our position and the wind howls. Dark clouds emerge overhead and Southern Colony Apologia stand blocking my friends.

"Wait, what are you talking about?"

"Justin . . . Justin, I didn't want you to find out this way. It's a bit unpleasant, but the redhead was caught undermining my authority with some colonials, and dearest Justin, you *know* we can't have that. They tried to reason with her, but she was absolutely defiant. You know it must be true what they say about redheads. Anyway, I just had her arrested and locked away, by these two gentlemen here," he says indicating to the Southern Colony Apologia. "She'll be fine, young prince."

"What are you gonna do to her, Foley?" I sternly question.

"Oh now, mate, don't look at me like that. She'll be given the Ocean's Wave until she calms down and rethinks things. I have every confidence she'll fall in line."

"And if she doesn't?"

"Justin," he asks, "have you had anything to drink today? Anything blue?"

"I haven't," my response comes and he looks disturbed. "Foley, what if Hope doesn't fall in line?"

"Well, I won't have a choice then, will I? She'll have to be dealt with like our Unbelieving friend here." I grip the back of my skull and pace around the cliff, wide eyed and mouth gaping. "But, don't worry about that, mate. It won't get that far." I scan the scenery and realize that Hope was right about everything. Despite the fact that he believes in some god or other, he lives up to the title of all the false Adonai. I can't go along with it. Much as I want it, I can't take vengeance either.

Grabbing the Unbelieving Apologia by his shoulders I stand him up and ask, "Can you swim?"

"W . . . What?" he asks in confused fear.

"Don't do this, young prince," Foley warns.

"Answer me," I command. "Do you know how to swim?"

"Of course, I, I mean . . ." guiding him over to the deep watery gap between the rocks I demand, "fight with us or jump." My eyes stay fixed on Foley as he watches intently. The murderer mumbles hurried profanities to himself for ten long seconds before finally disappearing over the edge. I glance down and watch the water until his head reemerges, and he begins to swim away.

"This is my last offer," Foley says. "Come back to The Colony with us and we will work something out. You will not be harmed." Ha! Uncanny.

"You're not the first of the Adonai to offer me that deal. Those are the very words my father spoke." Launching at the villain, our hands meet and we begin to wrestle on our feet. Courtney and Jack deal with the Southern Colony Apologia. Foley slips his knee under my thigh and we fall to the ground.

He raises his fist and strikes, but as I dodge he hits the rock and howls. In his pain I flip us both over and he shouts, "You were like a brother to me!"

"You pushed it too far, Foley. I saw it all for what it was. There's a lot I overlooked, but no one touches Hope!" Grabbing my throat he wiggles us both back up and I step away coughing. We both stand gazing at each other and the rain begins. Now I see that the two Southern Colony Apologia are down and have nothing left to give. Foley tackles me as Jack and

Courtney bind the thugs' hands. My back is again on the surface of the cliff and my head is half over the gap between the giant rocky arms. My former ally sits up and raises his side arm.

"What am I supposed to do here, Justin. You're a part of the prophecy."

"I'll tell you what to do Foley," I grunt. "Fall!" With everything I have left, I raise my knees against him and roll backward over the edge of the cliff making sure to grip the rocks. He yells as he ungracefully descends to the water. Jack and Courtney help me up.

"Listen guys, I don't . . . I don't know what to say. I'm sorry."

"I'm sorry too, Justin," Jack says.

Staring into my eyes, Courtney asks, "She meant something didn't she, champ?" I look at her as if I'm confused. I'm not. "Bailee, I mean. There was something there."

"I don't know. It doesn't matter now. We've got to free Hope and get out of here."

"We don't know where she is," Jack says.

Looking at him with a wrinkled brow, I respond, "Of course we do."

CHAPTER TWENTY-FOUR

We're halfway back to the Mansion when the sound of an old wartime siren begins to blare. Then a voice is heard over the speakers. It's Foley. "Colony, this is your Adon. Justin, Jack, Courtney and a girl named Hope have betrayed us. They are working against us with the Unbelieving Tribe. If you see them, stop them!"

Rushing through the Mansion I shout, "You two go get whatever supplies we might need. I'll get Hope." As they rush down one corridor of the Mansion, I yank a twenty-foot tall curtain down and drag it out into the yard. When I reach the hatch I look around sporadically until a large stone catches my eye. Perfect! Once, twice, three times I pound and the chain breaks.

"Hope, you down there, snowflake?"

"I told you so, you frostbitten sand flea!" Yep, she's down there.

The curtain is in and I feel her tugging it. I pull her with all my might and after a few seconds she's out. We hug tightly before she begins slapping at my chest for not trusting her intuitions. Jack and Courtney come rushing out of the house toward us. "How will we live, Justin," my girl asks. "Where will we go? No one is coming for us."

"I don't know how we're getting off this twisted patch of jungle," Jack answers for me, "but I know where we're going tonight?" In his hand he grips one of the old World War Two German landmines.

"What's that for?" I ask with shock on my face. I barely get the question out before what looks like the entire Colony emerges at the back of the Mansion. Foley strides in front.

"See. We need a diversion," Jack answers.

We run to a shallow point on the wall and vault over. Rushing through the woods deeply enough that no one will be hurt, Jack tosses the ordinance straight up and we keep sprinting. Over my shoulder I see nothing but dust, branches and smoke. "Don't stop," I shout. We reach the valley I first crossed when heading toward the Unbelieving Tribe three days ago. Jack hands a Hook-Slide to Hope and we all take off across the cable. I drop on the other side of the valley and look back. Foley stands watching. He knows better than to try. I retrieve the machete from my belt and strike the line until it breaks. The cord falls.

"Young prince," Foley shouts, "we will find you! You will join me in the end! I know it! It has been prophesied!" Without speaking, we turn to run.

***

"Here it is! Step only where we step," Jack

proclaims. Each time I think the Island has run out of secrets, I find something new. After two hours of jogging, we have arrived at what can only be described as a large sinkhole in the ground about sixty feet in diameter. A stream meanders halfway around the circumference and spills over in a couple of places creating two gentle waterfalls. Carefully approaching, we follow Jack's advice and tread carefully.

"It wasn't long after we got here, that Courtney and I decided we needed an exit strategy . . . or more like a . . ."

"A safe haven," Courtney says finishing his thought. "They usually either sent me and Jack, or the two other Apologia jerks."

Jack continues, "Every couple of days we had to scout out the Island to make sure no one from the Unbelieving Tribe was around."

"When we found this place," Courtney picks up, "we knew we had our retreat if we ever needed it."

"After the events of the Northern Colony we weren't gonna risk being stuck out in the . . ."

"Cold," Hope finishes. "I hate puns."

"Don't you mean euphemisms," I chide. They all laugh. I wish I could laugh with them. Bailee's death is still fresh on my heart.

"Why are we stepping only where you step?"

Hope asks. "Wait, dumb question. Landmines, right?"

"You got it. A lot of work went into this place. I told you I took one apart. I just didn't tell you why." Now standing at the lip of the hole, a large, beautiful, blue pool of water can be seen about forty feet below. The gentle waterfalls feed into it. A stream then carries water under the rock and, presumably, into an underground tunnel too small to enter.

Without explanation, Jack uncovers an old-timey rope ladder from the shrubs. It looks to be made of metal wire. He drops it and makes his descent. One by one we follow suit. When my feet hit the ground, I look around to observe the underground paradise. Plenty of sunlight pours in and concave walls make the space much bigger on the inside than the sinkhole would have indicated. The pool is the centerpiece of the hideout, but there is plenty of flat surface all around it for sleeping, pacing, sitting, or whatever else. A large boulder sits near a section of wall that, with everyone's cooperation, would serve as a great barrier behind which to change clothes. I'm sure Courtney brought everyone extra garments.

Courtney is preoccupied giving a tour to Hope when I notice Jack's fingers wrestling with a bag of Ocean's Wave. My heart races with desire, and even Hope seems drawn to the activity. "The cave is so full of memories," Courtney absentmindedly continues. "This area over here is where Jack first told me he . . ." She sees it. Rushing over to the spot where we, like zombies all stand, the blond smacks the open bag out of his hands and into the pool. Jack rushes over to the water and I feel despair fill the void where the blue addiction would have gone. As the only one of us equipped with enough discernment to resist ever touching the stuff, Courtney had to be the one to do it. "Don't hate me guys," she pleads. "It has its talons in you so deep. You've all got to get clean." Hope sits down with a look that indicates her acceptance of the lesson. Jack rests on his knees staring at the bag. None of us knows what to say. What can we say? After a few moments of reflection, the cravings momentarily pass, as the cravings of addicts do. I know the longing will return later, but we all quietly let the impulse fade. Once it does, conversation begins and the cheerful atmosphere returns to the roofless cave.

We all sit chatting about the predicament for about a half-hour before finally Courtney insists, "I can't take it anymore. It's hot, sticky, we're all filthy — let's swim."

"Uh," Hope wonders, "how are we going to do that without bathing suits?" Courtney digs in a bag while Hope asks the question.

"Oh," she says, holding up a tangle of modest swimwear. In a sing-song voice she reveals, "We've got bathing suits." Her grin is adorable. Hope squeals and everyone laughs. This time, I laugh too. A little. The smallest amount of enjoyment makes me feel guilty. Each time I start to think about myself I see . . . *her* face.

***

Hope is under the waterfall letting it wash the dirt and twigs out of her hair. Courtney and Jack are splashing each other and joking as if nothing of great importance is happening on the Island. I sit on the edge of the pool and grieve. Occasionally, Courtney locks eyes with me and makes a pouty face to indicate her sympathy. Clearly at some point, Hope had girl-talk with her about our . . . issues. I don't think she would have told her it was Bailee. If she had, Hope would have said something. No matter how mad she is, death would have brought the conversation to the surface again.

"Courtney," Hope says, "Do you mind if I deface your hideaway?" She grabs a black stone and moves toward the wall opposite the waterfalls and I turn to watch. She winks at me as she passes. Scratching away in letters as tall as her own body, she writes, "Wynfelt Manor III." Turning to face the group she sternly adds, "Just let one of you Apologia try to wreck this thing!" I love her. I always have, but my amusement is muted by our situation. Hope plops into the water next to me and the Apologia lovebirds swim over to our area of the pool. Maybe this is a good sign. Maybe she's getting over it.

"So, this cult that made that twisted version of the Bible," I ask. "Do they, I mean the people in that cult, all act like Foley?"

"No," Hope answers. "Foley doesn't look like any *one* cult. He's an amalgam of several. He believes in the burning in the chest as evidence of truth. He believes in violence to coerce belief. He believes in mind control, if necessary. He thinks demonic voices are really the voice of God. He believes in New Age meditation styles. One thing most cults of Christianity share that is true of him too, is that he denies the Trinity. Being on this Island with him just creeps me out."

"Maybe, but we're gonna make it out of this, guys," Jack says.

"Here we are," Hope summarizes, "caught in a world between a false religion and unbelievers. That's exactly where the church has always been. We're gonna make it."

"Yeah, we're gonna make it," I agree, "but how are we ever gonna get off of this Island. Even if we were all alone, and no one wanted us dead, we'd be marooned."

"Yes," Hope says, "but we've got a secret weapon."

"What's that?" Courtney asks.

Hope smiles and announces, "Julie Lyn, of course."

I shake my head and conclude, "She'll never find us, Hope. She doesn't even know where to look."

"You've got to have faith," Hope says. "If I know Julie, she's in the middle of a swamp somewhere digging for clues right now."

CHAPTER TWENTY-FIVE
JULIE

Textures change beneath me as the tires of the sport bike hit the dirt. A canopy of trees shields the road from the sun and creates a pattern of shadows and light on the path. Soon. My family is here. My enemy is here. The truth is here. The Australian outback is a place of extreme beauty. To my American eyes the strange marsupials, vibrant scenery and incredible people are mysterious and enchanting. For those who spend their days here, these sights are common. For me, though, they create an otherworldly atmosphere.

The ground changes again and I'm on sand. Grinding the bike's rear break with my foot, the rocket slides to a halt in the soft terrain. With my hand to my brow, I examine the holy grail of my search. The Island. A half-mile from the mainland beach where I stand the green trees and black rocks rise from the ocean. It's not in the shape of a crescent moon, even though that Lucas guy told me it would be. Perhaps if I saw it from above. For now, I can only trust I'm at the right place. Looking back from the Island to the trees I see that my informant was right. A narrow wooden boat is tucked away. Inside is one long pole with a paddle on each end. Perfect! Dragging the vessel to the beach, I feel the waves on my ankles and reality sinks in. I'm about to encounter the second Colony. I'm about to get answers.

***

Tall green peaks rise before me as I hit land on the beach. This spot seemed appropriate, as passage is visible between the rocks. Swiftly and cautiously I follow the trail that meanders through foliage and high cliffs. Suddenly, I feel the way I did on Porcher Island. It's like I'm in some young adult adventure story. This place would likely be a much more popular spot for campers and hikers if it didn't take so long to get here. We are nowhere near a large population base or landmark. It doesn't seem removed enough to provide the hiddenness of The Colony in Muskwa Kechika, but here it is nonetheless. This has to be it! Why else would Justin have a map of the place tucked away in his closet?

Suddenly, I shake my head as if to fluff off my thoughts and say, "Hello," to myself. Before me there is a large drop off to a grassy floor sixty feet down. The drop is in a circular pattern that looks to be about seventy yards in diameter. Creeping into my vision is a staircase that hugs the bluff and follows the circle down to the grassy earth below. No one is here. Descending the staircase I examine the area. Caves have been carefully dug out of the earthen walls to create what might be rooms or tunnels. Four spires stretch up from the center of the round area and extend a good eighty feet into the air, which of course means they would extend about twenty feet up from the surface of the jungle floor. It's good to keep track of such details, I remind myself. Always think like the journalist you plan to be.

Now, from the bottom of the staircase I approach the manmade spires in the center. Each one has a familiar phrase etched on it. One spire reads, "Freedom to Think." Another says, "Freedom to Live." A third says, "Hope to Seek." And not surprisingly, the last has, "Hope to Give." My enthusiasm hits a fever pitch. This is an Adonai Monument. I've found it! Almost as quickly as the dopamine rush is released in my brain, the fearful realization dawns on me. Just as the colonials mysteriously vanished from the Muskwa Kechika Colony, they have also disappeared from here. If Justin, Hope, Jack and their friend Courtney were here when The Colony moved, I may never find them. "Calm down, Julie." I tell myself. "Just keep looking, and keep taking pictures."

Approaching one of the caves that I now assume were housing units for the colonials, I notice that it once had a doorway of some kind that is now in pieces. Half of its frame is in place, attached to the cave wall, and the other half is on the ground and warped by water damage. It certainly doesn't look like anyone has used it in years. Moving deeper into the cave I reach for the flashlight in my green canvas bag and thumb the power button. Eerie. A picture frame lies shattered on the floor, and inside is a cross-stitch of the Adonai emblem with the words, "Home Sweet Home" below it. The cavernous hallway opens to a room and I see that there is an old couch, a pile of books and a few shelves amidst similar commonplace furnishings. This is weird.

***

After investigating five more cave dwellings which contain a library, a cafeteria of sorts, a classroom with blackboard and two more civilian apartments, I enter the sixth and am startled by the sound of movement.

"Yeah, I think so," a voice echoes from around the corner. I pause where I stand and kneel against the cave wall. "Um . . . no, I mean, this place is gonna need a lot of work. No one has been here in at least twenty years." Sounds like he's on a sat-phone. "It's incredible, though . . . No, no, I think it's perfect." Uh oh. His voice is getting closer. I've got to get out of here.

Five paces out of the entrance I see a second man walking in my direction with a backpack. We lock eyes. He's shocked. I run. "Ma'am, wait! Hey, is that a camera?"

I'm halfway up the stairs and he's giving chase. Bursting into the jungle, adrenaline courses through my veins. I know what will happen. Despite his repeated pleas that he has no intention of harming me, he's with the Adonai. He's got to be . . . Right? His footsteps pound the earth behind me and I'm almost caught when I hit a creek. Halfway across, I lose my footing and begin to be swept away by the water. I cling to a rock for ten seconds before a tree branch appears in my face.

"Take it," he suggests. "I promise, I won't hurt you."

Resolute I shout, "Yeah right, like you didn't

hurt the Departures!"

"What are you talking about?" he asks with a confused look.

"Say what you want, but I know all about the Adonai."

"The Ad . . . The what? Lady, I don't know what you're talking about, but if you don't get out of that water it won't be me you have to worry about." He seems genuine. I don't know what to think, but I can hardly argue with his logic. Begrudgingly, I grip the branch and wrench myself up enough to grip his forearm. The moment my foot meets dirt I shove him off and back up three steps and ready myself in a fighting stance. He laughs. "I don't know how you got here, but trust me . . . I'm as scared of you as you are of me."

"Yeah, you're afraid I'm gonna blow the lid on your secret Adonai Colony. Well, you better kill me now, cause you're right. I will!" I bounce on my feet like a prizefighter ready to go ten rounds.

"Again, I don't know what you're talking about. I'm afraid of your camera. This is going to be a hidden retreat for my organization, but it doesn't have anything to do with the . . . What did you say? The . . . Adonai or something?"

I drop my stance but with a skeptical eye sternly ask, "what organization?"

Tilting his head back as if to prepare himself for oncoming scrutiny, he admits, "Scientology."

CHAPTER TWENTY-SIX

Sitting on stone benches back in what was once an Adonai Colony, the two scientologists, David and Ron, explain their presence. From what they say, the information on the location was sold to them by someone who used to be a part of a confidential social science experiment. That's one way to describe what the Adonai are doing. From what they say, they have no knowledge of the history of the spot. They are also without any way to contact the informant. Their interests have to do with a planned retreat in a place where journalists and spectators will not disturb them. My presence was a threat. Having exhausted all attempts to extract information from them that might be useful in my search, I conclude that this is not the site of The Colony Justin was after. However, the horrifying realization that begins to sink in, is that there have been not one, not two, but at least three Adonai Colonies. How many more might exist?

"Okay, boys, I guess my curiosity has been satisfied," I say standing up.

"Well, wait. Do you want a free auditing session?" Wow, these guys are marketers of the first order.

Trying not to roll my eyes I clarify, "You mean the little device that's supposed to tell me how *clear* I am?" Thanks to a recent documentary, I'm aware of the auditing machines that basically amount to rudimentary lie detectors. Holding grips in each hand, subjects explain life events and watch as a meter indicates stress levels. I also know that their creation myth involves an evil cosmic warlord who was the head of a galactic federation. Seventy-five million years ago this, *Xenu*, sent the souls, or *thetans* of conquered peoples to earth. "No thanks guys, but why don't we skip right to the juicy stuff. You know about *Xenu*, right?"

Exhaling with a groan, David, who pulled me out of the river answers, "Yep, we know about Xenu."

"And, do you really believe that stuff?"

Looking at me with seriousness he answers, "Sure I do. No one else has to though."

"What does that mean?"

"Well, I mean, it's true for me, but that doesn't mean it has to be true for you." I immediately recognize the relativism.

"Don't get me wrong. I appreciate that you pulled me out of the river, but how can something be true for you and not for me?" He huffs a laugh as though the concept is self-evident. I clarify, "I mean, do you think that way about everything?"

"Yeah. It's fine. If you believe something, then it's true for you."

Readying myself, I sit back down again as

though I'm closing in on something big. I am. "So, do you think whether or not the planet earth actually exists is true for some people and not for others? In other words, is it a matter of opinion whether or not the earth exists?"

"Sure, why not," Ron says. I'm baffled by his answer.

"So, if someone maintained that the earth does not exist, they wouldn't necessarily be wrong? That's just what's true for them?"

David strokes his chin before answering, "You got it. Make sense now?"

Pursing my lips I respond, "Not hardly. In fact, I don't actually think you believe that yourself."

With an amused look, David utters, "Oh?"

"Think about it. Let's say you've got five hundred dollars in the bank, and you go to withdraw two hundred and fifty."

"Okay, I'm tracking with you. Go on."

"Great. What if the bank teller says, I can't give you the two fifty because though your truth is that you have five hundred in your account, the bank's truth is that you only have one hundred?"

"I guess . . . I guess that would be the bank's truth."

"Yeah, but you know good and well you wouldn't be cool with that." He grins. I raise my eyebrows and open my mouth wide with a smile. "And . . . The reason you wouldn't be cool with that is because you know that all this 'your truth - my truth' stuff doesn't work. There is only *the* truth."

"Okay, lady, I'll admit you seem to know a bit more about this stuff than I do," he says. Ron sits back, watching with amusement.

"So, I'll ask again. Is the Xenu stuff *true* or not?"

Realizing he has to bypass his typical answers he says, "I guess I don't know."

"Which means you don't know if the progenitor of Scientology is right or should be trusted."

"Fair enough, but do you really expect us to ditch what we believe after one conversation with a strange girl in the middle of nowhere?" he asks with a laugh.

"No, but I *do* expect you to think about it and after a week or so . . . yes, I expect you to do the reasonable thing and ditch what you've been told." I grin and bite my tongue in a teasing fashion.

For the next fifteen minutes I explain the Christian faith and why I believe it is *the* truth. Jesus claimed to be the divine Son of God. Was killed by

Roman crucifixion, buried, and rose again. People were willing to die for the belief that they had seen the risen Christ. Miracles still happen. The faith is defensible. Perhaps I was sent here merely to proclaim this truth to two skeptics caught up in a web of false beliefs. For the opportunity I'm grateful. Sadly though, I still don't have answers.

***

The bike hits pavement and my sat-phone buzzes. Pulling over I answer and hear the voice of Ben Ruth. After explaining my events he dictates, "I may know who tipped your new friends off to that Australian Island's location. I'll pay for you a flight. We need to talk. Just get here as quickly as you can. One of the Adonai from The Colony has broken radio silence, so to speak.

CHAPTER TWENTY-SEVEN

"There you go. One hot, double soy, triple espresso, mocha latte for, uh, Julie! Is that you?" The barista asks.

"Yep, thanks," I say. Moving through the corporate coffee empire's local franchise, I exit the door and slide into the rental car trying not to spill the piping beverage. I'm across an intersection in less than a minute and the campus comes into view on both sides of the street.

I approach a large regal looking home from a century ago. It matches the description. I check my notes as cars honk from behind me on the main road. Startled by a biker who sails past, I spill a bit of the coffee on my blouse and shout, "Awe, c'mon, Julie!" So much for impressing the academic community with my new studious look. This must be it. I park and enter what I now see is the Administrative building, and to my right a lady stands to greet me with a welcoming smile.

"Hi, sweetie! We've been expecting you," she says. "Gimme just a second?" Picking up the receiver of the in-house phone she says, "She's here. Are you ready for her? . . . Yes sir." She hangs up and moves across the room to open a garden door to my left.

As I enter, I find my professorial friend sitting in a cushioned leather chair, hunkered over a tablet, a laptop, a paper notepad and several folded maps. On the wall opposite his location the College's logo hangs. To my right and his left, are framed ancient manuscripts or something. To my left is a fireplace, which seems humorously large for the room, but gives the environment an academic flavor. Dr. Ben Ruth stands from his desk with an expression that appears to be a mixture of fondness for me, and concern for the situation. "Julie. I can't believe you're here . . . in my office." He gives me a sideways hug and I set his coffee down on the desk.

"I couldn't come without bearing gifts," I respond.

"Great! We're going to need it, my young investigator. I may have located someone with answers. Did you clear your schedule?"

"Of course. Where are we going?"

"Dr. Lorn Parson is alive and in hiding."

My eyes widen. "How did you find him?"

"In the good old days of our debates, I had occasional contact with him. He had an idea for a written dialogue that would be published in book form and thought it would be intriguing if we used pseudonyms instead of our real names . . . thought it would allow us the freedom to say things in a bit more straightforward way. That book never materialized, but his pen name was to be Norm Larson."

"Lorn Parson is Norm Larson," I repeat with a sour look.

"Trust me, I know," he agrees with my expression. "Knowing that he took off before any of the other colonials, I figured he might be on his own somewhere. I've been running standard internet searches for Norm Larson ever since."

"Smart."

"Well, Lorn fell victim to the vice of all intellectuals."

"What's that?"

He huffs a laugh and answers, "He couldn't bear to keep his mouth shut - literally, not even to save his own life. He made one simple comment in a public philosophy chat-room using the pen name. That was all I needed. I had one of our tech guys here at the college run a simple IP search and bingo - we've got an address in New York City. I'll bet he's the informant regarding the Island in Australia you just visited." Determination overtakes me.

"When do we leave?" I'm slightly annoyed that I just got off of a plane, but the possibility of a solid lead drowns out the frustration.

He stands and says, "The flight leaves in ninety minutes. Let's go." I grin ear to ear. Of course I want answers, I want to know that my brother is alright, but . . . I can't deny the realization that I love this stuff.

***

The streets of Manhattan are congested. Of course they are. Manmade canyons of concrete stretch before us as far as can be seen. Swirling outside the car is a mass of human diversity. Fashion, ethnicity, ideology and technology intermingle in a melting pot of activity. It's beautiful. The handiwork of the designer is brimming in the big apple.

"This'll do it," Ruth tells the cabby as he passes him payment. We exit onto the street and enter the river of culture that flows along the wide sidewalk.

"I don't see anything," I confess.

Squinting, Ruth scans the storefronts for a few moments before poking my shoulder and instructing, "Right there. I see it." The landmark is a bookstore or library of some kind that simply says, "Reading Room," on the sign. Next to it is an alley. Suddenly the world seems to slow to its normal pace as we enter the alley and no longer rush along with the rat race.

"What was that place?" I ask. "That reading room, what was it?"

"Huh," Ruth grunts half paying me attention as he looks around the alley. "Oh, it's a . . . a Christian Science thing. They're like . . . well, it's neither Christian or science, I'll tell you that much."

"Well?"

"Alright. They follow the teaching of a lady called Mary Baker Eddie. They've redefined every aspect of the Christian faith. The Trinity is no longer the Father, Son and Holy Spirit, but instead life, truth and love. The bottom line of their belief is that they teach that nothing bad - pain, heartache, injury . . . even death, really exists. It's all just mental illusion. This, of course, is incredibly dangerous since physical ailments are very real."

We continue walking and I say, "I've never heard of that one."

"Sure you have. You know those people that don't want certain medical treatments for religious reasons? You've heard of that right?"

"Yeah, okay. Is that them?"

"Usually. The problem is Eddie was demonstrably a liar. She claimed to be healed through her cultic beliefs, but in reality was plagued by physical ailments her entire life." I think through the concepts for a moment before my thoughts are interrupted. "That's enough about worldview issues. Help me look for the door." We round a corner and see that there is no entrance.

"I don't see anything, doctor."

"I don't get it. We traced Parson to an address

in *this* building. According to the available blueprints and floor plan, the Reading Room has no access to the rest of the building. There's just got to be a rear entrance." Looking up I see a doorway on a fire escape, but the ladder does not extend low enough to grip.

"There," I shout. "Can you boost me up?" He follows my gaze to the rusted grey frame of a door. It looks old, but solid.

He looks at me with pride and admits, "You're a true detective, Ms. Lyn. The Adonai never stood a chance with you coming, did they?"

"Comes with my family history," I offer with a wink. "And you keep forgetting. It's Julie *Harris* now. I'm a married woman." He chuckles as he laces his fingers together and kneels. In a flash I'm able to grip the black metal ladder and wrench myself up.

"There you are madam," my older friend says with class. Standing from my climb I examine the door and instantly notice its lack of a handle. Instead there is an alphanumeric keypad. Great!

"Big problem Doc," I announce. "We need a code or password or something." He stares at the scenery searching his thoughts and finally suggests, "Try C-O-L-O-N-Y." Seriously? You'd think with a PhD he'd be a bit more creative. Nevertheless, I enter the corresponding numbers. Nothing.

"No dice," I tell him.

"Okay, well, try A-D-O-N-A-I, M-A-L-O-R-Y, or . . . I don't know. Let me think . . ." I loyally attempt all the suggestions and come up empty handed. Finally, leaning on the rails I feel my plane ticket on the interior of my suit jacket. Pulling it out I see the word. D-E-P-A-R-T-U-R-E. Dr. Ben Ruth mumbles ideas to himself on ground level as I delicately input the possible answer. (BUZZ) An electronic sound is heard along with a loud (KUCHUNK) as the lock releases. Ruth is so deep in thought he doesn't even notice. "Julie, what about P-A-R-S-O-N?" Finally, he looks at me.

"You mean like Lorn Parson?" I ask. Only now does he see that the door is standing open. "Yeah, I think I'll go look for him now." I bite my tongue in a teasing sort of way and Ruth glares at me with sarcasm all over his face.

Entering the old structure it is obvious that, for the most part, no one has been here in decades. Brochures are scattered on the floor for *The Atheistic Advancement Society*. Someone left here in a hurry. Striding down the hallway I find an unlocked door - number three-one-five. Gently nudging the doorway it opens with a creak. Natural light streams in through the windows and the contents of the depressing room are revealed. Clutter is everywhere. Marketing materials and internal files for the forgotten organization behind the planning of The Colony clutter the room. In the corner rests a futon mattress, a pillow and a blanket. In another corner is the life-size cutout of Dr. Lorn Parson that I previously saw in his office at The Colony. Tell me this joker didn't lug that think all the way from British Columbia.

Leaning against the wall I begin to thumb through one of the old files when the artificial sound of a speaker crackles to life above me. The voice of the Adon presents itself audibly with, "Stay where you are. The building is surrounded. If you try to leave you will be killed." My eyes are wide as I consider the situation. I reach for my phone and realize Ruth is already calling.

Swiping the display I answer, "Ruth!"

"Julie, run!" His voice muffles and the call ends. They've got him. Peering out the window I see two black SUVs on the street. An African-American guy in shades and a blonde brute are paying way too much attention to the building. Parson's telling the truth. Craning my neck again I notice another voyeur. Across the street a wiry fellow nervously watches. I glance back and forth between the cardboard cutout of Parson and the stalker. It's him!

CHAPTER TWENTY-EIGHT

The banging on the door is getting louder. I couldn't call the police. If I had, Parson would have bolted. Next best thing? A New York City cabby. Always faithful. Fortunately, I was able to be patched through to the driver and it looks like . . . yep, he's gonna follow my instructions.

Getting out of the car in front of the building he shouts the phrase I told him to jot down, "Freedom to Think! Freedom to Live! Hope to Seek! Hope to Give!" It would be humorous if this wasn't such a dire situation. The two suits on the street move about frantically not knowing what to do. The pounding on the door ceases. Parson still watches from across the street. The confusion is my opportunity. Grabbing an old office chair, I shatter the window and vault through. Parson sees. I'm down the fire escape as the two Adonai guys approach the taxi. He freaks out and drives off as they chase him ten paces down the street. I'm across the road before they realize what's happening and run along an alley watching Parson above me as he races atop the edge of a roof. He's thought through his escape plan.

"Parson," I shout, but he doesn't stop. I launch over a short wooden fence and see him again. He's on another roof now, to my right. I head in that direction and realize my aerobic training is paying off. He's bound to run out of rooftops at some point. Finally I see a fire escape that's positioned just right and ascend as quickly as I can. When I reach the top he's already on the next roof. It appears he has positioned wooden ramps from rooftop to rooftop in preparation for this moment. Smart fella. "Parson, stop!" He looks over his shoulder, but keeps running. In reality, I don't know what I would do if he *did* stop. He could easily overpower me.

Reaching the edge of a roof it appears that his pathway ends. Suddenly he disappears over the edge. Whoa! I rush to the edge and see that he's injured himself, but is limping away. No choice. I drop and land in a dumpster filled with mattresses he clearly prepared. My landing is successful. Crawling out I see him turning a corner onto a busy sidewalk. Rushing to meet him I grip his arm and whisper, "Say or do anything and I'll scream, Lorn." He hisses in disgust at my words. "You don't want that, and I don't want that."

"What do you want from me?" he asks in an angry low voice.

"Not here, Adon. We need to get off the street."

***

In the back of a low-lit Thai eatery, I stare across at the injured scholar as he stirs some rice on a plate. He looks just as defeated as he did at The Colony. I'm keenly aware of an exit behind me to the right, and I observe the entrance on the other end of the room in a constant, obsessive way. So far, so good.

"Alright, Norm Larson," I say with mockery, "spill it."

Exhaling, he responds, "What . . . do you want to know?" It's clear he's given up.

"Where's my brother?"

"I honestly don't know." He looks up to notice that my face does little to disguise my skepticism. Posturing his shoulders up to a briefly sustained shrug, he raises his eyebrows and asks, "How could I? I mean think about it. I took off into the wilderness while The Colony was still burning." He lowers his voice and grimaces as if made uncomfortable by the memory. "It's a wonder I ever made it back to civilization." Raising his voice and looking up at me again, he finishes, "I nearly died out there, you know."

"Fine. Then how did you end up in the Adonai headquarters with a security detail?"

He chuckles a bit before his subtle laughter evolves into a violent momentary coughing spell. "You thought that was the headquarters? Ha . . . No."

"Well, what then?"

"It's a safe house. If an Adon is discovered, he heads there and waits."

"For what?"

Raising the left side of his cheek and furrowing his brow in confusion he answers with annoyance, "For orders. What do you think?"

"Orders from whom, the second Colony?"

"Second Colony," he says to himself in amusement. "I've really said too much." He stands. "I'm leaving, you don't know who you're dealing with."

"Sit down," I announce loudly enough that other patrons look our way. He intensely locks eyes with me and lowers himself to the seat. "Whose orders are you awaiting?"

Rolling his eyes he answers, "The Adonai, of course."

Looking around the room as I try to put it together, I continue my interrogation with, "You mean . . . some of the Adonai from The Colony?"

"There are others. They are some of the most powerful people in the world. They are benefactors. Who did you think funded the Colonies - professors, who make five figures? Come on, girl *think*!"

"What, like some kind of conspiracy theory or something?"

"Young lady," he says leaning in, "you have seen enough to know that some conspiracies are real."

"So you've been waiting around for all these months at the Adonai safe house and you still haven't made contact with them?"

"The policy is to wait at the safe house until the next Annual Assembly. Then, I am to receive my invitation. The waiting is important to assure I haven't been discovered. The problem is, I have been discovered and the grunts that are stationed here in New York now know that. I was just about to head off for the Assembly today when you showed up. How did you find me anyway?"

"I'm asking the questions here. What's supposed to happen if you're discovered?" He looks at me with fear kindling in his eyes.

"I must be . . . removed. Just like a Departure."

For a moment I feel sympathy for the former Adon. "So what's your move now?"

"I run."

"You said you were leaving for the Adonai Assembly today. So it's some gathering here in New York," I surmise.

"No. It's far away. I was leaving town to head there." I think things through and take a sip of water before realizing the obvious.

"You have the invitation . . . don't you?" He just looks at me expressionless. "What's the address, or coordinates or whatever?"

Clearing his throat he reaches into his jacket pocket and retrieves a handkerchief folded around something about size of a large watch face. "I guess at this point it won't do me any good, now that you've rendered me officially uninvited." Placing the handkerchief on the table, I open it with care. Inside is a device that resembles an old-fashioned pocket watch. It is golden, ornate and opens from a clasp. On the back the emblem of the Adonai is embossed. Inside I recognize a much more intricately designed model of the compass-like device that guided me to The Colony. A needle is pointing to the right, and the numbers at the bottom indicate the distance to what must be the site of the Adonai Assembly. "This is what you want, and you won't get in without it. They won't ask for your name and they won't expect to recognize all the guests, but I have no doubt you'll be caught. Young lady, my life is in serious jeopardy, but so is yours if you plan to attend. Don't do this."

"I found my brother once, Adon. I will not lose him again." He looks at the table pursing his lips and shaking his head.

Tossing a black domino mask on the table he says, "Then you'll need this, foolish girl." I stare at the eyewear and recognize it from films. It's the kind that covers only the eyes and the space between them. "Yes," he adds. "It's one of the *those* parties."

"Where are they taking Dr. Ben Ruth?"

"Your friend is high profile enough that the Adonai would likely not want to draw the attention that a search for him might bring. They may kill him, but I'd assume if they captured Ben, he'll be dumped out somewhere and forgotten - to live his life. Thanks to you, he already sounds deluded. Now he'll sound crazy . . . men in black, secret organizations . . . you can imagine where that will get him."

A long pause separates us from the discussion. Finally, one last question manifests itself in my thoughts. With a tired voice I ask, "How many, Dr. Parson?" How many Colonies are there?"

"I only know of two, young lady."

"Liar. I've been to the site in Australia."

He grunts the smallest of laughs and then says, "Australia. That was a prototype for our benefactors. It only functioned for six months. I lived there. It was never meant to be permanent. You went there, huh? You sure do get around, don't you?"

"Someone else has plans for it now."

"Hey," he says as if to avoid the shame of a nefarious transaction, "I had to make some money while living in the safe house. I sold information. It was risky, but I didn't have much of a choice."

As I'm about to stand, I say, "God be with you, Lorn."

"God . . . yes, well, I definitely hope so. Be careful, Daughter of Lyn. They will come for you even before you reach the Assembly." An atmosphere of intensity increases in the air as I reposition myself back into the seat.

"How will they know? You gonna rat me out, Adon?"

Leaning in with a grim look on his face, he assures, "I'm not your friend, little girl. I'll not tell them you're coming, but I need a plan B in case I'm caught. If I am, my only chance is to tell them I've tied off all loose ends."

"You can't chase me with a messed-up leg."

"I don't plan to. I have contacts in grey areas. Your threat will be . . . the Watchman."

"Arvin?" A lump appears in my throat as I think of the monster from Porcher. Mainly because of him I've been looking over my shoulder ever since The Colony.

"He's already on his way. That's right. I arranged for it while you were still in the safe house. Go for the Assembly and you're dead. Reach the Assembly and you're dead. Go home and Arvin will back off. Make your choice, but the Adonai Assembly is in two days. 7:00 pm their time."

The room begins to spin as the realization sets in. I stand and stumble toward the back exit in a full on panic attack. Scanning the faces of the restaurant, I compulsively look for Arvin. "Where is he," I say loudly to Parson, the whole restaurant looking now.

Stretching his arms out, palms up, he grins and reveals, "He could be anywhere, young lady." The blood rushes from my face and time seems to slow. "Run, Daughter of Lyn. *Run!*"

CHAPTER TWENTY-NINE

It's dark now. I couldn't take the time to stay the night in the city. I've got to get out of here as quickly as I can. With the city behind me, I follow the direction of the compass up I-95 toward the site of the Adonai Assembly. Four hundred and seventy miles. There is no telling where I'm headed, but it must be somewhere in Maine. Thank goodness for all night car rental services. Eyeing the mirror of my hunter green sport bike, I giggle a bit to myself that I was able to secure my favorite make and model. The giddiness quickly evaporates though, as I glance at the mirror in frustrated fear that I'm being followed. How far should I go before finding a place to spend the night? I won't get much further. It's too risky to get a hotel room, I've got to lay low. For all I know, Arvin and Lorn have means of monitoring my transactions. I don't know. I'm probably paranoid, but at this point who could blame me?

"Ben, I hope you're alright," I say out loud into my helmet as I fly up the interstate. All around me, every day citizens are going through their normal routines. I pass a car and see a family of four, both kids asleep in the back as the wife reads a book and the husband dutifully drives. Another car contains teenagers singing loudly to their music as they head back home after some adolescent night of revelry. An older man with a white beard guides his semi along and slowly looks at me with a smile as he sips from a mug. They all seem oblivious to the war that is going on just under the hood of this physical reality. Though I find myself in the midst of a very obvious conflict, unseen forces are attempting to ruin their lives as well. The demonic is real. Most casual Christians seem to think of the idea of supernatural agents at work as merely the stuff of horror films. Not so. If the story of Jesus is true, he certainly believed in angels and demons. It is a system dependent belief. All that is going on with the false Adonai is certainly the result of unseen forces, but so are many of the daily evils of this world. Any number of wars, afflictions, temptations and strife could be the result of the enemy's plans. This is certainly true of those worldviews and religions that involve the twisting of the Christian message. We are all in a conflict. Mine is just more obvious to detect.

Ripping me out of my daydreams, an exit sign creeps toward me and I decide to pull off of the road and search for a place to bed down for the night. There's got to be an old shed or an abandoned homestead of some kind. I won't be living in the lap of luxury, but what do you do? I'd give anything to see the McLeod house sitting in a field with fresh fish on the table, but they are a lifetime away from me on Porcher. There. That looks good.

***

The old barn sits at least one hundred yards from the closest house. I'm confident no one saw me, even though I had to walk the bike a half-mile. From up in the loft I will be somewhat safe from intruders.

At the very least I'll have some warning if they enter the room. The old bottles I've lined up in front of the two large doors at either end of the interior will rattle if disturbed. Resting my head on my canvas bag I stretch-out in what will be my unfortunate bed for the night. I just wish Rob were with me now. I shouldn't have sent him away. Retrieving my phone I see that its battery will soon be dead. Tomorrow I'll have to find a place to charge, but for now I need to talk to someone. Swiping his name brings Ben's face into the center position. I hope against hope he'll answer. Still straight to voice mail. Scrolling to Rob I see the happy smile of the man God brought to me. I ache for his presence. I can't have secrets from him. What I've done so far has been bad enough. I'm gonna tell him . . . everything. It's time. I swipe his name and a ringing sound emerges three times before, just as with Ben, the voicemail recording is activated. He's probably working on his plane, or out for an evening flight.

"Rob, I'm fine, but I miss you so much. I don't want you to come for me, but I wish you were here. Does that sound crazy? I know it does. Listen, I want you to know what's happening with me. I shouldn't have kept it from you." Tears begin to stream down my cheeks. I didn't see it coming. "I didn't tell you the whole truth. I'm on another wild adventure, but hey, that's how I met you, isn't it? I'm on my way to somewhere in Maine, I don't even know exactly where. The Adonai have got Ben, and I think Arvin is after me again." I realize that I'm rambling, but the emotion is too much. Isn't this the one man in the world I'm supposed to be able to break down with? "I'm close to finding some kind of Adonai annual get-together. I know that won't make sense, but I'm heading into the lion's den. I don't want you to get hurt so I'm glad you don't know where I am. I'm not going to call you until this is all over. If I do, you'll just talk me out of it or come up with some other plan. I don't have time for it. Rob, I miss you so much. I feel completely alone. I don't have Ben, I don't have Justin, I don't have my best friend Hope, and I don't even have you. Just know that I love you. And Rob . . . If something happens to me, I didn't want to tell you like this, but," The beeping emerges that indicates the message has ended. ". . . I'm pregnant," I finish to the lonely room. Lying on the wooden slats, and thinking of the chaos, I know that I'll be crying myself to sleep - that is, if I sleep at all.

CHAPTER THIRTY

Our enemies, in many ways, define us. They reveal our loyalties, clarify the limitations of our commitments, and force us to plant flags in faithful declarations of conviction. Life's dance includes them. While we should be at peace with all men, adversaries lead us deeper within ourselves to discover who we are. "Love your enemies," the Master said. And while this doesn't require the heart to sing at the sight of one's abuser, it does challenge a desire to do good to him in spite of an abuse. The Maker does not intend the attacker, but He can intend a use for the attack. We see it in the integrity of the victim. A good provoked by an evil. Faith provoked by faithlessness. We should not have enemies, but we should value what they teach us.

My enemy now races up the path toward my meager fortress. Arvin! "He found me", I say aloud. Backing away from gap in the sideboards, I immediately realize *how* he found me. The compass. There must be a GPS tracker involved. I've got to ditch it. I can't. Even if I plotted the coordinates to which it points on a map, according to Parson I can't get into the Assembly without the device. Shifting around the room like a squirrel in the path of oncoming traffic, I panic. "Pull yourself together Julie." He must have hidden his vehicle to approach me on foot for the same reason I walked the bike here without the engine running. Someone would have noticed.

I've never been a fan of driving a street bike off road. Loose soil and gravel is unnerving, but I don't have a choice. Shoving the doors open, Arvin and I lock eyes. He stops. We both stand staring at each other for three long seconds. He's forty yards or so out. Backing up with my eyes fixed on his position, I toss one leg over the seat and rev the engine. He's running. I release the clutch and the bike rotates cockeyed a bit as dirt sprays up behind me. Finally the back tire gains purchase in the soil just before Arvin covers the distance and I'm off. All I hear is a British accent shouting, "It's over, Daughter of Lyn!" Daughter of Lyn? I took no notice of the title when Parson used it. Apparently, I've developed a reputation among the Adonai and their sympathizers.

The uneven terrain of grass and mud makes for a rough ride. My sense of balance is heightened. If I were to drop the bike now, I'd be in trouble. Passing the house and turning onto the road I see an older man in a white undershirt and boxers running into the yard. His wife, with curlers and bathrobe, appears on the porch. Maybe they will slow Arvin down. If I can't find a way to mask the signal on the compass, I'll only meet the Watchman again. "Think, Julie!"

***

In the bathroom of a big box store after hours of travel, I struggle to crack the casing off the back of the compass. I've pinpointed the location of the Adonai Assembly somewhere in a community called Beddington, now only ten miles up the road. If I could only deactivate the device my location would be hidden. No such good fortune. It won't budge. Time for the backup plan. Reaching into my bag I retrieve the aluminum foil I just purchased, though I'm careful not to unnecessarily wrinkle the best cheap evening gown the lady's formal section had to offer. Wrapping the device in several layers, I can only hope the signal will be either muffled or completely blocked. Quickly, I change out of my dirty suit and into a new pair of dark jeans and a black T-shirt. Chucks for footwear round out my new look and I shove the rest into my bag. The beauty supplies I'll need later rattle a bit as I lift the bag, and in seconds I'm back out to my bike.

***

The exit for Beddington came without much celebration. A simple sign revealed "POP. 50." I don't know where I'll stay tonight, but I wanted to scope out my destination first. In some ways, the area reminds me of Porcher. There is a vast amount of wilderness, with homes only occasionally appearing. This must be one of the least populated towns in the state. The fresh air would be calming on any other day. It smells like relaxation. I reach the end of a dead end at the top of a hill and behind me I see a picturesque lake in the distance. Removing my helmet I scan the trees. Nothing. This is the spot on the map where the compass would have brought me. I fight the impulse to unwrap the foil to check my location, and instead opt for heading to a nearby residence I noticed at the bottom of the hill. Coasting back down, I turn into a yard with a gravel driveway.

I place the helmet on one of the handles and approach the house. I'm not even sure exactly what I will say, but determination transports me to the door and without a plan I knock. Thudding movement can be heard as someone moves through the interior. The door opens with a creek and I can smell the aroma of food wafting out. Before me stands an inviting older woman who reminds me of Gracie back in Endville.

Shielding her eyes from the sun, the grandmotherly lady says, "Yes?"

"Um, I need some directions," I explain. "I'm . . ."

"Interstate is ten miles back that way, dear." As she finishes the sentence she attempts to close the door.

"Oh, uh, no ma'am," I say with a nervous laugh. "I'm . . . uh . . . actually not looking for the interstate." She observes me closely with a bewildered stare. By the looks of her nightgown, she was expecting a quiet day without visitors. "I'm trying to find a . . . a . . . like a large meeting space. I'm supposed to meet some people at some sort of office building, or event center or . . ."

"Mansion. You're trying to find the mansion," she says. Not sure what I'm looking for, her suggestion is as good as any.

"That's it. The mansion," I say through a smile. "I don't know what I'm thinking. Can you tell me where it is?"

"You don't want to go to the mansion."

I pause with a blank look for a moment before responding, "Why not? I mean . . . I'm supposed to go there. I . . ."

"Why you goin' to the mansion?" She asks with interrogation all over her face.

Playfully I retort, "Why do *you* think I'm going to the mansion?"

"Don't know. Don't think you belong. Run along now." She knows something.

"I'm going to that mansion, whether you take me or not."

Shifting her eyes back and forth around the trees she whispers, "They're watching now."

"Who?" I say loudly, without thinking.

"No one she says straightening up. No one is watching. Run along now, dear. I'm an old woman with old things to do." She moves through the house and I slide along the siding to her kitchen window. She runs the water and my head pops up from the outside.

"Hey," I say with a toothy smile. She shrieks and places her right hand over her heart as if ready to pledge.

"What . . . What are you doing, girly? You want to give an old woman a heart attack?"

"Sorry, but I need to know. Who's watching us and why?"

Giving me a now-now sort of message with her eyes she caves with, "Wait for me in the truck."

***

Driving along a country road that circles the point I placed on the map, Evelyn explains her actions. "I don't mind telling you everything, dear, and I don't mind showing you. You're the type that needs to see for yourself and that's just fine, but once you see the mansion and hear what I have to say, I'll expect you to have gotten it out of your system and leave Beddington while you can. First, you need to tell me what you're doing here."

"You wouldn't believe me," I honestly say.

"Adonai," she says with a mockingly menacing tone. She watches for my expression and I can't fake ignorance. Seeing that I don't protest, she continues, "Oh I know all about em'. Secret Colonies and social experiments, I've seen or heard it all." I'm relieved on the one hand that I'm in the right place, but terrified that my cover has been blown. Maybe it hasn't. "No need to sit there in your own thoughts, girly, I know that's why you're here. The question is, are you for or against?" This is, indeed, a defining moment in our minutes-long relationship.

"I'm . . . uh . . . for them."

"Ha! No you're not. You couldn't fool me for a second." She's right, I'm not a good liar. I feel bad for it anyway. I silently breathe a prayer. "What are you doing now? You prayin'? Nope, not with the Adonai. Sugar, I don't know if you are aware, but the Adonai do not pray."

"Okay, well I should ask you the same question."

"With the Adonai? Me?" She frowns in amused consideration. "No, but I know how to stay alive. Play along," she finishes as she shifts the truck into park.

We exit the truck and begin walking up a path. Evelyn carries a walking stick and I follow like a lamb led to the slaughter. We reach the top of a hill and I see it. A large and rich home . . . no . . . mansion is right. It spreads out over at least three acres, and sits on a bluff above a beautiful, rocky misty river. The river breaks into a fifty-foot waterfall as the river continues on. Across the waterfall is a solid stone bridge held up by archways over the water. It is wide enough for two cars to sit side by side. This regal estate is nestled grandly among tall trees, high hills and beautiful earth tones. Across the bridge from where we are I see a private landing strip complete with a passenger jet of some sort.

"There it is, girly. Come over this way and you can get a better look. We move to the edge of a high drop-off above the river, and holding a tree I lean out to get a view. Looking to Evelyn again my back is to the cliff and she asks, "So dear, have you had enough adventure? Are you going to make me proud and go home while you can?"

We stand there staring at each other for what feels like an eternity while I think of how to respond. "Evelyn, I can't. I've got to find my brother."

"That's too bad, dear. I didn't want it to be this way." As her words trail off she turns her back to me, but before I can react she thrusts her walking stick into my chest and I tumble over the cliff. Gripping the roots I hang far above the rocks along the edge of the river. I want to scream, but if I do I'll be heard. Whimpering I struggle to hold on. She leans over to look at me and a necklace falls free from the inside of her shirt. It bears the Adonai emblem. In a maternal tone she urges, "You'd do better, sugar, if you'd just let go. You'll sleep forever, but it'll be worse if they find you."

"Why . . . (_umph_) . . . why are you helping them?"

"I can tell you now, can't I? My daddy was an Adon. In fact, he was one of the first. It's just the way I was raised, I guess." What? She must be eighty years old. The Colonies don't go back that far. I can't consider it now. I hear the waters rushing below me and I know I can't hold on for long. Static briefly is heard and I look up to see Evelyn working a walky-talky. "This is the owl's nest for home office, over."

A voice speaks through the static, "Come in, owl's nest."

"We've got a looky-lou, here. We're on the . . ." Suddenly she's silent and I hear scuffling from above. A hand appears over the edge reaching out to me. Then I see that face. The monster from Porcher Island. The Watchman. Arvin.

He says, "Daughter of Lyn, you have found your way home."

Our enemies define us. Life's dance includes them.

CHAPTER THIRTY-ONE

I'm in Evelyn's garage before Arvin removes the gag from my mouth. Tied to a chair, I can barely move. It took a while to get me and an unconscious Evelyn back here and tied up. There must be some hope for him if he couldn't bring himself to kill a woman in her eighties. She's likewise tied up in the living room.

"Haven't you missed our time together, Julie?"

Hissing my words, I demand, "Tell me how you found me, you snake." He overacts his hurt feelings by recoiling two steps with his hands over his chest.

With a sour face, he responds, "Aluminum foil? What were you thinking my dear? American television has led to everyone thinking they understand how to circumvent technology."

"So, what are you gonna do, take me to the Adonai?"

"My understanding is that you know full well why I'm chasing you to the ends of the earth again. I've no intention of handing you over. I'm here to tie up a loose end for Parson. He's promised me half of what's left from a recent lucrative venture."

"It doesn't make sense. If you're doing this for Lorn Parson and not the Adonai, how were you able to track the compass?"

"Because I put together the compass' original design. Why else do you think I had the one you stole from me on Porcher. I made them! That's why your father paid me any attention in the beginning. Granted they have modernized the design, but the program is still the same. To find you, this time, all I had to do was bring up the locations of the compasses and locate the one fleeing New York in the middle of the night."

"You sound proud," I point out with an angry face.

Raising his brow he answers, "Yes, I suppose I am."

"Tell me, have you been exercising your . . . proclivities since being back in the real world?"

His face darkens and he warns, "What I do is none of your concern."

"You have. You are still the troubled soul who is a troubler of souls."

Slamming his hands down on either side of the chair he roars, "I didn't want to kill you, dear, but you're making it easier."

"There's an answer . . . The true Adonai can save you."

Slowly straightening back up he announces, "I'm passed saving, my lady."

"You're not. You can be made whole!"

He readies a blade and raising it says, "Time to go away with the fairies my young friend. Just close your eyes . . . and fly away with the fairies."

My heart is beating a mile a minute when suddenly Arvin hits the wall and crumples to the floor groaning. In his place stands the image of happiness, and though it is night it feels like sunlight has flooded the room. Rob! A solid slug to Arvin's face puts him out, and my knight unties me.

"Rob! How did you . . . I mean, what are you . . . . I mean, how?" He hugs me tightly and we kiss. When he finishes he steps back and stares at me with a stern look.

"I oughtta tie you back up and finish the job for what you've put me through, doll. Australia, Maine . . . I mean I can understand those, but New York City," he says with disgust on his face.

"Rob, honey, I can explain."

"No, no, no ma'am, you can't. Have you or have you not been chasing the Adonai again?" He says it as though I'm a teenager being lectured by my parents for staying out too late.

"Well, I mean . . . It's complicated."

"I'll ask again. Have you or have you not been after the Adonai?"

With my toes together, my hands clasped at my waist and my head down I begrudgingly answer, "Yes."

"How many times have I told you not to try and take down the Adonai yourself? Huh? How many times?"

I come alive again crying, "It's Justin and Hope, Rob. They're out there somewhere."

"What?"

"I'm sorry I didn't tell you, but I got a letter from Justin. He followed a lead, but I haven't heard from him in a while. I got scared, okay?"

Hugging me again and stroking my hair he says, "Okay, baby girl, but tell me now, is there anything else I don't know?"

Stepping back I look at him and a few stray tears roll over my cheeks as I sniffle and rub my nose. "Yes," I say with the widest of smiles. "Rob, I'm pregnant." His eyes go wide and he slowly lifts his head.

Jumping, he shouts, "I'm gonna be a dad?" I nod. "You gotta be kidding me, Wooohooo! I can't believe it!"

All the commotion causes Arvin, still unconscious, to groan.

Turning to him, Rob says, "You shut your mouth you rotten animal!" Lifting the monster into the chair, Rob begins to tie him up. He slaps his face swiftly until Arvin rouses from his slumber. "Arvin! Arvin! Wake up!"

Arvin's eyes open and he rolls them as he observes the situation. "Don't be away with the fairies now," I tease.

"I'll figure this thing out," Rob says to me. Then turning back to the Watchman, he demands, "Arvin, Where's Justin? Where'd they take 'em?"

"Yukimura . . . (*cough*) Yukimura knew. I didn't go with them. I don't know where Justin is."

"Okay, where's Yukimura now?"

"He never returned. Let me go and I'll get you inside the Adonai Assembly," the villain bargains.

Positioning the gag in his mouth I explain, "Sorry, Arvin. You'll stay right here till this is all over. I finish tying the gag in place when I think to ask, "Rob, wait a minute. How did you find me? How did you know where I'd be?"

Laughing he says, "simple. I stuck a GPS tracking device in your wallet." His hands are on his hips and he smiles wide with a proud look.

I ball up my fist and hit him in the bicep, halfheartedly three times, grunting with my teeth clenched, "You didn't trust me."

He laughs again and says, "Hey, I didn't bother to check up on you till Ben called and told me he lost you."

Snapping back to reality I ask, "You spoke to Ben?"

"Yeah, he called me this morning. Said some Adonai boys dropped him off in the middle of nowhere. He's probably back home now. Said he tried to call you. I did too. You're phone must be dead - goes straight to voicemail." I grab for the device and see that he's right. "I landed at a private airfield about ten miles away and paid the night officer to give me a ride out here."

Taking a deep breath with my hands on my hips I look at Arvin as most girls my age would assess a new coat of paint on a bedroom wall. "You think that'll do?"

With his arm around me, Rob grins and nods before answering, "Baby girl, I think that'll do just fine." With that, we head into Evelyn's house to get some sleep.

CHAPTER THIRTY-TWO

After a night of constantly interrupted sleep, thanks to Evelyn in the living room, we spent most of the day laying out our plan. I guess I've always been the type that believes it's better to over prepare. I worry a bit about our two prisoners, but I don't have much of a choice. If we call the police the Adonai may scatter. If we let them go they'll alert the Assembly. We would never kill them, so we're stuck with the only other option - keep them tied up.

We crouch above the Mansion four hours before the Adonai Assembly is set to begin. There is a bustle of activity. Vans drive across the stone bridge, tables are being brought in, decorations are carefully moved, and catering services are arriving in preparation. To our right, across the bridge, a private plane lands and begins to taxi toward an appropriate position. My nerves rustle up as I realize what is about to happen. Actually attending has just been an abstract concept until now.

"Looks pretty big," Rob says, stating the obvious. He lowers a pair of binoculars and hands them to me to take a look.

Inhaling deeply I reply, "We can do it. We *have* to."

"Explain to me again why you don't think you'll be recognized." I lower the binoculars and hold up the domino mask between two fingers. "Oh, right. This is weird, babe. They don't do that kind of stuff where I come from."

"It makes more sense than most would realize. It's a domino mask. 'Domino' is from the Latin 'dominus,' which means 'lord' or 'master,' just like the Hebrew word 'Adonai' does. 'Mask' is from the medieval Latin 'masca,' meaning 'specter' or 'nightmare.' Those who wear these things tonight are Adonai nightmares."

"Yeah, okay. I'll take your word for it."

"We don't have a tux, nightmare mask or compass for you. You'll never get in through the front door. You'll slip in with the service crew. We'll hide the bike . . . here and cover it with bushes." Suddenly I feel fear for my husband. That's what it means to truly love. You're more concerned about the object of your love than yourself. I'd die for my boyish pilot. "Rob, you've got to be careful. I can't live without you. I've learned that over the past few days."

"Baby girl, all I know is crashing this party is what you want. You love your brother. It might not be the way I would handle things, but what do I know? If this is what you want, then this is what I'll do. I'll be fine. Besides, I've got a son to think of now."

"How do you know it's a boy?" I ask with a gaping smile.

"I just know. I been thinking, Julie . . . Why don't we name him Malory - either way, boy or a girl? You and Justin were a part of your father's redemption. We've got to help undo his messed-up legacy. Besides, Malory sounds like it could go either way."

Beaming, I begin to cry. "It's perfect, flyboy."

"I thought so, baby girl."

***

Approaching the massive estate with my mask on, I feel . . . pretty and . . . and . . . pretty nervous. It's hard to keep my thoughts straight as I remain completely ignorant of what stands before me. One side of a massive and ornate wooden double door is open and guests in masks similar to mine move carelessly along a red carpet. Steady streams of formally dressed attendees meander across the bridge and toward the front door. Everyone seems to be in good spirits. A tall blonde woman in a slinky black dress spins her compass on a chain as she walks arm in arm with an older man, her flirtatious attention obvious. A longhaired eccentric with a neatly kept goatee immediately catches my eye as I recognize him despite his mask. I'm no good with names, and I can't be completely sure, but I think he's an A-list actor. Now I know I'm right as his pop-star date becomes visible. This is crazy. The masks don't totally mask anyone. Instead, they just render you not completely sure. For this reason, I can't be one hundred percent certain that the short white-haired fellow in front of me is a famous politician, or that the African-American man over there is the popular level science guy that hosts his own cable television show, or that the redheaded fellow in the wheelchair is a recognized physicist. As a journalist, I couldn't report it as a fact, but personally, I know who they all are.

"Welcome to the Assembly," the doorman says without smiling. "Please have your invitations ready." Producing the golden object I try not to make eye contact, *but don't look like you're trying not to make eye contact, Julie,* - I tell myself. "Thank you," the doorman dryly says.

Stepping into the foyer I see that I am in a large open space. The walls are mahogany, the fixtures are marble and the whole thing is rich as chocolate cake. In various alcoves guests are huddled in groups munching hors d'oeuvres and enjoying the social dynamics. To my left is a lush sofa flanked by matching chairs. Gorgeous women recline laughing as they discuss philosophical and religious opinions with men. To my right, a pair of older fellows seem to be arguing a finer point of something in an animated way. Directly before me I see that I am on an oversized circular balcony that overlooks a ballroom twenty feet below. Descending the stairs, I find myself in the midst of a crowd. The scent of expensive perfume and cologne is undeniable. Now on the ground floor, I can see that beneath where I stood on the balcony is a stage. Expensive art hangs on the walls and large vertical banners hang behind the stage that each bear a different tenet of the Creed of the Adonai. The whole thing strikes me as reckless. How could all of these people be trusted to keep the secret of the Colonies?

"Welcome everyone," a voice says from the stage. "Please, please, keep enjoying the evening's festivities. If you're in the midst of some fascinating dialogue, ignore your jester of a host. For those who need a distraction from aimless banter, allow me to introduce myself. I am known as The Director. In a moment you will experience one irritating necessity of our annual Assembly. Our servers will be waving wands over your general area to ensure that there are no listening devices on your person. Hey, that reminds me of a joke. You know what really . . . bugs . . . me? Hidden microphones."

The guests lightly chuckle and a heavy-set man behind me shouts "Boo! You had better icebreakers last year, Director!"

The Director laughs from the stage as a server works his way through my section with an electronic device. He says, "No hecklers, now. For those of you with the Adonai emblem engraved on the back of your invitation, please move through the doors to *your* right, and *my* left at your earliest convenience. The rest of you are free to enjoy the festivities including the exploration of this beautiful residence. However, if you venture into the rooms down the hallway to your right, do not enter the last door unless your invitation bears the engraving. Ta ta for now." The ambient noise of conversation spreads from wall to wall again. Eyeing the compass, I see the emblem, but my age would likely give me away. I'm no Adon. Still, I'm getting in that room.

I quickly pace the hallway before anyone else has a chance to enter. Inside I'm alone. The room is not large. I'd say it's twenty by twenty. Seven chairs sit facing each other. To my right is a wet-bar and an oversized painting takes up almost the entirety of the back wall. It is a grand painting of my father's Colony. A large gold tile plate is screwed to the center of its bottom and reads, "A World of Hope." Lining the wall to my left are busts of each of the Adonai I know, plus a few others. The room has no windows and is lit by candles. Footsteps! I've got to hide. The large wet-bar has a cabinet just spacious enough to slip inside. Pulling my knees to my chest I position myself as best I can and close the cabinet door. A few bottles rattle and I struggle to quiet them just in time for the Adonai to enter the room. I hear them sit and ceremonially recite the Creed. I don't know if I can hold this position for long. Hopefully, the Adonai do not speak in vain repetitions.

"Greetings," a deep and resonant voice says. "For our new members, I am the Supreme Adon of our movement. You are each here because you have been appointed an Adon of our order. You are all privy to information that represents the most vital of all secrets. Few outside of this room are aware of our projects. They affirm atheism, but don't really know what they're funding or supporting. They're not ready. They could not handle it. Our forebears have left us with a lofty mission. One day, our Colonies will survive a true and genuine Great Darkness of *our* orchestration. As you know, it will be followed by an opening of our Colonies' gates. It will be a different world. You, in this room, have either already been a part of our efforts or have been chosen because of what you have to offer. After almost one hundred years, we now have everyone we need to realize my grandfather's vision."

"Hope to seek," they all say, as one might voice an amen.

Clearing his throat the speaker continues, "But we are not without our setbacks. As you know, The Colony you see in this painting has dissolved. It is a sad loss. Two Adonai were killed in those events. One of them was my right hand, Malory Lyn. We will, however, recover from this tragedy. The Son of Lyn, who was responsible for this rebellion, has been caught and sent for execution at the Circle Island Colony and all other loose ends have been discredited or otherwise eliminated." Execution? Justin!

A woman's voice enters the conversation with, "Forgive me Adon, but I'm uncomfortable with this news. As I understand it, Adon Yukimura has given no communication in some weeks."

Another unfamiliar voice speaks up - this time a man. "My fellow Adon is right, and how do we even know what's happening at Circle Island? What if the Son of Lyn has led a second rebellion?" The suggestion makes my heart sing. "No one has been there in ages."

A younger man, judging from his voice, speaks up next with a Russian accent. "And what of the Daughter of Lyn? This is my first meeting, but I've seen her interviews."

"Calm down," the leader urges. "Let me take each of these concerns in turn. It's true that we have not heard from Yukimura, but I've been in regular communication with the Circle Island Colony's Adon. He assures me that Yukimura is still there, and that everything went according to plan with Malory's son." Oh, this is like a rollercoaster of emotion. "As for the Daughter of Lyn, she's become a laughing stock and conspiracy theorist in the eyes of the media. She has no knowledge of us." But I do. "Harming her would only provide evidence of her claims. Now, let me assure you that the majority of the colonials from the Northern Colony have been transplanted, and are settling in nicely to their new homes. The swift relocation was not easy, but thanks to this Adon," he must have motioned to someone in the room, "we had all the vehicles and organizational support we needed to . . . clean up, so to speak. However, for those of you who are still concerned about Circle Island, I plan to leave for Rio the day after tomorrow. From there I will arrange for a boat to The Colony. I will report to you via the normal channels of what I find. Will that put you all at ease?"

"Hope to seek," they all chant in agreement.

"Well, alright then, Adonai," he says with satisfaction. "We'll meet again later tonight. I knew you couldn't enjoy the evening with these questions on your minds. For now, go enjoy a celebration of things to come."

***

After a few moments of pointless banter, they

leave and I collapse on the floor next to the wet-bar. Moving out of the room, I see that much of the crowd is heading toward an arched doorway on the other side of the ballroom. Not wanting to tip anyone off, I decide to follow them. The Director announces, "That's right, ladies and gentlemen, I hope you're not a pretender. If you are, you're about to be discovered."

CHAPTER THIRTY-THREE

Denial has come to refer to many things in the modern world. One may deny involvement in some crime, deny the advances of an admirer, or live in denial of some truth. For believers, the term retains a heaviness regarding the faith. Throughout the history of the church there has been a recurring temptation to deny the Master when trials come at the mention of His name. In the face of death, the faithful, right up until today, have stood firm in their commitment and fallen by the sword. It must cross every follower's mind at some point or other, "Why not deny just to live. All will be forgiven." But there is a mysterious reluctance. The hearts of God's children scream against the temptation. With such a great heritage of loyal martyrs, Stephen's blood inspires us. We will not deny.

I am three guests back from a black velvet curtain bearing the Adonai emblem in red. It does look menacing. Nevertheless, the only way I'm going to be discovered is if I verbally confirm my intentions here, and I hardly see how that is going to happen. Two more attendees stand before me, now one. A somber atmosphere has descended on the stone hallway. It is dim in here . . . no. It's dark. My turn.

I'm surrounded by the curtain. It forms a black circle around me only a little wider than me. (KACHUNK) the lights go out. It's completely black.

My heart is racing so fast I can't be calmed. Suddenly an almost growling voice violates the space saying, "Do you know the Creed, traveler?"

Stuttering, I will myself to speak, "F . . . Fr . . . Freedom to the Think, Freedom to Live, Hope to Seek, Hope to Give." That wasn't too hard. Calm down, Julie.

For a moment I think I've passed the test, but there has to be more. After all, the Creed isn't much of a secret. It was displayed at the main stage for all to see. My fears are confirmed when I hear the voice again. "Do you deny all false religions and gods?" I ponder this one for a moment. I wouldn't be lying. I do deny all false religions and false gods. I decide the parameters of conscience and honesty permit the answer.

"I do."

"Do you deny the God of the Christians?" Are you kidding me? An internal struggle swells. I *could* justify this. I need to find out the truth about my brother. I need to stop the Adonai. I'm like . . . undercover or something. Three times, I open my mouth to meet the request with a denial. Three times something inside me won't allow it. The only way they would find me out is if I verbally confirmed my intentions. That's basically what I would be doing. Clever. It has always been this way. The enemies of the faith play on our commitment.

"I do . . . not." Five seconds of total silence passes before violent wind rushes down from above.

It's so loud I hear nothing else and the heavy velvet curtains fan out at the base, only visible because of an erratic red strobe light that flickers without rhythm. The deepest fear I've ever known swirls into the deepest panic. I don't know what to do. I try to move forward through the curtain, but it's a tangled mess. I can't find an opening and it seems that solid walls exist two feet beyond the velvet in every direction. Unable to resist the base response, I scream. Suddenly it stops, the darkness returns and a firm hand tightly grips my bicep, yanking me out. I'm not in the hallway where the line of Adonai guests wait. I'm in an empty, arched, stone passage that is illuminated by red light. A loud metal cranking is heard and a door opens to the evening moonlight. Tossed out onto grass, I land on all fours and hear the door shut behind me. I'm alone. Did they just . . . kick me out? Am I free to leave?

"Stand," a young male voice says. It is the voice of the younger man in the Adonai private meeting. I fail all attempts to manually control my breathing. The anxiety is out of control. I'm in full-on fight-or-flight. With my hands clutching the earth, I raise my head to see what new horror is before me. I'm in a courtyard of some kind. It's about twenty feet wide and fifty feet long. On either side of me the same repetitive archways stretch to the other end, but behind them are impassible walls. Twenty feet up, on either side of the space, six Adonai look on from behind their masks - three on each side. The seventh is at the other end of the courtyard staring at me. He wears a weathered Apologia uniform - the same I recall from The Colony. Chin-length blond hair further hides his face. "Remove your mask," he sternly commands.

Slowly I rise to my feet and brush off my dress. I have no choice. Sliding the eyewear over my head I raise my chin for all to see. The sounds of whispers echo down from above the courtyard before I hear a female Adon reveal, "It's her. It's the Daughter of Lyn."

An older man says, "Julie. Her name is Julie Lyn."

The masked Adon wearing the Apologia uniform takes three long paces toward me but still stands a good thirty feet away. He removes his mask and I see a long scar diagonally stretching across his face. "Tristan," I can't help but gasp before covering my mouth with both hands. Moving toward me, the greatest warrior of the night watch has retribution on his face. I back away and scan for something to climb. Nothing. Even if there were, I would find myself with, not one, but six Adonai to combat. Circling the space, I can't help but think of so many who have faced a similar fate before me because they would not deny.

Grabbing me by the hair as I try to shift away, Tristan forces me to my knees again. Raising some sort of ceremonial blade, he looks to the Supreme Adon for a command. Crying, I look up and know that nothing I could say would help. The Supreme Adon nods one time.

CHAPTER THIRTY-FOUR

Just as the Apologia is about to strike, the metal door swings open and a disheveled Rob, with a much too small tuxedo enters the courtyard gasping for air as if he's just run a marathon. All attention turns to him as he briefly stares at the scene and then rushes the Apologia. Tristan turns from me to face the oncoming threat and Rob grips his wrist just below the blade. They spin, wrestling each other, until the ceremonial weapon falls to the ground, sticking hilt up in the grass. Glancing to the roof I see that the Supreme Adon has disappeared. Through the door of the courtyard, four more able-bodied Apologia spill out. No time.

Distracted by Rob, Tristan isn't watching me. Standing behind him, I prepare to deliver my one good jab. It's the same maneuver that took out Brent at the Northern Colony. Here we go. With a shout, I pound against the back of the Apologia's head with the knuckles of my index and middle fingers, just as Hope taught me. He stumbles. It doesn't put him out of commission, but it creates enough of the desired effect for Rob to grab the blade and join me at the far end of the courtyard where Tristan first stood. Knife raised to threaten Tristan, all five Apologia freeze as we slowly back away toward the arched exit. Once we reach the outside, we break the stare and run.

"Fast," Rob shouts as we descend a rocky

staircase and find ourselves on an expansive back patio with more tables and about one hundred guests. Beyond the patio is the gorgeous river, and above, the bridge can be seen. Servers, who may well be Apologia officers in disguise, block our path. Hand in hand Rob instructs, "C'mon," and we vault from a chair onto a white linen covered rectangular table that stretches halfway along the porch. Guests squeal and gasp as we cover the distance. The Director tries to maintain order with another lame joke.

"Don't be alarmed ladies and gentlemen. How . . . How bout an atheist pickup line? Are you a deity, because you look unreal? Ha ha! Get it?" His attempt to maintain order isn't working. Glasses, bottles and candles go sailing as our feet tread the unlikely runway without elegance. My path is momentarily blocked as Rob trips and lands chest down on the table. He recovers quickly, and continues the chase as Apologia cover the distance in like manner.

"Rob," I scream. He looks back and I shout, "You're on fire!"

"Now's not the time for flirtation, sweetheart!"

"No, Rob," I exclaim with an insistent look. "You're actually on fire."

"Whoa," he wails as he notices his left sleeve is flaming. Still running, he removes the jacket and tosses it wildly, toward the house. Visitors part to miss the formalwear fireball as it enters the large garden doors and collides with a curtain.

"Whoops," I say out loud. The last thing I see is the trail of flames working its way up the long stretch of fabric. No time to worry with that.

Dropping off the table, the end of the patio comes into view and we take no time to discuss our plan. We both drop over the edge and land rolling in the grass. Standing we see that to our right is the bank of the river with rounded stones. The waterfall rumbles. To our left are the woods. "There," Rob says pointing to a door underneath the patio. "It must lead to some kind of storage area. "I'll lead them into the woods. GO!"

"Okay," I huff and slide into the doorway. I wanted to protest, but there was no time to offer another plan. I'm not entirely sure what the plan is.

Watching from the cracked door, I see Rob with a decent head start. Four Apologia land and roll in the grass and expertly maneuver back into a run. Four. That's not right. Then I see it. Boots hit the ground ten feet outside the door and Tristan watches the chase. He doesn't follow. His hand goes to his face for three seconds and then he begins looking around. He's figured it out. Approaching my hiding spot he mumbles something unintelligible to himself. I've got to move.

***

The shadowy interior smells like aged cardboard and sawdust. I'm crouched behind a high stack of crates in a back corner, hoping against hope that the Apologia gives up and assumes I fled elsewhere. Slowly moving through the long basement, Tristian speaks. "I'll find you, Daughter of Lyn." The fear begins to creep back in. "It would be best for you to reveal yourself. No one believes you." He's creeping closer. "Your father is dead. I'm told your mother is senile. Worst of all, we've killed . . . your brother." Two tears, in quick succession roll down my cheek. "The Lyns are a weak family." Along the wall to my right, I see an old-fashioned laundry shoot. If I could get inside, I could ascend into the house. "We will remove the very name, Lyn, from the history of the Adonai." He's right on the other side of the crates now. This is my chance.

Throwing my weight into the tower of crates they begin to fall and Tristan is, at least for the moment, incapacitated. "The Lyns will be the end of the Adonai," I declare before rushing up the laundry shoot. With arms and legs pressing against each side of the oversized shaft, I climb. I'm ten feet up when he joins me in the passage and mimics my movement. We both grunt heavily. He's gaining on me. A hatch is visible in just ten more feet. I keep moving. Is that smoke I smell?

Popping out of the shoot, I land on the floor of an exquisite bathroom. Two ladies are touching up their lashes when I cross the room like some sort of dolled up zombie. Grabbing a bulky purse from one of them I move back toward the shaft. "Hey," she says, before watching me dump the totality of her bag's contents into my point of entrance. Clanging is heard as beauty products, keys and other assorted items fall on Tristan's head. While I trudge to the door, the women back up to the sink, scared to interact with me further.

"You two don't smell that?" I ask. I open the door and smoke fills the room. They both shriek and I order, "Get out! The place is on fire." As they scurry past, I follow. Before shutting the door I see a leather clad arm appear at the shoot.

Racing down the hallway, I see that I'm now back at the foyer that overlooks the ballroom. Guests push their way through the main entrance, but a traffic jam has developed. "Dummies," I say to myself. Sliding a window open with ease, I step out onto dark mulch and begin jogging again. Only now do I see that Rob is Approaching on the back of the motorcycle. "Rob!"

"C'mon baby girl." I'm on the back of the bike in a snap and Rob revs the engine to warn the crowd. People are everywhere. The fire is raging. We ride.

"Rob, wait! Cross the bridge!"

"Are you crazy? We've got to run for our lives!"

"I know, but the Adonai inner circle - they might be heading for the landing strip. They have no escort. We've got to try!"

"*Ugh*," Rob moans. Turning the corner of the house, the bridge appears and we jet past the running overdressed Adonai benefactors. Across the river now, we ramp onto the private runway and speed toward the area where several private planes are positioned. The guests had arrived in style.

"See anything, flyboy?"

"I don't know, don't pressure me."

"Wait . . . there!" The Supreme Adon is hurrying toward his own plane. No one is with him. "Pull over next to the service building." Whispering to each other, we make a plan.

***

"Supreme Adon," I call. He turns halfway up the stairs and I see Rob slipping behind him a good distance away. "I am the Daughter of Lyn, and I'm here to find my brother." Wind picks up and I push my hair over my ear. "I don't care about your plans. I just want my family back."

"Young lady, your brother is dead, and if you've any sense, you'll thank whatever god you believe in that you survived this night. Run away, Daughter of Lyn."

"You don't know that . . . that my brother is dead." He turns to continue up the stairs. "Take me with you to the Island." He stops again, and out of the corner of my eye I see Rob's head poke up in confusion. This was not part of the plan.

"How do you know about . . . It doesn't matter. You want me to take you to the Island, where you'll be killed like your father and brother were, all on the off chance that somehow he's still alive? No, dear. I'm going to ignore your youthful stupidity." With that, the stairs raise and in minutes, the apparatus is down the runway and into the sky.

Rob jogs up to meet me and says, "Well, we're tracking him now. The same GPS that led me to you will lead us to your brother."

CHAPTER THIRTY-FIVE

It took all night. With the Supreme Adon's plan to leave for the Island in two days, we couldn't waste time. We cut Evelyn loose, left her to deal with Arvin, headed for Rob's beloved plane and took off. It looked like the destination was somewhere in Arizona. Halfway there we settled down in a small town and slept on the aircraft. With the light of day, and the nightmare of the Adonai Assembly behind us, it was a more hopeful flight to the GPS destination. Now, five miles out, the target is in view.

"Just looks like a massive cluster of rock," Rob says, as we view a mountainous red mass of earth protruding at least the equivalent of thirty stories up from the flat desert topography.

Squinting in the cockpit I examine the scene. "No, look," I say pointing to a metallic tower of some kind, situated in the midst of the giant natural structure. "There's something here, Rob! We found it!" I hop up and down in my seat clapping my hands together with enthusiasm.

"Yeah, okay," he says, turning the plane away from the site so as not to be noticed, "but how are we supposed to get into that thing?"

"Well, we'll just have to come up with a plan."

"And," he continues, "once we get in, what are we supposed to do, say we're here for the first flight to the secret hidden Island Colony? How's that supposed to go?"

"I don't know, but he's not leaving till tomorrow. We'll wait till night and sneak in."

"Again, baby girl, how?"

"Well, I've never asked you this before, but do you like rock climbing?" He looks at me as though I've seen too many movies.

"We'll come back tonight and set her down a few miles away. It'll have to be a pretty long hike. If they see the plane, they'll know we're coming. And just so you know, I've got no intention of losing another plane on one of your crazy Adonai adventures."

***

No fence surrounds the base of the rocky face. Now at least a hundred feet up, we continue our amateur climb toward a natural opening. It took dealing with a lot of Rob's protests to convince him that this death defying escalade is no more threatening than trying to infiltrate the location to begin with. That, of course, was a point of agreement that led to more protests about the whole project. Nevertheless, I like to think my careless charm and cute face had something to do with his begrudging acceptance of the plan. Here we are, clutching the side of a mountain in the desert.

Looking down at me, my loyal husband announces, "Just a little further and we'll make it."

"See. I told you it would all work out." No sooner do I say the words than loose rock falls free under my foot and I slide a few inches before regaining a solid position. He doesn't speak. He just looks down at me with raised eyebrows and a serious gate.

After Rob crawls through a gap in the surface of the rock, he grips my wrist and lifts me to his side. We both take deep breaths and I stare down at the dizzying drop. It would've meant death. He glares at me again with one eyebrow raised. I grimace and move past him through the passage. He follows. A good thirty feet from the outside we sit on the balls of our feet and view the interior of the mountain.

"There's the jet," Rob says, motioning to the metal bird sitting just inside a cavernous opening carved out of the rock. A few vehicles are scattered around the floor of the interior, and stretching up from the center is the tower I spied from the air. At its base there is a larger more traditionally shaped building, but above it, the spire reaches to the lip of the mountain's highest peaks. Four ten-foot-wide metal supports maintain the stability of the tower and reach out like artificial arms from the huge cylindrical building to the rocks around us. Toward the top of the building there is a wider section with large windows that slant inward from top to bottom.

"That must be the Adon's office, at the top," I surmise.

"I'd say so. You know there's got to be some serious surveillance in this place . . ." He's cut off by my movement toward one of the large supports. "Awe, Julie," he groans.

Clambering up a slanting, rocky outcropping, I approach the giant arm. It takes another half hour of climbing to reach the location. Tapping it with my knuckles, I notice that it makes a slight clanging. We'll have to tread lightly. "Gimme a boost, babe," I say.

Rob lifts me enough that I'm able to squirm on my belly to the top. With outstretched arms and bowed legs I carefully stand. My partner follows, hopping on his rear up to the curved surface. The area, illuminated by moonlight, is silent. The deadly distance from here to the floor below causes biological sirens to blare in the brain. "Just move slowly, baby girl." I bite my lip as I begin taking steps. A tightrope walker would find the balancing act hilarious, and rightly so. It's not the width of the support that necessitates our caution, but the certainty of death if we fall.

Halfway across the forty-yard distance, I hear a sound echo through the environment from above. Risking my equilibrium, I glance forty feet upward to see the windowed top of the tower. Nothing. Keep walking, I tell myself. "You okay, flyboy?"

"So far so good."

"Talk to me. I need a distraction for my nerves."

"What do you want to talk about?"

"I don't know, something mundane to take our minds off the threat of immanent death."

"Gotcha . . . Okay, well, I have been meaning to talk to you about the cabinet situation."

"What? What are you talking about? What cabinet situation?"

"Well, I notice that when you put glasses in the cabinet, you put em face up."

"Yeah. That's how you do it."

"See, that's the thing. I'm not so sure."

"Um," I begin, "what idiot would put them face down?"

"This one."

"Yeah, but then the rim of the glass is touching the surface."

"But . . . with the glass up, dust can gather inside. I'm allergic to dust. Gotta pick your battles, babe." Fortunately, from behind me, he can't see me rolling my eyes. "Julie," he adds in an excited tone. "Down!"

"I got it, Rob, face down. Don't get so worked

up."

"No! Get down!" I look back to see a rope hanging between the two of us from the overhanging windows, now above us on the spire. Dropping to my belly, hugging the surface, I look back up in time to see boots hit the metal with a loud and echoing thud. An Apologia! "Easy, fella. We're not here to . . . *umph*." The Apologia pushed him to a sitting position on the support. "Hey," Rob says, "I . . . I know you." The Apologia doesn't stop approaching as Rob crab walks backwards on his hands. I've got to do something. Tossing caution to the wind, I stand and rush the remaining distance to the main structure and turn to shout.

"Hey, look at me! I'm getting away," I warn the leathery soldier. He takes the bait and turns to face me. "It's Brent!" He takes four long paces toward me before stopping to turn his attention back to Rob, who is on his feet and has the rope in his grip. Without much concern, Rob swings out over the empty space and makes a semicircle around the enemy's position. Landing back on the support next to me, he wobbles a bit before stabilizing. Brent tries to follow as we rush around the circumference of the tower looking for a doorway, or a ladder or something. Nothing. "What do we do now?"

"You answer for challenging the Adonai," Brent says as he turns the corner and we back onto another support.

"Brent," I say, "you know you're doing the

wrong thing here. Justin is as much your brother as he is mine. You grew up together."

"Justin *was* like a brother, before he turned against us. Now he's dead. I regret nothing." We continue to back away along the arm.

"You know," Rob begins, "you guys have got no sense at all do you? Running around in your dumb little uniforms like you're some kind of rugged ninja rock stars made sense when you were the only people in the world. You know the truth now, Brent. Grow up and put that stuff to bed."

"I am an Apologia and an Adon, you don't know what you're talking about."

Rob answers, "You're an Adon, huh? Did you even know you weren't invited to the secret Adonai convention in Maine two days ago?" He looks confused. "You don't even know what I'm talking about do you?"

"They're using you," I add. "You're just a goon to them, Brent." He stares at the ominous empty space. "You already know it don't you? Leave this place with me. Help me save Justin, Hope, Courtney and Jack." For a moment I think I'm getting through to him.

"Jackson," he says to no one in particular. "What a dope." There is a nostalgic smile on his face. Looking back to us, he says, "It's too late. This is what I am now."

Rob speaks up, "It's not too late, bro. You can still make this right. Just take us to the head honcho."

With a solemn laugh, Brent answers, "He'd have me killed."

With palms raised, Rob approaches Brent and says, "Don't attack me, pal." Brent looks anxious. His eyes shift wildly as his thoughts are conflicted. When Rob is on solid footing, two feet away, he delivers one solid slug to Brent's stomach. The Apologia heaves deeply and crumples to the deck clutching the point of impact. Quickly, Rob gets the Apologia hand restraints and attaches Brent's left wrist to a railing. As he finishes he explains, "Now you can just say we overpowered you. See how that works, bud?"

We head back to the rope and I fear what the solution might be. Rob ties it around my waist in a secure knot before free climbing the rope to the window. Once there, he begins pulling me up. I squeeze my eyes shut and clutch the rope, trusting Rob to do the work. It seems to last forever, but finally his arms hoist me through the window. Looking around, I see that we are on a lower deck of the dizzying architecture. Easels stand at various points around the space, with architectural renderings of installations that I imagine are the Colonies. One is in a jungle. Another is on an icy peak. A third is in a desert. Do these already exist or are they plans for the future? Wrapping around the center beam is a staircase that stretches like a snake diagonally toward the ceiling. It's time for a private meeting with the Supreme Adon.

CHAPTER THIRTY-SIX

Ascending the stairs, we find ourselves in a plush living space with windows all around. The air is cool and it smells like books. The center beam of the tower now has a circular bookshelf from the floor to the ten-foot high ceiling. A brass and wooden ladder is fixed to a track at the top of the shelves. Potted plants are expertly placed at various points near the windows and busts of various individuals are positioned every ten feet or so. I immediately recognize the face of my father on one of the statues.

Rob leads as we circle the center beam and an office arrangement comes into view. The Supreme Adon sits with his back to the windows behind a very large carved wooden desk. Outside, the rock face is visible. On either side of the desk, at the windows, four large stone tablets rest on easels. They are of the same reddish stone visible on the mountain outside. The Creed of the Adonai is carved into them. At the top of each is the emblem of the Adonai. They look old.

"Infiltrate an Adonai Assembly," the Adon begins, "track the Supreme Adon to his very hidden office, bypass all security and overcome my personal Apologia guard. You certainly do the Lyn name proud young lady."

"What is this place?" Rob asks.

"None other than the site of the very first Adonai Colony, my friend." I feel my eyes widen and my mouth open. "Obviously, this tower was not here at the time, but in nineteen twenty-five, my grandfather began a mission within these rocks. In fact, these stone tablets were a part of the first Adonai Monument. Every day, those colonials would recite the Creed of the Adonai, just as our colonials do now."

"But why?" I demand to know.

"Well, originally, The Colony was established so that a community of unbelievers could be free of any religious influence. Back then it was even more unpleasant to live as a skeptic than it is now. Over time, however, my forbearers thought it made sense to locate influential leaders who longed for an atheistic utopia and invite them to join our movement. We grew. As we grew, so did our ambition. To say the least, it is no longer our desire to merely live separately. We have big plans."

"What are you gonna do?" Rob asks. "Take over the world?" he laughs.

The Supreme Adon puckers in consideration and ponders his answer. "It is a secret of the Adonai. But, you know, that's not really why you're here is it? What you really want is to find young Justin."

"That's right. I want to go to the Island. If he's dead I want to see it for myself."

"Yeah," Rob adds. "Better yet, just tell us where it is and we'll handle the rest."

"Tell you where it is," the Adon repeats to himself, "I'll do no such thing, why would I?"

"Because we'll sell you out. Plus, I'd say I could make you talk," Rob threatens.

"Ah, violence as a motivation for information. I think you'll find I'm quite willing to endure such things, however, at the push of a button, ten Apologia will be on their way. I simply see no reason to notify them so long as things remain civil."

With passion I say, "Then take me with you."

"You don't know what you're asking."

"I don't care . . . I'm ready for anything." He sits considering my words for a few long moments before standing to cross the room. From a hutch, he removes a wooden tray with two glasses and a small pouch. Placing them on the desk he measures out an exact amount of bluish powder and then pours it into two glasses. Then gripping a pitcher of water, he fills each glass and stirs the powder in.

"What's this all about?" Rob asks.

"This is a substance brought back from the Circle Island Colony where Justin was sent. Ten or so years back we exported a stockpile of it for our purposes. When you drink it, you'll immediately be rendered unconscious. Then, I'll transport you to the Island."

"How do we know you won't kill us the minute we're out?" Rob asks.

"Oh, you don't. I'm not pressuring you. By all means, leave. You're the ones who are so obsessed with going to The Colony."

"If we leave," I ask, "aren't you afraid we'll tell someone about this place?"

"Why should I be? I'm a legitimate businessman with various streams of profitable and legal income. The US government is perfectly aware of my personal residence here. Listen, you two . . . you've . . . got . . . nothing. As you have already seen, no one will ever believe you. So, make your choice, I really don't care." A long pause follows the Adon's explanation. I pace the room trying to imagine every possible outcome.

Finally, I pick up the glass and stare into Rob's eyes. He shakes his head. "Pick it up, flyboy."

He breathes heavily with his mouth closed. He raises the glass and says, "It's . . . it isn't . . . ."

"Shhh," I say with tears welling up. "I'll never be at peace till I know." The blue liquid flows into my mouth and I become dizzy.

"Sit down, Daughter of Lyn," the Supreme Adon says. I do. Rob drinks and sits in chair in front of me. We grip hands.

"I love you, Rob."

"I love you, baby girl." It all fades to black.

Debris flies up all around them as they sprint across the valley below. A trail of explosions chase after my fellow Apologia. Above, I sail along the zip line clutching the Hook-Slide, now with familiarity. Behind us is Oleth and the Unbelieving Tribe. Before us is Foley, on the run from everyone. The explosions stop. Jack's security measures have come in handy, but they almost meant his own death. Dropping, I land and steady myself with my fingertips against the earth before launching forward next to he and Courtney. Ahead of us, the Adon . . . no . . . false prophet of the Southern Colony shows no signs of tiring out. Over my shoulder I see a snarling Oleth emerge from the smoke and dust with an army of young men behind him. This could be the end. For several days we've tried to distract either Oleth or Foley from the blood lust of annihilating each other. So far we've been successful as red herrings to drag them off the scent of the opposition. Today, unfortunately, we've become caught in the crossfire.

"We're almost to the bridge," Courtney urges.

Huffing, I shout, "Just don't stop running!"

The rope bridge that extends sixty feet across and forty feet above the deep and rough river appears almost ancient. Several slats are missing, but we race across to see Hope has Foley with his hands raised, palms up. Her new homemade bow is retracted with a handcrafted arrow aimed at Foley's head. Is it just me or does she look proud to have finally found a practical opportunity to make use of the weapon besides hunting? Joining her, I quickly retrieve Foley's blade and cut one side of the rope bridge free. Instantly the bridge twists at our end like the DNA double helix and I move to the other side to repeat the action.

"Wait, Apologia," Oleth shouts from the other side of the river. "Give us the false Adon and we will pursue you no more. As much as I look forward to gutting you, it's that worm we are after." His followers cheer and shake their fists.

"What do you think, Foley?" I ask with a gruff voice. "You've made your bed. Perhaps we should make you lie in it." He squints as he looks to each of our faces in turn. It's like he sees something.

"You Northern colonials don't look quite right. You're still experiencing the withdrawals from the Ocean's Wave aren't you?" None of us answer, but I grit my teeth. "Irritability, inability to fully concentrate, increased aggression - you ache for it don't you?" Courtney looks at us with worry.

Shaking it off I growl, "Quit stalling, Foley!"

"Send him over," Oleth barks.

"Young prince," Foley responds, "I've no

problem surrendering to that barbarian. In two hours I'll have complete control of his camp. In fact, if you'll be so kind as to lower your weapon, Ms. Wynfelt, I'll head that way now." He slowly sidesteps toward what's left of the bridge as Hope lowers her bow.

"Foley, don't . . . he'll kill you," I say. I can't help but feel some connection to the monster, even now.

"Don't worry, Justin. See I know the truth. I've seen the prophecy, and you have as well." He places his feet on the bottom rope and holds on to the top one as he balances and begins to cross the river. Oleth draws his sword, an obvious indication that he plans to immediately exact his vengeance.

"Foley, look at him! Think about what you're doing!"

"Justin, I told you, I've no concern at all for this beast. It's not possible. His blade would not penetrate my flesh. As I've said, I've seen the prophecy. It cannot be undone."

"You mean the one that includes me standing at your side? You think after all this, I'm gonna join you?"

Halfway across he answers with a confident lopsided grin, "I know you will." With that, he drops into the water below. We all rush to the edge and watch for his body. His head reemerges and he is carried downstream by the current. Five members of the Unbelieving Tribe begin crossing the bridge toward us and I swiftly cut through the remaining rope. Three of them hang onto the bridge-turned-ladder and two fall into the river. They all survive. Looking back to Oleth, I see that he is gone. His followers trail behind him as he tracks Foley from the solid ground.

"Let's slide, crew," I instruct.

***

Jogging through the jungle, Jack stops and we all stop with him. "What is it?" Hope asks.

He turns his head sideways as if to weigh his words. "I know this won't be a popular opinion, but maybe we should consider the possibility that . . ."

"What? Just say it," I demand in irritation.

" . . . that we should never have left the Southern Colony." He takes both his lips between his teeth and raises his brow in a there-I-said-it sort of way.

Before I can reply, Hope marches over to him and sticks her index finger in his chest insisting, "Of course *you* think we should have stayed. It wasn't *you* that was left at the bottom of a hole in the backyard!"

"Back off, snowflake," I say. "We've all been in that hole, you weren't the only one." She looks at me with her mouth open in shock. "Sorry, but it's not the craziest idea. There's safety in numbers, and the Southern Colony colonials may have killed the older Adonai sympathizers, but now they are peaceful for the most part."

"That's all I'm saying," Jack agrees, with a shrug. Hope's irritation calms as she thinks through the proposal.

"You're not actually considering this are you?" Courtney asks Hope. Looking to me and Jack she argues, "You're all just looking for your next hit."

"What," Jack says.

"Ocean's Wave," she continues. "You can't live without it." At her words, I exhale with my hands on my hips and stare upward. "No. Don't brush me off, Justin. You're all jonesing for the Nazi-sauce!" No one says anything. "Just admit it." After a few somber moments, Hope caves.

"I am." We all look to her. "I'll admit it. I've never had a physical craving like it . . . But, Courtney," they lock eyes, "that's not what I'm thinking. We're going to get killed out here. Maybe we shouldn't go back to The Colony, but we can't keep getting involved in this war either."

"As long as we're all confessing," Jack says, "I'm struggling with my commitments here. I . . ." Tears well up in his eyes. "I can't help but see the logic in it, Justin. I don't mean the belief stuff. I mean the self-defense. I mean the capital punishment. We're alone out here. I can't blame Foley for doing what he has to do to protect his Colony." I place my hand on his shoulder. He admits, "I can't defend what he did to

Hope, throwing her down in that pit, but maybe we could negotiate something."

Courtney says, "I don't like watching you three suffer, but . . . if you decide to go back there, you'll go without me."

With my right hand still on Jack's shoulder, I put my left on Courtney's and say, "We needed to get this stuff out, didn't we? Let's sleep on it tonight. Tomorrow we'll be thinking more clearly."

Jack looks up through his tears and adds, "Let's just get back to the new Wynfelt Manor and go swimming. We need a sense of normalcy."

"Don't start," Hope says, punching his arm in a sisterly way.

CHAPTER THIRTY-EIGHT

The scene is set in the cave lagoon we now lovingly call Wynfelt Manor. Candles sit around the space, their lights reflected on the pool of water. Though they are common in the real world, these rare commodities were a gift to Courtney from the Veritas girls. She's been saving them for a special occasion. We sit on appropriately sized stones at a table Jack fashioned from planks discovered around the Island, and prepare to eat the results of Hope's bow hunting and Courtney's foraging. We're doing alright out here, I guess. Roofless, the cave allows the moonlight to provide more ambiance. I can't say this is as comfortable as life back at the Mansion, but it's not unpleasant.

"Tonight," I say, "I must violate the policy of our special meals. In the Wynfelt tradition, we never discuss Colony matters here. But, I have a plan, and time is short."

"I guess I'll allow it," Hope judiciously says with a wink. She seems to have gotten past the issue with Bailee. Although she doesn't know the whole story, or what I've been dealing with since the Veritas girl's death.

Inhaling the misty air, I declare, "We've got to

get off this Island. We all know the truth. Even if there were no Southern Colony, or Unbelieving Tribe, we're marooned out here. We need to think about our exit strategy."

Jack pipes up, "Well, fat chance of that. What do you want to do, swim for shore?"

"I see two options. First, we know that boats end up here occasionally. When I first met Jack, they were dismantling one in a grotto filled with broken down vessels."

Courtney perks up, "Yeah, you ever wonder what happened to their passengers?"

"I know what you're getting at, but I can't believe Bailee would have been complicit with killing unless they were Adonai. Regardless, my point is that we *could* try to salvage one."

"No chance," Jack says. "Foley would have to be okay with it, and I think we all know the reason those boats were destroyed was out of commitment to maintaining The Great Divide."

I continue, "That's just it. This plan would involve convincing Foley of his false beliefs and getting his help. I admit it's a long shot, but it's one we have to try." Courtney rolls her eyes at the idea. "Listen, I said I saw two options. The second relies on the distraction of the first. Even if Foley won't help us, he'll talk. While he's talking, I'll sneak into the Mansion."

"Why?" Hope asks.

"What did we find beneath the map at the Northern Colony in the Administrative Lodge?" They all look puzzled. "A phone, remember? 'Come in Northern Colony, this is the Southern Colony' . . . Remember? There's a phone somewhere in that Mansion, and if I can find it, maybe I can get help?" Their eyes widen as the realization dawns.

For an hour, we lay out our strategy. Jack and Courtney will try to convince Foley to side with us and organize an escape. I will sneak in under the cover of darkness and try to find the phone. It's all set.

The rest of the night is filled with laughter and friendship as we ignore the seriousness of our situation. We eat, we swim, we dance with no music, and we pray. Tomorrow night, our mission begins.

***

Dusk. A single arrow with an attached message sails through the air and thuds into a wooden column at the back of the Mansion. Having made her only contribution to the project, Hope retreats toward our underground fortress. The message was simple,

Foley,

It's time to talk. Meet us at the old schoolhouse at dark.

Sincerely,
The Apologia of the Northern Colony

If it works, I'll only have one chance.

***

From my spot on a branch, a good distance away, I see that Foley took the bait. With a hand on his sidearm he cautiously creeps through the woods with one of the Southern Colony Apology twins escorting him. Time to trust my crew and take off. Twenty minutes will place me at the Mansion. "Move, Justin," I tell myself.

***

Approaching from the woods on the far side of the Mansion, the side with Foley's library, I scan the area. There's no apparent threat, but the other boneheaded Apologia twin must be lurking somewhere. Wait, what's that? Just a Veritas girl heading home for the evening. Now! Crossing the distance to the side of the structure I slide in the grass next to the exterior wall and crane my neck to see through the window. The kitchen. Raising the window I slip in. It's dark and silent. The Mansion may well be vacant, but I can't trust that. With careful steps, I move through the space and cross the hall to the library. No lock. Good.

Inside the room, I begin moving books around on the shelves, careful to remember their original positions. Nothing. I open a hutch with great confidence. Still nothing. I know it's not in the Nazi underworld through the secret passage. I saw everything there. Besides, it would need to be someplace Foley might hear a call. His personal quarters!

I'm down the hall and halfway up the stairs when I hear the shower running in the bathroom. Down the hall opposite Foley's suite. Perfect! The opportunistic thug is supposed to be guarding the house, but he's indulging in 'me time' while his Adon is away. I feel myself grin as I walk more freely into Foley's private world. A massive bed with swanky pillows and a gorgeous comforter stretches out from the wall to my left. The dresser and armoire are beautifully carved and mimic the size and design of the bed. Another doorway leads into a gorgeous bath. Artwork hangs about the room. I can't resist the urge to examine a particular painting more closely. The initials? "A.H." It can't be. I look around the room, mesmerized. I've got to focus. A shadowbox rests on a table and I open it. IDs. A lot of IDs. Each one is fixed below a photograph of a boat. Courtney was right! He's been killing them. Suddenly the Veritas ceremony before the destruction of the boats makes sense. They've made a Great Divide sacrament of the destruction! My thoughts are interrupted with a ring. The phone. I look to the armoire. There!

Opening its doors I see the yellow rotary phone with no numbers. Timidly I pick it up. "Adon," an older man's voice asks. "Adon, are you there? This is the Supreme Adon."

The voice snaps me back to reality and I realize the need to improvise. I've got to impersonate Foley, impersonating one of the Southern Colony Adonai he killed. He's been a pretender for years. With my best fake Australian voice, I respond "Here, Supreme Adon."

"Good. This will come as something of a shock, but we're going to meet soon. I'll be visiting you at Circle Island." I know that aside from Yukimura's visit, the Adonai never check up on this place except by phone. Foley would find this strange. What would he say?

"Sir, I find this most strange. To what do we owe your illustrious presence?" Illustrious? That might have been too much.

"There has been some concern about Damian Yukimura. You said he left after delivering the Son of Lyn and the Daughter of Wynfelt, but he hasn't reported since. On the other hand, the Daughter of Lyn has become a great nuisance. But . . . she willingly surrendered. I'm going to be able to settle everyone down once I can assure them all that Malory's offspring are out of the way." Julie! He must be bringing her here. Stay cool, Justin. Foley wouldn't care about that news. How would he react to the Supreme Adon's doubt that I'm . . . out of the way?

Channeling Foley, I add, "Supreme Adon, I assure you . . ."

"No, no, Adon. I don't doubt you. It brings me great peace that thanks to your leadership, I never have to worry about Circle Island. That said, the other Adonai need assurance. I'll be there tomorrow night just after dark."

Thinking on my feet I advise, "Uh . . . Supreme Adon, you'll need to enter through the opening in the cliffs. That will place you at the beachfront of The Colony."

"Yes, of course, Adon, I know. It's not like I didn't choose the site myself." Wrinkling my lip in disgust I rock my head back and forth in mockery.

"Of course, Supreme Adon. We will be waiting with great anticipation and fanfare."

"Fine. Freedom to think!" With that, the communication ends.

***

I'm halfway back to the cave lagoon when I hear a familiar voice. "Dope has conquered *lust*, reason now to *hope*, preach the truth he *must*, no longer he a *dope*."

"Aldo," I say with surprising satisfaction.

"Aldo here. Aldo will advise you."

"What do *you* want in all this, Aldo? Are you hoping these two Colonies will destroy each other so you can have your solitude back?"

"Hee, hee, ho . . . no. *Aldo is pure, peace-loving, considerate, submissive, full of mercy and good fruit, impartial and sincere.*" A new possibility dawns on me. I have to ask, though I might sound crazy.

"Aldo, are you . . . God?"

"Ho, ho, hee, hee . . . no. Maybe you still a dope. Hee, hee, ho, ho! Aldo is not God, but names sometimes have meaning. I Aldo." Okay, well, whatever that means.

"What then? What am I supposed to do?"

"Speak truth, and . . . escape Island. Take no vengeance," he says with a truly somber look. "Take no vengeance," he says again. "Vengeance belong to God. And . . . *for you*, ends not justify means."

"I don't know if I can keep going, Aldo. Bailee is dead. The Island is tearing apart. I'm burnt out."

Placing his hand on my shoulder he whispers, "Remember Aldo's words. If you remember, you survive." Then pulling my ear so close to his lips that I can feel his whiskers, he passionately demands, "*Do not forsake wisdom, and she will protect you; love her, and she will watch over you!*" Then, releasing me, he steps away.

"What is that, Aldo? Is that some kind of riddle?"

"Proverbs chapter four and verse six. Aldo, not God, but . . . Aldo serves Him." He turns to leave again. When I saw him before I would have stopped him if I could have. Now, though, I let him leave. I imagine I'll see him again.

Disappearing into the woods he encourages, "Dope has conquered *lust*, reason now to *hope*, preach the truth he *must*, no longer he a *dope*."

CHAPTER THIRTY-NINE

Seekers of truth, that's what all the world should be. It is unlikely that any man has acquired for himself a worldview completely free of all inconsistencies, contradictions and falsehoods. Even the followers of the true Adonai, the God of Abraham - revealed in Jesus Christ, are not always without doctrinal confusion springing forth from faulty interpretations of texts, experiences and sagely advise. Knowing this is the beginning of intellectual humility. Without the willingness to be corrected, the awareness that one might be wrong, a man is committing himself to the lottery of his birth. He has cuffed himself to the beliefs of his community. He will not change. If the community is right, he is right, but only by dumb and blind allegiance. If the community is wrong, then he is wrong and in his blind acceptance . . . will never know.

Have Foley and Oleth bound themselves to their beliefs, or are they willing to listen and change? Thanks to Jack and Courtney, I'll find out. Sending Courtney with Jack was the right move. Having never allowed herself to become addicted to the Ocean's Wave, she thwarted Foley's predictable attempt to entice her man with the blue temptation. As expected, he would not listen to their plea to help us, but they found success in securing a second meeting. If Oleth agreed to it, the opposing Adonai would meet with me at a summit in the Cave on the peak. Another hopeful arrow carried an invitation into the Unbelieving Tribe, and Oleth now approaches. I feel naked. On one side of the mountain, the Adon of the Southern Colony climbs a new cable. On the other, the Adon of the Unbelieving Tribe ascends. Jack awaits Foley, and I stand above Oleth. As instructed, they both drop their weapons. They have no choice. Refusal would mean we would cut the lines. With angry stares we all enter the cave and Jack stands guard outside.

The summit begins with my words. Cautiously, I say, "I'm pleased and grateful that you both agreed to meet here. The tiny world of this Island does not need to be torn apart with war."

Oleth interrupts, "This is a waste of time. My tribe waits at the bottom of this rock to attack even now."

"I welcome it," Foley responds. "My colonials are here standing watch too."

Breaking in, I attempt to calm them with, "Is there no compromise that can be met? Can't you both agree to live peaceably on separate ends of the Island?"

"No," Oleth grunts. "The fine structures and Colony estate he possesses are meant for an Adon, an unbeliever. We share the view of our fathers. That makes us the rightful heirs of the proper Adonai Colony."

Foley answers, "You have no right to that which belongs to my god. He is a warrior and will exact judgment on you with my blade." Oleth stands at these words.

"Wait, Adon! This is why we're here." He begrudgingly sits. "Foley, you're misunderstanding the scriptures. God is described as a warrior. You're right about that. But the Old Testament believers who killed to take over their promised land, did so as direct and revealed judgment from God against a people who had rebelled for centuries. That's not all. They had direct communication from Him regarding what they were to do. You don't have that."

"I do! Naturally, I do. You know this, Justin. My vision - the prophecy. What are these, but direct communications from Him?"

"There," Oleth argues, "do you see what this brainless narcissist believes?" I hold out my hand to indicate it's not time.

"Your beliefs and what you teach are based upon a cultic translation of the Bible that teaches Jesus was a god, and not God in the flesh - incarnate." He shakes his head in disagreement. "Listen, Foley, I know what I'm talking about here. Your whole framework is built on twisted scripture, ancient Germanic-occultism and personal experience with . . . something."

"What do you mean, 'something?'"

"Foley, how do you know that your visions and voices are from God and not the demonic?"

"Because they're real." As Foley speaks, Oleth puts his hands behind his head and stares up in frustration.

I contend, "I don't deny that they're real, Foley. I deny that they're from God. There is an entire cult, back in the real world, that is gaining acceptance in the United States. They claim to know what they believe is true because of a 'burning in the bosom,' as they put it. Another group, the ones who commissioned the publication of your mistranslated Bible, has tried for over a hundred years to convince the masses that Jesus was a god rather than God in the flesh. You have fallen into a trap set by a crafty enemy. It's not because you're a fool. It's because you were a target - a target of an incredibly intelligent deceiver."

"These ideas you spout," he answers, "are the reasons we kill to protect The Great Divide."

Oleth breaks in, "I've no problem with killing. In fact, it makes no difference to me if he accepts what you say or not, Apologia. One believer is as bad as the next."

"Okay, Oleth," I begin as I turn my attention to the Unbelieving Adon, "you say you reject all morality - all right and wrong, good and bad."

"It is all an illusion. There is no God, and without one, your morality is meaningless."

"Then, we have a point of agreement. You see, Oleth, I think you are more consistent than most skeptics. You realize what the best atheist philosophers admit. It is the same truth that dawned on Nietzsche. In the absence of God, Adolf Hitler was not worse than a beloved grandmother who gives to the poor. They are just both people doing what they please. Better, worse, good, bad, progress, regress - these are all meaningless words without God. Am I right? Do we agree?"

"Yes. Tell me this is not the reason we are meeting. It is a waste of my time."

"But deep down, Adon, I don't think you believe that. Deep down you *know* that it is wrong to rape, kill, steal and destroy." As if on cue, a thunderous rumble meets my ears and dust falls from the roof of the cave. Foley and I look around erratically and stand.

"Do you hear that, Apologia?" Oleth asks. I meet his gaze with my mouth open. "That is the proof that you are wrong. I am not troubled by killing. We have placed the mines where the false Colony stands."

Hunched over to fit through the opening, Jack wipes the sweat from his eyes and shouts, "Justin, an explosion like you've never seen! Half the Southern Colony is crawling away! I . . . I don't know about casualties!" Foley and I rush through the entrance to peer down at the wreckage. A shout is heard from the side of the mountain and then a mass of the Unbelieving Tribe is seen charging toward the Southern Colony survivors. We rush back to restrain Oleth, but he's gone.

Foley grips me by the throat and yells, "You

fools! This is your fault!"

"Foley . . . (*cough*) . . . We've got to save them."
He releases me.

"You'll fight alongside me? Of course you will.
The prophecy is taking shape."

"I don't . . . I don't know about that. I won't kill
anyone." Jack is shaken up and alternates his attention
between our conversation and the action on the
ground.

Foley responds to my disclaimer with, "We'll
see."

CHAPTER FORTY

I've never been in a fray like this. Blades swing all around me. The occasional blast of gunfire is heard. Land mines placed in the area by Oleth's men sporadically go off sending dirt and debris high into the air. My senses are heightened by the seriousness of the activity. Everyone is trying to kill everyone.

I duck to dodge a sword from one attacker and bring my palm up to collide with his chin. Without time to process the small victory, I realize the need for a swift sidekick in the other direction to stop a guy charging me with a knife. Catching his wrist prevents a third man from sticking me with another blade and we wrestle around on our feet for a few seconds before Jack clubs him with a chunk of wood. Our eyes meet and we realize a deep fear.

"Foley," I shout to the gleeful warrior who is caught up in his own battle. "The Southern Colony has too few men! We've got to retreat!" A mine detonates near our position and we all hit the shaking earth. I'm glad Hope and Courtney aren't here. Again I shout to Foley, "And we don't know where they've placed these ordinances!"

Convinced by the explosion, the Adon returns, "Expedient idea, young prince! Let's go!" We turn our attention to the tree line and begin to run, dodging steel death and visible landmines as we go. Reaching the cover of the jungle we only find that more Southern colonials struggle against more soldiers from the Unbelieving Tribe. "FALL BACK COLONIALS!"

***

We hit the river with at least ten from the Southern Colony. Some leap to grab the zip line and move across hand over hand. Most, though, just splash into the water and try to swim across. This is a horror show. A loud battle cry exits Oleth's lips from deep in the forest and reaches our ears on the bank of the river. It's all the motivation I need. We splash into the river, but are quickly swept downstream. Stupid! Jack, Foley and I fight the current, but wildly flail. "Jack," I yell, but I no longer see him. The Adon, though, is still bobbing in front of me.

"Justin," Foley calls in a manner that indicates he's in control. "We're heading for the eastern side of the Island!"

"Great! What does that mean?"

"It means, we're about to drop off the lip of our largest waterfall! See the clearing ahead?"

"I can't get any footing!"

"Stop trying! When we spill off the edge, straighten your body. A drop from this height could kill you. You've got to hit the water standing straight - feet first!"

"What about Jack? I don't see Jack!" There's no time. The Adon is already over the edge. I'm next. Suddenly the aquatic environment is gone and all I hear is the wind rushing up past my ears. The drop seems never ending. Am I about to die? For only a split second I hear the splash of my feet hitting the water, then the sound is silenced when water fills my ears. They pop and I spread my legs to stabilize myself. Pulling my body back to the surface, I look around for . . . there. "Jack! Jack, Are you alright?" He isn't. The world somehow feels dark as I see my fellow Apologia face down in the river. With the current now more timid, I swim to him and pull his body ashore.

"Jack! Wake up!" I slap his face a few times. Nothing.

"Aside, mate," Foley says before dropping to Jack's lifeless body and blowing into his mouth. I've heard of this technique, but never seen it done. "C'mon, my friend," the Adon says, pushing against his chest with one palm atop the other. He returns to Jack's mouth and forces more air into his lungs. I can't help, but feel some renewed appreciation for him in this moment. Jack is more than a brother, and Foley . . . well . . . at this point I feel a sympathetic concern for him. He's a villain, but . . . he might be savable. I'm shocked back to reality, with the realization that Jack is not waking up. "This isn't good, mate." Foley repeats the action several more times with increasing aggression. Genuine emotion emerges on his face. Finally, he rests back on his haunches and wipes his nose with his forearm.

"What are you doing?" I demand. "Keep trying!"

"It's no good. He's gone. Justin, I . . . I'm sorry, but there's no way to . . . I'm sorry." I shove him onto his back and he does not attempt to prevent the action.

"No," I shout while trying to mimic the Adon's life saving tactic. After three more attempts, Foley pulls me away by my shoulders and I weep. We both sit on the sandy riverbank for a few moments before Foley stands to walk around in thought. Across the river and downstream a few dozen yards is a boat of some kind with two decks, upper and lower. It's been lying there for years, from the look of it. Inside there is movement. Foley runs. I stand, somewhat disoriented by grief and watch him, wiping my tears away. He issues a battle cry as he pulls himself out of the water at the edge of the vessel and enters. Oleth!

CHAPTER FORTY-ONE

With or without Jack, I don't have much time. The Supreme Adon will be here soon, passing through the rocky entrance to the Island. Now, though, my world is in a tailspin. I came here to save Jack and Courtney. Jack is dead. I can't even bring myself to fully accept it. Forced by the action of the day, I have to hold the plan together at its seams or else . . . no one will make it out of here.

Climbing onto the outside deck of the boat, I peer through the window in time to see the action begin. "Take this, false Adon," Oleth says as he tosses Foley a sword. "We will finish this here." Foley readies himself, taking a stance. He looks afraid. I've never seen this look in his eyes before. They cross blades and the dance begins. I'm still too dazed by Jack's death to think straight. Glancing over my shoulder I see his body still positioned lifeless on the opposite bank. I look back to the action through the window. Foley deflects several of Oleth's attempts to skewer him and finally gets nicked on the right bicep. He grunts and grips the spot backing away.

"Time to die," Oleth calmly announces. Sliding around to a door, I launch down the aisle in the middle of the space and wrap my arm around Oleth's neck. Before Foley can react the killer flops me over his head and onto my back in front of him. He grips my throat and lifts me with brute strength tossing me like a rag doll out the window and onto the exterior deck. I try to recover, but see that the two are at it again.

Foley commands, "Leave, prince Justin. This animal cannot defeat me. It has been prophesied."

"Foley, you'll die!"

"Don't be a sticky beak, Justin." Three more deflections occur.

"What!"

"A sticky beak, mate. It's what Australians like me call someone who sticks his nose in where it doesn't belong. Now don't be a sticky beak. Leave. The colonials need you. The Unbelieving Tribe is heading for The Colony." He never takes his gaze away from Oleth. Two more deflections and an unsuccessful stab passes before Foley finishes, "The Unbelieving Tribe. You must fulfill your end of the prophecy. Vanquish them!" Not because of a belief in the prophecy, and not because I'm worried about the lapse in etiquette that would result in my being labeled an Australian sticky-beak, I leave Foley and Oleth to themselves and head toward The Colony, only . . . Jack's body is gone! With renewed hope, I pull myself out of the river and race toward the cliffs beyond The Colony. The Supreme Adon is coming. I have to be there. Maybe Jack will be there too.

***

Vaulting logs and ducking branches, I sprint through the jungle. One of the Unbelieving Tribe has separated from the battle and is giving chase. He's right on my heels and I don't have time for this. Reaching a zip line, I flick open the Hook-Slide and take off. He follows suit. Mid-slide he kicks at my back and one hand falls free. I dangle, spinning by one hand until we both collapse on the edge of a steep hill and struggle against each other. Without thinking, I instinctively place my foot on his chest and kick him over. Startled by my deadly action I stand and view the hillside where he tumbles to the bottom and begins to pick himself up. He's fine. It looks like he's given up and headed in the opposite direction. I've got to keep running. Only, another image captures my attention.

"Jungles fill with *blood*, valleys echo *screams*, but evil like a *flood*, cannot threaten *dreams*." Behind a tree I see Aldo sitting on a log.

"*Oh*, Aldo! I don't have time for riddles now! I've got to get to the cliffs. I . . . I've got to . . ."

"Escape? Yes, you must escape. Soon Aldo will disappear with the Island. Don't forget Aldo's words when you gone."

"What?" I ask while heaving from the chase. "If I escape you'll be free! We'll send help. I mean, I guess you can stay here if you like, but without all the danger of the Unbelieving Tribe or The Colony or . . ."

"Dreamer, you not see Aldo again. This your last advice. When you meet leader of Colony again . . ."

I cut him off before he can finish.

"Aldo, I won't meet him again. We're leaving this place. You should come too!"

He breaks in with, "When you meet leader of Colony again, *do not let kindness and truth leave you; bind them around neck, write them on tablet of heart. So you will find favor and good repute in sight of God and man. Trust in Lord with all heart. And do not lean on own understanding. In all ways acknowledge Him, and He will make paths straight. Do not be wise in own eyes; Fear Lord and turn away from evil.* Men on Island cannot kill dreams God has given dreamer. Dreamer will survive." I begin to plead, but Aldo slips away as he always does. His last rhyme echoes, "Jungles fill with *blood*, valleys echo *screams*, but evil like a *flood*, cannot threaten *dreams*." I want to try and convince him to go with me, or ask more questions, or . . . something, but I don't have time. I've got to move.

***

At the back of the Mansion I find that the horror has reached The Colony. Inside, I can see that the Unbelieving Tribe is pillaging the place. The remaining Veritas girls are tied up in the back of the garden against a wall. Rushing over to them, I loose their restraints and order, "Follow the beach away from The Colony! Get as far away as you can!" Sobbing, they do as instructed.

Turning my attention back to the Mansion, I refocus on the plan. Kicking off of the side of the structure, I wrench myself onto the balcony outside Foley's room and slowly open the door. A member of the Unbelieving Tribe intentionally smashes a painting before leaving the space. I enter and see the yellow phone sitting inside the armoire. I can't allow anyone to call for Adonai assistance once we're gone. Ripping the cord out of the back of the device, I follow by smashing it on the dresser. That should do. Thirty seconds pass and I'm back outside heading for the cliffs. In the front yard of the Mansion where the Unbelieving Apologia was killed by Foley, I can almost see the cliffs. It's getting dark. Then I hear his voice.

"Young prince!" I stop in my tracks. Turning to face him, I see an injured Foley, holding his arm. "We have work still to do."

"Foley, I . . . where is Oleth?"

"Oh, he's out there somewhere. You've got to know when to abandon ship, mate. That fellow knows his way around a sword. I can't compete," he says with a laugh.

"You've got to run. We've got to split up. They'll kill us, there are too many of them."

"No. You and I will complete the prophecy now."

"Foley, even if I believed all that, how is it even possible?"

"Come back inside and I'll show you." My

impulse is to run, but I can't let him know the plan. That boat can never reach shore. I've got no choice.

***

In the Mansion's hidden underworld we stand in the room where the history of the Island hangs in aged photographs on the wall. The Ocean's Wave sits in boxes, and the doorway to the secret bunker is to my left. Removing some old crates, two levers are revealed. "This is it, young prince," The Adon somberly reveals. "We throw these levers and the Unbelieving Tribe will be destroyed."

CHAPTER FORTY-TWO

"What do you mean, they'll be destroyed?"

"The Island's . . . former inhabitants set ordinances beneath The Colony. That's precisely why this Mansion is set on the hill a good distance away."

"Why would they do that? It doesn't make any sense."

"Obviously, in case they were ever discovered."

"But . . . Why? Why would *you* want this? You'll kill your own colonials in the destruction."

With a look that conveys Foley knows something I don't, he reveals, "The Unbelieving Tribe has control of the beach. It's sad. Many of my friends are no doubt gone forever. But . . . the women and children are safe on the western edge of the Island. If we throw these levers, Justin, we can start again. We can build The Colony the way it should be. If we do this, we can fulfill the prophecy right now, together. If we don't they'll kill us all." My thoughts are clouded by circumstances. One act of killing and the killing will end. Once Julie is here, the people I care about the most will all be on one Island. The scent of the Ocean's Wave stimulates my thinking. Because of its constant preparation in this room, it's in the air. My friends are far away on the cliffs by now. They'll be safe. Something about it makes sense. Is it the Ocean's Wave affecting my judgment? Do I care? Maybe the prophecy *is* communication from God. "Remember the words, Justin? 'Together the two saviors will birth a paradise safe from the world across a great divide. Gott Mit Uns!' that time has come. We cannot resist. Vanquish them!" My hand creeps to the levers as I, with conflicted thoughts, explore the possibilities. "Look at us, Justin! With our hands on these levers we are the very image in the painting!"

"STOP," another voice yells. It's Jack. "Justin, don't." He's alive. I feel my breathing increase.

Foley says, "Not another sticky beak."

"Stay out of it, Jack," I demand. "I know what I'm doing!"

"You don't! This isn't the way! It's . . . what I'd have done only days ago. But you, Justin . . . You found me and talked sense into me. This isn't what God wants. The killing has got to end." His words kindle something inside of me. The spark grows into a flame as I recall Aldo's words, and consider how they bear on the situation.

The funny little fellow had said, "*Do not let kindness and truth leave you; bind them around neck, write them on tablet of heart. So you will find favor and good repute in sight of God and man. Trust in Lord with all heart. And do not lean on own understanding. In all ways acknowledge Him, and He will make paths straight. Do not be wise in own eyes; Fear Lord and turn away from evil."*

Slowly, I move my hand away from the lever.

"Justin," Foley protests, "don't listen to him. This *will* happen. You don't even have a choice. The prophecy cannot be wrong."

Staring at the cement floor for a moment I look up at the confused Adon and declare, "If you *claim* to be a prophet, Foley, you *are* one. It's just that you're either a true prophet or a false prophet. In this case, it's clearly false." I turn to leave and am halfway up to the exit when I hear the rattle of wood. Before I can react, Foley grabs a board that stretches the distance between the levers and forces it evenly against them both.

"WAIT, NO!" I scream, but it's too late. Rushing to him in anger, I initiate a sleeper hold and wrestle him to the floor until he's unconscious. "Jack, quick!" my friend helps me to pull the slumbering Adon through the wall and place him on the cart that leads to the bunker. I work the operation and Foley disappears into the darkness toward the small cavity in the earth. "He'll be fine there until we're gone."

"Justin, I don't hear anything. No rumble, no destruction."

"Maybe it didn't work. Let's go!"

***

With the Mansion in the background we race

toward the cliffs. It's almost over. Our feet hit rock and we rush along the long grey arm that separates the ocean from the massive cove. Suddenly, as if the whole earth were violently awakened, The Colony erupts with flames and the ground quakes. We hit the stony surface as chunks of rock fall away and crash into the sea. Debris, flung all the way from The Colony beach lands all around us. Jack and I stand to see The Colony burning in the night. What buildings remain are set ablaze. Surviving members of the Unbelieving Tribe scatter. In the distance I see the Supreme Adon's ship approaching the entrance between the cliffs.

"Jack," I say with a traumatic tone, "we should have warned them! We should have abandoned the plan and warned them!"

"No, Justin," he says gripping my shoulders. "If we'd tried, we would be dead too. This is not your fault. Foley would have done it regardless!" I scream to the sky and stumble back to the ground. Jack grips my arm and pulls me back up.

"It was you, Jack. If you hadn't come, I might of . . ."

"You didn't, Justin. You didn't do it. Now you've got to think of Julie, Hope and Courtney."

"Julie! You're right." I glance over my shoulder to see the ship approaching. It's close. Dusting myself off I begin to run with Jack beside me. Hopefully, the Adon won't see the destruction until he's at the entrance. That will give us time to get aboard before he can turn back. "Hope, Courtney!" I shout. They're lying on the rocks so as not to be seen. We land next to them and watch as the ship grows closer.

Hope begins, "What happened?"

Courtney adds, "Are they all dead?"

Jack answers, "It was Foley. The Unbelieving Tribe is decimated, or on the run." Courtney rolls over on her back and cries. "We don't think any . . . or many, colonials were on the beach when the bomb went off. The women and children are safe, if Foley is to be believed."

"He's not," Courtney screams through tears. "We should have killed him!"

Hope speaks up, "Courtney, you're angry, but that's not our way." She brushes the Apologia girl's hair as she speaks the truth.

"Well, maybe it should be! How long do we put up with this kind of thing? Whatever they believe, Foley and Oleth are both Adonai. This is what they do. They kill!" Regaining my senses, I cover Courtney's mouth and crane my neck over the rocks to see the ship below. It's passing through the rocky entrance and barely fits.

"It's time." We unfurl two cables Hope and Courtney attached to the rocks and briskly repel toward the large vessel beneath us. Landing on the deck, all four of us rush to the front to find a well-dressed man I presume to be the Supreme Adon. His salt and pepper beard matches his hair. He looks to be about sixty years old and holds a cane in one hand and a drink in the other. He looks equally shocked by our presence and the destruction now visible at the beach. Two other individuals, who I presume to be Adonai Apologia, stand by. Thinking on his feet, Jack is already inside the boat instructing the captain to stop the vessel. We each have blades ready to toss and no one moves.

"The Supreme Adon, I take it," I say.

He gazes at me and steps two paces closer. "The Son of Lyn, I suspect. You have your father's thin lips." I squint for a second. "Now you have destroyed not one, but two of my Colonies, young man."

"This? I didn't do this. Your sitting Adon is responsible. Of course, if you'd paid more attention to your projects you would know that this Island has been at civil war. The man you've been communicating with is an imposter." He just stares at me, not sure what to believe. "How many Colonies are there?"

"I don't answer to you, Son of Lyn. Where is the Adon?"

"Oh, he'll crawl out of his hole soon enough. You can talk it over with him all you like. You should know, though, he kills Adonai for sport. He'll see you as a pretty big fish."

"What are you planning? Are you going to maroon me on this Island?" He takes a drink as if he isn't troubled by the thought.

"As a matter of fact, I am."

Ignoring my comment he looks to Hope and says, "Which of you ladies is the Daughter of Wynfelt, you or the blonde?" He waits for Hope to answer. "It's you. I can tell. Your father never knew how far reaching the Adonai influence was. The old fool thought his Colony was the only one. I never met him, but I understand he's dead. My condolences, ma'am."

"Enough," I growl. Looking to the two Adonai Apologia I command, "Overboard!"

One of them says to the Supreme Adon, "Sir, we can't . . ."

Cutting them off he interjects, "Can you swim to shore alright?"

The other answers, "Well, yes sir, but we can't leave you . . ."

"No, no, it'll be fine. I'll work things out. Please be careful though." I can't believe how complicit he's being. They both climb over the edge and begin to swim. Courtney retrieves a sidearm from the Supreme Adon's belt. "Now, let's see if we can come to some sort of an arrangement."

CHAPTER FORTY-THREE

Temptation is powerful. This entire experience has represented different modes of enticement to do evil. I was tempted by Bailee. There's nothing wrong with physical attraction, nor the desire for romance. The Veritas girl may have had no ill intention. At least not in her love for me. I was tempted, though - tempted to betray, and indulge in carnal immediate gratification. The Ocean's Wave seduced me in a different way. I was tempted to ignore my responsibilities and be ruled by a substance. Foley coaxed me. Though he thought I would be drawn to the position of prestige he presented, I was not. I was drawn to the friendship. The appeal was brotherhood. It was a temptation to go my own way and design a peaceful, but pointless kingdom on the Island. It would take a stronger bait from the Supreme Adon to reel me in.

"Where is my sister?"

He sits on a built-in couch as The Colony burns behind him. "What do you want, Justin Lyn?"

I chuckle in amazement at his question. "What do I want? I want to know where my sister is. I want to know how many Colonies are. I want the Adonai to be brought to justice for their lies. What kind of question is that? What do I want? I want it to end."

"I don't think so. I don't believe you want it to end, Son of Lyn. If we break it down, what you want is your family and friends. You want them safe. You want a place to call home. You want all of them there. You want an environment where you can worship your God without the fear of Adonai involvement. I can offer you all of that." He takes a sip of his drink as if he's just out boating with friends. His confidence annoys me.

"What . . . What do you mean?"

"I'm talking about your own Colony - The Colony of God." My fierce expression fades. "I can offer you that, Justin. Imagine it. All of you could be free to live your lives just as you did at your father's Colony. The difference? You could run it however you choose. It will need a wise ruler. You don't have to call yourselves Adonai. Believers might find that title blasphemous, but the four of you could serve those roles well. I can arrange everything. I can provide you resources, support, and protect your secrecy." I stare at the flames as he speaks. "Come on, young man. You know that vast world of swirling ideas is no place for you. If I had to bet, I'd say that you were a bit relieved to be on this Island - back at a Colony - separate from that world. Just say the word and it will all be yours."

"Why would you do such a thing? I thought the whole point was to get rid of belief."

His lips turn up as he considers the question. "I'll settle for compartmentalization. Besides, I had a certain fondness for your father. Indeed, I ordered your deaths, but I'm feeling benevolent tonight. Besides, I apparently don't have many options. Here's what you do, son. Kneel to me, accept me as your Supreme Adon and we'll have a deal." Something about his words evokes memories of my time studying the sacred text before embarking on this adventure. I can't accept his terms.

"It is written: '*Worship the Lord your God, and serve him only.*' I can't bow to you, Adon." We stare at each other. We are at an impasse. "Now, I'll ask one more time. Where is my sister?"

Before he can respond the boat slightly shifts and a large (THUD) is heard. Spinning on my heals I see the shadowy figure of the Adon of the Unbelieving Tribe. Oleth trudges toward me as Courtney and Hope flank the Supreme Adon. Courtney looks traumatized, as though whatever she experienced in that Unbelieving Tribe dungeon is rushing back to her. I have no confidence in my abilities here. Jack can't leave the captain. It's all on me. I stride toward the murderer.

The mountainous enemy demands, "Am I a dog that you come at me? Get off this boat or I'll feed your flesh to the birds and wild animals of the Island."

With surprising peace I respond, "You come against me with a sword, but I come against you in the name of the true and Almighty Adonai." We rush each other and he swings his blade. I duck and launch my whole body against his torso. He does not fall, but only staggers backward, off balance. I rush him again and this time his knee impacts my gut forcing me to heave. Gripping my throat with his hand, he prepares to toss me overboard, but when I kick against his stomach he drops me and my feet hit the deck. I spin, half to get away and half to strike. The back of my hand connects with his head and he drops his sword. Kicking against the side of the boat I spring past his body intending to wrap my arm around his neck, but the warrior deflects the maneuver and I land belly down. Pushing hard against the boards I begin to rise. Looking back, I locate his shin and strike with the ball of my foot. He's down. Not much time! On my feet, I grab his sword and hold it toward him where he is positioned on his back. "You're beaten!" We both breathe heavily. The waves lap against the side of the boat. In a moment I'll demand that the Supreme Adon, the captain and Oleth all disembark on the beach away from the action. Then, I hear it! A gunshot! I'm startled and for five seconds my ears ring. Everyone gasps. Oleth is dead! Courtney holds the Supreme Adon's pistol!

Snatching the weapon out of her hands I shout, "What are you doing, Courtney? What have you done?" Hatred is on her face and then she begins to weep. "You've killed him! He wasn't even a threat anymore!" Reality clearly sets in as the Apologia girl cries into my shoulder. I embrace her. Jack and Hope are now at our end of the boat.

"I couldn't let him live, Justin! You don't understand what it was like with him! And the Adonai won't stop! You can't let them get away with it!" She continues to cry. "Don't hate me, Justin. I couldn't take that!" I want to comfort her, but I can't affirm her choice. "Just tell me that we still have *each other*. Tell me things won't be changed forever."

"They won't," I tell her, but somehow I'm not sure. "We'll figure it out." I hug her again, but Oleth's body is visible in my field of vision. "Courtney, sit down. I've got to go deal with things." She sits and buries her face in her hands, continuing to cry.

"Justin, they're gone," Jack says. I rush to the front of the boat to find that the Supreme Adon and his captain have vanished. I don't see them in the water. Maybe they climbed the cliffs. It's unlikely, but they don't appear on the boat. Finally, my concerns for them are washed away by the realization that Julie may be inside this vessel.

"Julie! She's got to be here," I insist. Moving through a doorway into the space where the captain had been I open another door and step down into the interior of the ship. There are narrow doors on either side of the slender hallway. I open each of them. A bathroom, sleeping quarters, a closet - but no sign of Julie. I continue into a spacious living area with plush furniture and a rich decor. Then I see a crate at the back of the room. It's large enough. Even two people could fit inside. Hurrying to the spot I begin to look for a way to get it open. A smile creeps across my face. It's got to be her.

CHAPTER FORTY-FOUR
Julie

"Rob . . . Rob, wake up," I say as we lay flat on our backs in some sort of a crate. "Rob, there's someone here." I nudge him until he rouses.

"What," he says.

"I guess we're in some kind of a box or something, but there's someone outside."

"What a headache, baby girl. Well, we must be on this . . . Island or whatever." Light spills in as the crate is opened. I can't see anything at first. It's too bright. It's cold. It doesn't feel right for a tropical Island. My eyes adjust and I see a face. I see a shaved head, and an athletic build.

"Justin . . . is that . . ."

"On your feet," the voice orders. It's not Justin. My vision completes the transition and I see mountains in every direction. Everything is covered in snow. Conical tents made of leather and other fabrics speckle the vicinity. The man giving orders is wearing an Apologia uniform.

Rob demands, "Tell us what's going on! We're

supposed to be at an Island! Where's the Supreme fella?"

"You don't ask questions," the man says in what sounds like a Swiss accent. "You do as you're told." A cocktail of fear and anger swirls in my blood. He lied to us. "Follow!"

"A spear is pointed at us and we begin to walk. A stone pathway protrudes from the snow. Moving along, we descend a staircase that snakes down from the icy shelf on which we were standing. More tepees speckle the area as do buildings made of stone and plaster. Lines bearing various flags of varying colors swoop down as they are strung from one building to the next overhead. They look like the Tibetan prayer flags I've seen. We continue downward until a massive circle becomes visible sitting in the midst of the mountain peaks. It's as though The Colony is situated in a bowl, like a crater or a dormant volcano or something. Around the circle and sloping up the hillside are stone benches filled with a crowd all the way around the floor. There must be five thousand people seated there. Past the crowds there are shops, then what look like residential dwellings. It's all one big circular community reaching upward from the stone circle like an amphitheater. To my right I see that a path leads through a valley toward more buildings that trail down a slope. Where are we?

"Move along," the escort says. "As we weave through the crowd along the edge of the circular focal point, we approach the alternate side. The atmosphere is festive. High lamp stands hold rock edifices with burning pyres that illuminate the blue-tinted scene with orange light. On the opposite side of the circle we are led into what looks almost like a castle set into the slope. Passing through the large wooden doors we find ourselves in a wide hallway flanked by archways that stretch the length of the passage. Beyond the arched dividers are expansive spaces with large fireplaces, tables and seating. Blue banners hang along the walls with the Creed of the Adonai on them. My mind is scrambling to process it all. Finally we enter what can only be described as a throne room of some sort with three oversized wooden chairs on a slightly raised platform. Four Apologia officers line the walls and two large figures, wearing uniforms I've never seen, stand at the door. Seated on the thrones are two women and one man. The man sits in the middle and wears a blue velvet cloak with its hood raised. He would look medieval were it not for a pair of thick-rimmed modern glasses and an almost trendy goatee. The women wear grey cloaks and with the raised hoods not much can be seen. They appear slender and athletic.

"Welcome to your new home, Daughter of Lyn," the mysterious male figure says, "I assume this is your suitor."

Intimidated I utter, "He . . . he's my husband. Where are we?"

"You are at the largest and most secure of the Adonai Colonies. We call it Berget."

"Where are we geographically?" Rob asks.

The female Adon on the right answers from within her cloak, "It is a secret of the Adonai. No colonial knows."

With passion I ask, "Do they know that The Great Darkness is a lie?" Instantly my eyes move across the faces of the Apologia and the two unknown guards whose life roles I do not know. No one reacts to my words.

The female Adon on the left says, "They all know that The Great Darkness has not yet happened."

"Your father's Colony," the male Adon begins, "was the only to have introduced the belief that The Great Darkness had already occurred. It was an experimental Colony. We needed to see how a generation with that belief would react. It failed, because of Noah Wynfelt. Here, we let them know the truth about the coming Great Darkness. However, the belief in supernatural superstitions is presented as antiquated. It should be. In your new life at Berget, you will be free to talk about the concept of God all you like, though we will discourage it, but you will be seen as radicals. You will be seen as freaks. You will be outsiders living among us."

Rob can't resist the question, "What do you mean this is our new home! We're not staying here!" The strange figures by the entrance readjust as if preparing for action.

"Rob, don't . . ." He cuts me off.

"No, ma'am! I was prepared to die! I was prepared to go to some Island to find Justin, but this aint gonna work!" The Adonai all stand, and when they do, the Apologia officers grip our arms as Rob struggles to free himself. The Adonai move in single-file order out of the room followed by the ominous guards. We are led behind them.

Exiting the Adonai structure, we are led directly into the middle of the massive stone circle. The crowds roar with enthusiasm at the sight of their leaders. Rob and I are prodded by spears to our backs, nudging us ever forward. Finally, the male Adon raises a scepter of some sort and the colonials fall silent. His voice echoes through the expansive area when he says, "My beloved Colony, are you all well fed and in good SPIRITS?" Their combined cheers sound like a thunderstorm. "I'm glad my friends. Today I want to introduce to you the newest members of our community. This is the Daughter of Lyn, and her husband."

Rob moans, "Don't I even have a name?" A guard prods him with the end of his spear. "Okay, okay."

The Adon continues, "The two of them are deluded. They believe in superstitions. They believe in the great lie!" Shouts of detest rustle up from the crowd. "No, no. They will serve as living reminders of the delusion of belief. It is our hope that they will come to accept the truth. This one," he says, motioning to me, "Is the daughter of Malory Lyn. As you all know, Dr. Lyn was one of the greatest and most brilliant of all the Adonai. His Colony was destroyed. The

341

Daughter of Lyn contributed to its fall." More angry shouts. "I want you to see the mercy of the Adonai. We will allow them to live among us, eat among us, and if they like, raise children among us. In this way, we will both honor the memory of Adon Lyn and punish the crimes of his daughter. Perhaps she will be rehabilitated. I expect no colonial to do them bodily harm. I expect no colonial to speak to them. I expect no colonial to regard their existence. Do you understand, Colony?" More cheers erupt.

The guards lunge forward and grab my arms as I rush to the Adon's side and ask, "Why are you doing this to us? Why not kill us now?"

Looking down at me he answers in a low voice, "You *will* die, Daughter of Lyn. You will die at an old age after a lifetime of seclusion. Your God will not help you. You're mine now." The crowds continue to roar as Rob and I are taken away.

"Baby girl," Rob proclaims, "I love you! We're going to get out of here! This isn't the end!"

"We will, flyboy! I have you and," announcing to anyone who can hear, "I have the true Adonai!"

CHAPTER FORTY-FIVE
Justin
Three Days Later

Despair is not possible for the believer. It's not that believers should not despair, nor is it the case that it is sad when believers do despair. It is simply not something a believer can do. The child of God can be depressed, grieve, and even regret, but cannot sorrow as others who have no hope. Desperation is a state of being without hope. For the children of God, no matter what calamity may come, there is the promise of everlasting life together. We have assurance of justice. The believer can be certain that *Truth Will Triumph!*

Will I ever see Julie again, this side of eternity? I don't know. I don't know if we'll ever even make it back to civilization. We are lost at sea. Figuring out how to handle the ship was no real problem. Jack came in handy. We could not prepare, though, for the loss of the navigation system. We don't know where we were, we don't know where we are, and it has been three days. There's no fuel. What little food was in the kitchen on this boat is now gone. Little water is left. Now we merely take turns watching for assistance. I'm up now. It's the middle of the night. I lay sprawled out sloppily on the back of the vessel as it ebbs and flows with the current. In every direction during the day I see the grayish-blue water meeting the grayish-blue sky on the horizon. Now I see only black, but for a column of light reflected on the sea.

"It's your turn to go inside with the others, Justin," Jack says in a fatigued voice.

"Jack, do you believe God answers prayer?"

"Yeah, of course I do. I prayed that we would get off that horrible Island, and guess what? We're off." His eyebrows slope downward. "Although, from the looks of things, maybe that wasn't an answer to prayer." We sit silently for a few more moments.

"I think it was." He looks up at me expressionless to hear what I might say.

"I just don't think we asked for enough. Look up at the stars, Jack. Remember when you became curious about the universe and how it all came to be?" He nods. "Jack, when God gave us stars to admire, He could have given us just one. We would look up at the night sky and say, 'Just look at the star God gave us! Isn't it magnificent?' But when He made the stars, He made trillions. My understanding is, we don't even know how many there are."

"Justin, are you okay?"

"Yeah," I say with a laugh. "What I'm getting at is . . . He knows how to give good gifts to His children." Jack stands and slowly walks to the edge of the boat resting his hands on the rails.

"Justin," he turns. "Courtney is not a child of God . . . not like us." I just stare at him listening. "Will she ever be? *Can* . . . she ever be?"

"I believe she can. What's she been saying?"

"She goes back and forth between indignant demands that it was right . . . to deep and foreboding remorse. I don't know if she'll ever be the same."

"She won't. But she can be forgiven. She can be redeemed." More silence meets us on the deck.

"I wish I knew what Noah would say."

A grin creeps across my face. "I know what he would say." Jack sits next to me. "He'd say . . . pray." Without any more talk I lead, "Master, we are lost without you. We need someone to find us. We need someone kind. Julie needs you wherever she is. Courtney needs you. Please have mercy on us in this desperate situation. You are the true Adonai. You are the Veritas - the truth itself. Deliver us, Lord. In the name of Jesus, amen." An atmosphere of peace descends on the ship like a blanket. I stand and take a few paces before looking back to Jack. "Hey, buddy. What was that song you sang at the Northern Colony, just before Julie and Rob found us?"

"What?"

"Come on, you remember. It was some dumb song about she'll be at the mountain or she'll see the mountain or . . . what was it?"

"Oh, yeah. Wait. Justin, I don't feel like singing."

"Yeah you do. Get me started and I'll sing it."

He groans and begins, "She'll be coming round the mountain when she comes. She'll be coming round the mountain when she comes." He stands and we both sing, "She'll be coming round the mountain, she'll be coming round the mountain, she'll be coming round the mountain when she comes. There you happy now?"

"No. How about, she'll be crossing a big blue ocean when she comes?"

"Awe, man. Fine . . . She'll be crossing a big blue ocean when she comes. She'll be crossing a big blue ocean when she comes." Now we've lost all inhibition and are screaming the lyrics to the night. "She'll be crossing a big blue ocean, she'll be crossing a big blue ocean, she'll be crossing a big blue ocean when she comes!" Courtney and Hope, roused by the noise appear on the deck.

"What are you guys doing?" Hope asks with a tickled grin.

"Losing our minds, snowflake! Join us!" She looks at Courtney for a moment who actually seems delighted by our activity.

Hope sings with us, "She'll be crossing a big blue ocean when she . . . Wait! Look!" Sure enough, the lights of a large ship seem to be visible on the horizon.

We all begin to cheer.

"Jack, get the flare gun!" A moment later a ball of light ascends high and bursts into four bright red chunks. After a few more minutes it becomes obvious that the ship has altered its course and is heading toward us. Again, we all celebrate loudly. "Listen, crew, whatever happens, we still have it."

"What?" Hope asks.

Courtney speaks for the first time in days without tears, "Each other." I smile and nod. We all rest on each others' shoulders and chant, *Truth Will Triumph!*"

***

On board the large military vessel, we have tried for an hour to explain some elements of our story. Some of it we have kept secret. Now knowing how far-reaching the Adonai influence is, we have to be careful. These soldiers are, no doubt, safe, but the ears of the Adonai could be anywhere. It was a good idea, I think, to tell them that we were kidnapped and taken to a remote Island. I'm leaving it at that. Once the Island is located by the authorities it will speak for itself. Then I'll feel comfortable elaborating. If the Adonai are not discovered for some reason, then the remaining enemies will be after us.

We all eat sandwiches and soup as a seasoned officer goes over the notes he's taken. "So, you don't know how far from this Island you drifted. Right?"

I answer, "That's right, but we suspect it was somewhere off the coast of Rio De Janeiro. That's where we were taken from."

He looks confused. "It's just . . .The problem is, son, you're off the coast of . . ."

Hope says, "Where? Just say it!"

"Calm down, miss," the man says. "We're off the coast of Madagascar.

"Madagascar," I say with a wrinkled brow. I guess it's possible, but it doesn't make sense."

He purses his lips with a sympathetic look. "I'll tell you what folks. You get some sleep for a couple of hours. We'll be ashore soon enough. Then you can sort it all out with the authorities.

"Ben Ruth," I say as it occurs to me. "I need to call someone in the States. Can I make a call?"

He thinks for a few seconds and says, "Of course. Absolutely." He momentarily leaves the room and I turn to address my friends.

Before I do, Hope asks a painful question - Painful to ask and painful to answer. "The girl you were infatuated with." I look at her with wide eyes. "She was the one who died wasn't she?"

What else can I do but answer, "Yes."

She offers a friendly smile but says, "That changes things, hero. I'm not sure exactly why, but it does." All I can do to prevent tears, or an argument, or a defense, or whatever . . . is to give her an understanding smile and address the group.

"This is only the beginning," I say. "We now know that the false Adonai have much greater influence than we ever imagined. They'll be after us. Ben Ruth can help, he's a close friend. If the Island is found, the lid will be blown off the enemy's plans. If, on the other hand, the Island's inhabitants disappear like the Northern colonials, no one will believe us. It'll be the same nightmare all over again. The Adonai will be after us. We'll have to go into hiding. I'll never end the search for my sister, but it will be dangerous."

Hope responds, "We'll get through it together." My eyes swell a bit at her words. "We'll find her, hero."

"Truth will triumph," Jack adds.

In unison, we all agree, "*Truth will triumph!*"

The wheels of the plane hit the ice and it slows to a stop. Every time I fly this thing I think of Rob. Then I think of Julie. They're always on my mind. I should have known the boy scout would have already made a will. I step out onto the snow-covered world and begin trekking toward the train tracks. The environment is quiet. Snow falls. In the icy landscape, I can't help but feel at home. Passing through a tunnel I think of the train - the original Wynfelt Manor. My life changed. My existence changed. I had found the truth there.

***

Meeting a river I begin to follow it downstream. At one time I was swept along with the current after plummeting away from Noah and Hope at the Chapel. It's as if this entire region is dead. It's eerily quiet. Aside from the occasional chirp or flutter of birds, I see no animal life. The scenery evokes thoughts of some former civilization now destroyed by a nuclear winter or something.

***

After several hours of hiking I have arrived. Before me, trailing up the mountain is the Northern

Colony - my Colony. I stand staring at the place I once called home with nostalgia. Sometimes I feel as though I could almost convince myself it has all been a dream. Here, however, the memories come flooding back in. Worst of all, the vanishing of The Colony was not the end of something. It was a beginning. Now, years later it still hasn't been resolved.

***

I thought this would be difficult. I thought I would have to will myself up the street in a struggle against my memories. Nevertheless, walking up toward the Life Circle, it all feels somewhat inviting. It should, I guess. After all, I used to walk these streets daily. Life was happy. Life seemed good. Standing in the midst of the Circle I reveal my presence. "Jack! Courtney! Are you here?" My voice echoes in the dead space. Moving up the path toward the Adonai Monument, I look in the windows of each structure hoping to find some sign of activity. Nothing.

Arriving at the Monument I become lost in thought. "It is disrespectful to ignore the words of the Creed," I say to myself out loud as I recall the day it all started. Looks like they missed something during the cleanup. My father's dry blood still clings to the granite beneath a section of the carved stone. I wish I could hear his voice now.

"Justin," a voice calls, but it isn't my father. It's Jack. He slowly trudges over. He bears a smile that includes its own nostalgia. "What are you doing here?"

"Awe, man," I say. "Thank God you're still around. Where's Courtney? Is she okay?"

"Yeah . . . well. She's in good health. Most days everything is fine. She's off foraging in the woods. We have to do that kind of thing now."

"You've never run into anyone else?"

"No. Occasionally a plane flies overhead. Whatever the Adonai had done politically to prevent that has apparently changed. But no, no one ever bothers us. We've been in solitude for, what? A year and a half, maybe."

"Well it's time to come out of hiding."

"What are you talking about? Did you find Julie? Have the Adonai been exposed?" With eyes that demonstrate he's deeply disturbed, he asks, "Is it over?"

"No. But I have something I need you both to hear. When will she be back? Can we go get her?"

"Let's walk down to the old Life Circle. She'll have to pass that way heading for her apartment."

"Apartment?"

"She hasn't wanted to look at me in a long time. She feels bad about it, but she says I just remind her of . . . everything. Remember, she had friends here like we all did, but she also had friends at the Southern Colony. They may be dead now. A lot has been taken from her.

She killed Oleth, or murdered him or . . . whatever you want to call it. She knows the Adonai will always be after us. I just don't understand it, Justin. Why couldn't anyone find the Island? It can't be *that* hard. It's a pretty darn big Island. And it's not like the Adonai could pick it up and move it.

"I know. I ask myself the same questions everyday." I also wonder about Aldo's comments that he would disappear with the Island and what that could mean. Did he know something? "I'll tell you this, though, pal. I sympathize with your lady problems."

"Not you and Hope."

"Yep. We still talk, but Bailee did change things. She feels like it can never be the same as it was. I proposed when we got back from the Island, but . . . let's just say it didn't go well. We've both been in hiding, but not together. We check up on each other, but that's it. It's like a business relationship or something."

"I just can't believe it. It's been hard for all of us I guess, Justin. You chose to stay and continue the fight. We went into hiding. I would have stayed with you, but I couldn't let Courtney come here alone. This is as secluded as we could get. After all, for better or worse, it's our home."

"No. It's not. You can't go back to Egypt when the promised land is ahead."

"What promised land?"

"A world free of their threat."

"I guess, but that won't solve my problem. The worst part is, before, I didn't have Courtney. Now I have her, but she can't bear to look at me."

***

At the Circle of Life Cafe, we sit without tea or coffee. I used to love this spot. Walking up from the stables, Courtney stops when she sees me. Then, she jogs to us.

"Justin, what are you doing here?" She lightly hugs me in a halfhearted way.

"I need you. I need both of you."

"Why?" Jack asks.

"I know where they are - Julie and Rob."

"You do," Jack says. Courtney grimaces.

"Well, kind of. I know how to find them, but I need your help." They both look at the sky thinking. Actually, they look plain nervous. "Listen, guys, I could never have gotten off that Island . . . in fact . . . I could never have gotten out of here without both of you."

"Well, you got that right," Courtney says with a bit of her old sarcasm.

"Yeah, but you know what? I don't think you

could have done it without me either." They both sit there and smiles grow on their weary faces. "I believe we can rescue Julie and Rob. I also believe we can stop the false Adonai, for good. But . . . we can't do it without . . . *each other*."

"Justin," Courtney confesses, "It's just too big. The enemy's influence is too far reaching."

Placing one hand on each of their shoulders, I reveal, "I know it feels that way, Courtney. But listen guys, a funny little man once told me something that has kept me going. *Jungles fill with blood, valleys echo screams, but evil like a flood, cannot threaten dreams!*"

www.ingramcontent.com/pod-product-compliance
Lightning Source LLC
Chambersburg PA
CBHW050919030726
47503CB00007BB/2373